The Opposite of an Empath

charles tyler

The Opposite of an Empath

of an

Empath

charles tyler

A catalogue record for this
work is available from the
National Library of Australia

https://www.nla.gov.au/collections

Title: The Opposite of an Empath

Author: Tyler, Charles

ISBNs: 978-1-7635713-2-7 (paperback)
              978-1-7635713-3-4 (ebook – epub)

Subjects: FICTION / Literary; General; Psychological; Family Life /
              Marriage & Divorce.

Cover design and layout by Charles Tyler
Cover image by Charles Tyler

published by inspirationism

for the empaths

knowing and unknowing

The Opposite of a Psychopath

Part 2

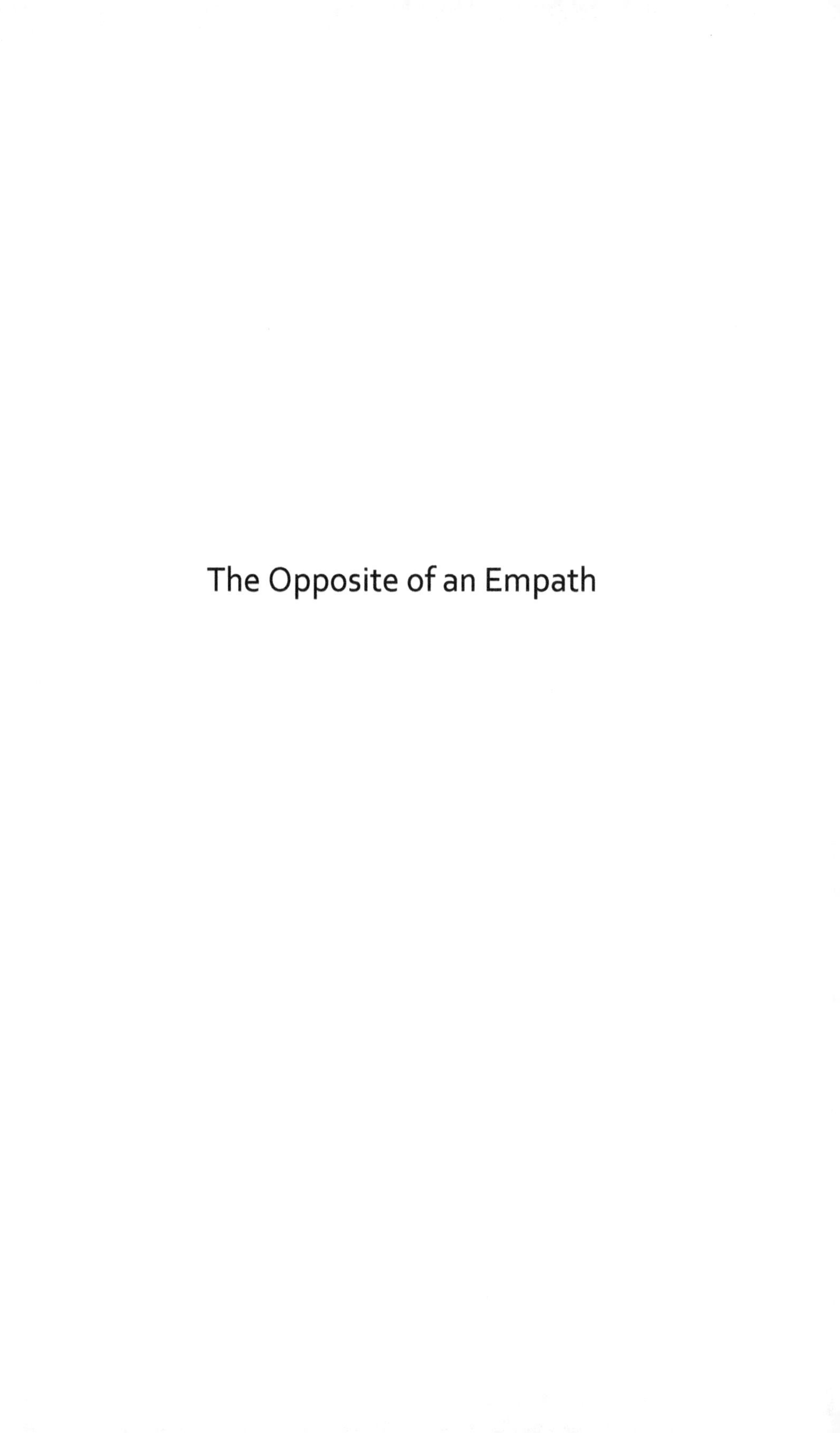

The Opposite of an Empath

Chapter 1

The Dutch counsellor's whole body burst into smile and a mirage of golden light flowed into the space between us. She had built me up to this moment as a percussionist would a drumroll – her final flourish not a *ba dum tsh!* but a complete revelation: a new word, new concept, and new theory.

My opinion of her scattergun-approach during our past session-and-a-half was proved wrong, and I could now see that her aimless meandering from one subject to the next, disjointed tangents, and double bouncing were there for a purpose.

Microscopic spotlights flashed from the ceiling and walls, a hallucinatory manifestation of the figurative sparks ignited by her punchline-posed-as-a-question – *'do you know what is … the opposite of a psychopath?'*

Her questions, videos, scenarios, and speculations were all part of a cleverly orchestrated plan to corral me towards exactly what she wanted me to know, and what she wanted me to know, was that the opposite of a psychopath was an empath, and that she believed I was one and the same.

Not bad for someone with English as their second language!

Her azure eyes continued to hold mine; projecting pride with her clever wordplay; or were they seeking assurance pride was warranted?

My bemusement must have presented as amusement because her smile remained in place, gradually stretching beyond what I thought was humanly possible.

What was going to happen next? Was she going to rock back in her chair and slap her knee in delight?

Was she going to chortle?

Was she going to say more?

I waited a moment. *No.*

Was she expecting me to respond?

It was a rhetorical question, wasn't it?

Did I need to provide her with an answer?

Perhaps I should say something – anything – just to break the silence …

My lips opened to speak, but nothing came out, my words and thoughts simultaneously frenzied and frozen.

I must have looked ridiculous.

She'd confounded me with the simplicity of her question, but I wasn't buying it so easily. How could I be sure of her theory, and that it wasn't just hypothetical hyperbole? How could I know if it was true? Was the opposite of a psychopath an empath, or was she fusing two disparate ideas at opposite ends of a spectrum that didn't really exist?

Or was she just embellishing the truth for effect in an effort to have me see my life in a new light; to teach me something new?

Was this part of the holistic view of the mind, body, and spirit she claimed to be expert in, or just another idea to rattle my thinking, and to − how did she put it − 'help promote new ways for me to process problems and information'?

That's why I was here, wasn't I?

But if the opposite of a psychopath was an empath, why hadn't I heard the word empath before now? Why hadn't it been a part of my university studies?

Was it because this empath thing was new psychology; a new theory formulated in the years since I'd graduated? Or was the concept pseudo-psychology, or was it possible that it wasn't even psychology at all?

I needed more information.

She'd described an empath as 'an emotional sponge who absorbs the feelings or emotions of others as their own', but how could that be true?

How could any person feel the feelings of others as their own, and not just their own feelings about someone else's? And, if an empath *could* do this, how could they tell the difference between the two sets of feelings anyway?

Sure, I'd had some bizarre experiences in Hong Kong with the chef and maître d' during the chopping ceremony, and again at the night markets with the distressed pets in cages and live seafood tortured in buckets, but anyone in those situations would have had felt the same.

I knew myself, and I was sure I didn't absorb and project others' emotions as my own … or did I?

Was my empath'ness the reason I couldn't answer the questions about what I enjoyed doing or what made me happy, or why I'd fallen into the relationships I had?

Had I merely been sponging emotions from others for my whole life, believing that their feelings were my own?

But how could a person *feel* the energy from people, animals, and the environment, and what if anything, did this have to do with the Dutch counsellor's discussions on eastern philosophy, dimensional perceptions, hypersensitivity, micro-expressions, and my dislike for reality TV shows?

I'd thought this empath concept was as simple as investigating my feelings and paying extra attention to them, but it was now appearing more complicated than that.

The clarity she'd intended to impart with her revelatory *ba dum tsh!* was starting to have the opposite effect, and her drumroll of questions, videos, scenarios, and speculations were now making as much sense as a record playing in reverse.

Sure, it made sense that psychopathy existed at one end of a spectrum just like everything else, and that it would have to have its opposite at the other, but wasn't the opposite of a psychopath simply a normal person; a normal person like me?

I was normal, wasn't I?

I continued to think on her various comments. Why was

she using the words psychopath and narcissist interchangeably? They were different disorders, weren't they? And if they were, how did narcissists play a role in all of this?

She'd said that the word empath was just a label, and that labels didn't matter; but she was still using it as one. She'd identified herself as an empath not just a minute ago, and it felt like she'd now identified me as one too … or was this a diagnosis?

Wait a second, was this actually a diagnosis?! Fuck!

Was this why the blue-suited counsellor suggested I come here? So that I could be diagnosed with my very own personality disorder?

I couldn't stop the questions and thoughts flooding through my mind.

If psychopathy was a personality disorder, then surely its opposite was too.

And if the opposite of a psychopath was a personality disorder, was there a cure? There wasn't a cure for psychopathy that I knew of, so surely there wouldn't be one for this either.

Did I need to be cured?!

I wasn't prepared to deal with this!

More questions surged through my brain, and my synapses exploded like fireworks, spewing chemicals to form new connections and obliterate old ones; recalling, recounting, and dissecting my experiences and learnings from the past nine or ten months, and then to the forty years before that, to determine how I'd ended up here, hearing what I was hearing, and thinking what I was thinking.

Stop!

I was doing it again, exactly like I'd done on the rooftop in the mall in Tokyo, when my now-ex-wife told me she wanted to live on her own, reacting instinctively, shutting out the present, and disappearing into the murky depths of my own mind.

I needed clarity to extricate myself from this quicksand, and I needed it quickly.

I refocussed on the smiling face sitting opposite me; faintly surprised that her eyes were still locked to mine.

How much time had passed? Was it a second, or was it ten? It felt like hours.

Say something! Anything!

I was on the precipice of a fall, teetering on the brink of an unknown abyss, holding on to the one thing I could be sure of. This silence had dragged on for long enough.

What could I say in response to her theory?

The idea of an empath was new to me, and I had so many questions to ask, but how could I ask them without sounding like I was challenging the idea, or being resistant?

Was I being resistant?

Less thinking, more talking!

"Ahem."

I cleared my throat to untangle my words and ideas, and to transition me back to the here and now, into her living-room-counselling-suite, and into the armchair I was sitting.

"I'm sorry, but can you please explain all that again? I don't think I understand this empath thing, nor how it differs from empathy, and isn't the opposite of a psychopath a normal person?"

Fuckkk!

My mouth was still tangled, and my words hadn't resembled any of the ones I'd wanted to say. Worse still, I'd popped her smiling bubble, and the golden cushiony glow generated by her adroit wordplay had been sucked from the room around us.

She was going to end this counselling session without answering my questions and banish me from ever returning.

She took a slow and purposeful breath and switched her stare to the space over my left shoulder; the ocean blue in her eyes transitioning to a darkening stormy grey.

She exhaled just as purposefully, preparing herself to start over.

"Let me ask you a question."

Please do! Ask me anything!

She paused to inhale and exhale again, seemingly arranging the words in her mind.

"Actually, rather than a question, let me try an analogy for you, but not a literal analogy … an analogy you can be lateral with. Do you know what I mean by this?"

Her voice was calm and patient, prompting me to sigh in relief. "Yes, I think I'm quite good at being lateral."

She flicked a sardonic glance my way, causing me to cringe at my over-confidence. It was a clear indication I'd need to prove myself before either of us could believe what I'd said was true.

She inhaled again to start over.

"Earlier, when I was in the kitchen, making us a pot of chamomile tea and you were out here, in this room; when I was pouring the hot water into the teapot; if I was to have an accident, and spill the hot water onto my hand and scald myself and shout out in pain, then you may have one or more different reactions."

I leant forward and nodded along, practicing all the active listening techniques I could muster to assure her I was keeping up with her this time.

"You may have a reaction, where you will feel sorry for me or pity for me that I burnt myself with the hot water; and you will know it will be painful for me. You will be sorry that it happened to me; and you may also be happy it did not happen to you. You may or may not offer to help me, but you will ask me if I am alright."

She looked at me with pleading eyes. "Do you understand this reaction, and do you have this picture in your mind?"

"Yes, yes I do, but it seems a little bit heartless."

A simple 'yes' would have done!

"I ask you to suspend your judgement as it does not yet matter if you think it is heartless. The reaction I described is called sympathy, and some call it condolence. It is your feelings about my experience, or someone else's experience, but in this scenario, it is your feelings about my experience of me burning my hand."

I didn't agree with the part about a person being happy

about her misfortune, but I kept nodding in agreement, wanting her to continue.

"Okay, yes, that makes sense. Sympathy – mine about yours."

"Empathy or an emp-a-thet-ic response is different as it will relate to your own knowledge of my experience, or a related experience, or even an imagined experience, and an emp-a-thet-ic response will usually have some sort of kindness. Not everyone has empathy, and those that do have it, have it across a wide spectrum. To replay the scenario, when you heard me yell out in pain, you may remember a time when you burnt yourself, or you may imagine what it was like to have scalded your own hand, and because of this, and because you have kindness, you will jump out of your chair to offer some assistance to help me, or you will ask me what I need to be better; or you may remember when someone close to you burnt their hand and what they did, or what you did to help them stop the pain.

"This is empathy. It is your imagined or recalled feelings about my experience as though my experience was yours, or that you were in my situation."

"To walk in your shoes?"

"A common way of describing empathy, yes."

She'd slowed her sentences, drawing out her words and had become staccato in the delivery and pronunciation of her syllables. Her eyes were again missile-locked onto mine, analysing my expressions and reactions to what she was saying, searching for the additional assurance she needed to feel confident I was keeping up with her.

"Yes, I think that makes sense, but I still don't understand where the empath bit comes into play."

Her face softened and she pushed her hands towards me, a gentle request for patience.

"Okay, so in this scenario, which I remind you is an equivalence only, and not real; in this scenario, an empath will have an emp-ath-ic response and will feel the sensation of the scalding hot water on their own hand, as if it is happening to them, as if their own hand is burning; and because of this physical sensation, they will have a reflex reaction to stop the pain in themselves by stopping the pain in the other – or maybe it is the other way around, but either way, it does not matter, and the result will be the same. An empath will feel the sensation – how you say – viscerally, real, in their own bodies, but they will not know it is not real for them, and because of this, they will act intuitively and immediately with what needs to be done."

"Are you saying that an empath—"

"Remember, I asked you to be lateral. I am not saying this happens in real life with something like burning hot water, although it can with clairsentients, and I do know people who feel the physical pain of other people. But if we put that to one side for the moment and turn our focus back to feelings and emotions; what I am saying is an empath feels the feelings and emotions, and energies for that matter, of other people as their own, whilst not knowing that these feelings and emotions and energies are not their own, and because of this; because they do not distinguish between what is theirs, and what is someone else's, they are quick to react, quick to jump in, and quick to help and fix things without being asked, to alleviate the pain that is not theirs to allev—"

She brought her hand to her mouth and coughed, two, three, four, five times. It was a long sentence and she'd run out of air, her larynx compressing beyond its limits.

I looked around the room to see if she had a jug of water nearby, which she didn't.

"Where is your kitchen? I'll grab you a glass of water."

"It is okay, I will be fine."

She coughed again and persevered to force the last few words of her sentence out. "Empaths are quick to alleviate pain that is not theirs to alleviate. In my example, if you can replace the physical burning with emotional burning, then you will know what I am talking about and I suspect you can now better relate to and understand what I am talking about."

Nope.

I didn't, and my lack of understanding was pulsating across my forehead from temple to temple, and back again so violently I expected she could see it through my skin.

To me, her telling me that I might be able to feel the feelings of others as my own, without being able to tell the difference, was the same as telling me that my thoughts may not be mine, and that my entire reality might not be real. And if either were true, then how could I possibly know what was true and real and what wasn't?

Despite my best endeavours to conceal my inability to understand her, she sensed it and continued. "As I said to you earlier, an empath feels someone else's feelings as their own. Empathy is remembering or imagining, and having feelings about those memories or imaginations, but empaths feel other people's feelings as their own, as if they are the ones having them."

I shook my head in frustration. Repeating the same words in a different order wasn't going to help with my understanding.

"If you remember my earlier point, it is important to understand that empaths may have empathy in this particular situation, or they may not. For example, in my analogy, an empath may think I am silly for not being more careful, but they will still act to help, but they will do so with or without kindness."

It was a fourth dimension to her analogy I didn't need, as the third still had me stumped.

"Empaths will believe what they are feeling is *their* feeling; and unknowing or unaware empaths have no idea it is not. 'Knowing' empaths learn to distinguish between their feelings and those of others, and more than this, they learn how to make conscious decisions about what they are feeling."

I needed to interject. "If what you're saying is true, how can they make a decision?"

"'Knowing' empaths learn to choose how they want to react. In many ways, whether the feeling is empathetic or empathic is irrelevant, but knowing how and when to react, or what we want to do next, is very relevant. It is not easy, but it must be done."

Her expression showed motherly concern.

"You are an unknowing empath, and I am here to open the door for you towards knowing. You can choose to walk through the door to investigate some more, or you can decide to do nothing with this information, and this will be okay too. There is no right or wrong way, and it is your choice; it will always be your choice."

I thought about what she'd just said, and it made no sense. "I'm not sure you are giving me a choice!"

"Think of me as offering you a red pill to uncover an alternative truth to your life, or a blue pill for you to remain exactly where you are. Which pill do you want?"

Without hesitation, I responded. "I'll take both pills please!"

She sighed. "I do not think it works this way."

I gave her an animated grin to let her know I was kidding, amused by my own joke, even if she wasn't.

She ignored me and looked towards her right, and through the leadlight window. "One last thing, and to complete my analogy; if we introduce psychopathy into this scenario, a psychopath will not care if I burned myself and may even be happy I did. They have no empathy, no kindness, and no conscience. They may laugh at my misfortune or do something else to cause me more pain, like hiding the bandages or pain relief."

Her deepening tone of voice suggested she was finished discussing this topic and that if I didn't grasp it this time around, then she had no other way of explaining it to me.

I desperately needed my laterality to kick into gear, but her analogy still sounded like science fiction, when what I wanted was more science fact.

I couldn't accept that some, or all of the feelings I'd felt until now, might have been other people's and not been mine at all, and I couldn't accept that my relationship failings could simply have arisen from me misappropriating the emotions of my partners, absorbing them as my own, or even worse, projecting them as mine towards them.

I needed more information so I could buy into her otherworldly premise, but before I could focus my thoughts on asking her a better question than my last, she got in first and asked me another one.

"Have you ever had the experience where you see someone hanging from a cliff by their fingertips and your own hands become tingling or sweaty? Or when you see spicy or salty food on a billboard or television commercial, and your mouth starts to water?"

Her mention of the words 'hands', 'cliff', 'spice' and 'food' were enough to trigger perspiration to wet my palms, and saliva to flow from my gums and into my mouth.

She spied me scraping the moisture from my hands onto my knees, her lips parting into a broader smile. "Seems you know exactly what I am talking about!"

I was familiar with what she was talking about and had a long list of physical reactions and sensations hardwired to images, words, and imaginations. My mouth drooled at the thought of salty fish and chips, and my face broke into sweat at the thought of any food that was spicy. My heart raced with an athlete's during a race, and I physically recoiled and winced in pain at seeing a hard knock, or injury.

But didn't everyone have these reactions?

"These experiences are heightened for empaths, but they do not have anything to do with *being* an empath. They simply demonstrate how thoughts, or observations, or feelings can bring on a physical reaction without needing to have an actual physical experience, and the same can be said for the emotional side. These types of reactions and sensations are to do with the autonomic nervous system and maybe being an empath does too …"

Her voice trailed off to silence, and she raised her left hand to her throat, possibly to prevent any more of her thoughts from being said.

Was this the science fact I was craving?

I needed to take greater control of the conversation, but my mouth was still a couple of steps behind my brain.

"You mentioned earlier that it doesn't matter what you think, and that the word empath is just a label and that labels don't matter, but what does all of this mean for—" Before I could finish my question, I slipped off the edge of my armchair, my knee hitting the floorboards, and my hand whacking the small wooden table between us.

She sprang towards me and grabbed the handle of the half-full teapot to prevent it from crashing onto the floor; leaving us both to spectate as the two empty teacups spun on their saucers until they came to a safe but skewed stop.

In my eagerness to know more, I'd converted my figurative precipice into a literal one.

"Are you okay?"

I looked up and smiled to let her know I was, and she responded with a full belly laugh, rocking back, and slapping both her knees.

"It seems I have your attention now!"

I levered myself back onto the armchair and grimaced in humiliation.

"You've had it since I arrived here for my first session last week!"

It was the truth, and regardless of how I felt about what she was saying, or my misunderstanding of the concepts of empaths and sponging emotions, a wisdom within her commanded my full attention, and my willingness to learn more.

I patted myself down, and after a few seconds of composing ourselves, she leant back in her seat, and I retreated into the safety of mine, pushing my spine hard up against the backrest to prevent another embarrassing incident. And then the words flowed, unstoppable.

"I want you to know that in the space of these past nine days, it feels like I've learnt more here than I've learnt during the past nine months, or possibly the nine years before that, but I can't say with any certainty that I understand any of it, or even if I did understand it, how am I going to apply it to my life. It's all new and interesting, and even if it doesn't make sense to me now, you've opened my awareness to my possible hyper-sensitivity—"

"Probable hyper-sensitivity," she interrupted, holding her right index finger to her lips. Was she shooshing me or shooshing herself?

"Okay, *prob-a-ble* hyper-sensitivity. And to the idea that there is no right or wrong, and to the notion there are different dimensional realities, and to the possible, or is it *prob-a-ble* narcissistic personality disorder in my ex-wife, and to this whole new empath thing, and whilst you've given me lots of information, and lots to think about, I still want to know more about what it means and what I need to do about it. How do I use it to change?"

The last remnants of her amusement at my slip and fall disappeared in an instant, and her expression again turned serious. What had I said to cause this abrupt reaction?

"What makes you think you need to change? You continue to search for answers on 'how' to be, when you just 'need' to be. You keep looking for the black and white, and right and wrong, when you could be focussed on the spectrum between them, and the full spectrum of life."

I was being lectured, and she wasn't yet finished.

"As I said to you last time, you do not *need* to do anything with this information; and in many cases, the best thing you can do, is nothing. It is what it is, and you are here to increase your awareness and be introduced to new ideas so you can consider them as they apply to you. I am here to show you new ways to process information. Think of me as a signpost at the fork in a road, an opportunity for you to walk a different path; but it is up to you whether you want to walk it or not. If you do, you might learn something new, but if you do not, then this is okay too, as I am sure you will learn something else. And if you do walk down one path, there is nothing stopping you from turning around and walking back to where you came from, or even creating a new path. Empath is just a label and labels do not matter."

She paused, allowing herself to catch her breath, and to give me a chance to process what she was saying.

Her repeated use of the word 'path' stirred memories of my walk down the Philosopher's Path in Kyoto. The lime-green sunlight dancing off cherry blossom tree leaves; the fire-engine-red window frames of the unexpected café; the children fishing for carp with tree branches, and the cicadas' vibrations through my body.

Their shrill shrieking had beckoned me from the Heian Shrine and accompanied me from the start to the end of the Philosopher's Path and back again, fracturing my thinking and alerting me to patterns of behaviour in my ex-wife that had been hiding in plain sight, patterns I'd not been conscious of, or had been ignoring and not paying attention to.

It was in the Heian Shrine gardens that I encountered a fork in the road with two signs on a post, one pointing left and the other pointing right. Both said the same thing, 'This Way'. Each path was different, but both led to the same destination.

I'd travelled to Kyoto begrudgingly that day and had felt as though the sun was setting on me, when in fact, it was just starting to rise.

Perhaps today was all about fracturing me again and alerting me to my own patterns of behaviour.

"I think I understand what you mean."

She smiled with a glimmer of hope.

"You cannot speed up this journey and you cannot fast forward your experience. You have heard new words and ideas today and this is the time for you to process them and tune into what they mean for you … or not.

"Let yourself experience the things I am talking about, rather than trying to make sense of them with words and explanations."

Easier said than done!

"Patience is not my strongest virtue," I protested. "In fact, it's probably not one of my virtues at all!"

"Good. This will be practice for you. To acquire patience, you need to practice it. Does this make sense?"

"Unfortunately, it does, but I still wish there was an easier way."

Patience aside, I still wanted her advice on what to look out for on this new path, and hoped she could point out a shortcut or two, just to hurry things along.

"If all this empath stuff is true, can you help me to identify when a feeling is mine and when it isn't?"

"Before we continue, can you please do something for me?"

Double bounce … or was it?

I stifled a sigh. "Sure, what can I do?"

"Can you stand up for me?"

Had I been slipping again?

I obeyed her command and stood up quickly.

"Now, close your eyes and relax your shoulders. Let them drop to where they feel natural and comfortable. They are currently too high, way up near your ears."

I did as she instructed, surprised by how much they needed to fall to be where they were supposed to be.

"As you do this, unclench your hands and stretch your fingers as wide as they will go, and as you do that, breathe in, to a count of three, hold for a count of four, and breathe out to a count of five." Her voice had become whisper-quiet. "Hold your head high but let your body relax. Think of a string tied to the crown of your head gently pulling you up."

I opened one eye to see if she was reading instructions, as the meditation teacher who guided me through my first class in New York a few months ago had used a similar phrase, except he'd asked us to imagine it was a fishing line. It seemed some aspects of this trade were global.

I did as she requested and as I relaxed and stretched myself out, it became apparent she'd noticed something I hadn't.

My body had been contracted and contorted, and as I tried to release it, I could feel my tension all over. My arms and legs had been folded, and folded again, and my hands had been tightly scrunched into fists. My hips felt fused to my pelvis and my torso felt like it was cast from concrete.

I squeezed my eyes tight and used her three-four-five breathing method to relax and breathe into what I was now feeling as full-body soreness.

After three cycles of breath, she interrupted the reverie I was drifting into.

"Okay, this is better. You can sit down now, but not too close to the edge. I like my teapot in one piece." She giggled.

I did as commanded, but as I settled my back into the chair, she directed her gaze towards my hands and knees.

My fingers had curled back into my palms, and my legs had automatically crossed as soon as my thighs had hit the seat. I hadn't consciously done either, but I guess that was her point.

Somehow, her silent instruction compelled me to override this reflexive action; to spread my knees and my hands wide across my legs, splaying my fingers as wide as they would go.

"Do you know how tense you are, and that you hold your tension in your neck, hands, and legs?" She used both her hands to gesture to the base of her skull, her waist, and knees.

Head, shoulders, knees, and toes, knees and toes …

"I do now."

The left corner of her mouth flicked upwards as she again dropped her gaze to my legs – crossed again – and my re-clenched fists.

Fuck!

"Sorry!"

She smiled more fully, and I tried again, reconfiguring my body into an alternative pose with my hands under my legs.

"Remember, mind, body, and spirit are connected. When one is out, the others will be out, and our body is very good at letting us know when something is not right. Your tension in your body is a sign of tension in your mind, and your clenched fists are defensive and fighting, resisting new information or maybe just holding on to the old. Your crossed legs are tying yourself in knots, or maybe I am tying you in knots as you try to make sense of something that does not yet make sense."

"You're right about that. I'm already struggling with this new path."

"Anyone who embarks on a new path does. It is unknown, and this creates tension because you want it to be known. Tension exists between where you are and where you want to be. Logically, if you accept where you are right now, then there will be no tension."

If only it was that easy!

Only now, as she was describing it to me did I realise how my physicality during our sessions had been unconsciously revealing. I didn't agree I was being defensive and fighting, specifically, but I was now alert to the tension and resistance in my body she was creating.

"Have I been like this the whole time?"

"Yes, much of the time, in both this session and the last, and you are like this again now."

I looked down and unfurled, increasingly frustrated that something so simple was proving so difficult to correct.

"You can rest your body to rest your mind. You do not have to do it the other way around."

I'd heard something like this before.

"Smile to be happy, not just when we're happy, yes?"

"Yes, a person can awaken happiness by smiling or better, by laughing. And you can relax by relaxing!"

"Fake it until you be it, hey?!"

She smiled and lowered her eyes for a third time, to my re-crossed legs and re-clenched fists.

Fuck it!

Of all the things we'd covered today, how was it that keeping my legs uncrossed and hands unclenched seemed to be my biggest challenge?

"Sorry, so back to the empath thing, and how it applies to me—"

"Oh yes, the empath thing as you call it. Have you read the Allegory of the Cave?

Am I ever going to get a straight answer from you?!

I shook my head. "No, I don't think I have, at least not that I recall."

"But you know of it?"

I wasn't going to guess. "No, I don't think so."

"Please look it up. Read it. It is relevant to you and will explain where you are right now, and what you are feeling."

"Really? It's a story about me being tense and confused in a cave?"

She smiled. "Your cave is built from what you think you know, and what you think you believe, but maybe you will not be there for much longer."

She shuffled in her chair and made herself comfortable.

"This is my version of the story, so it is not the same one you will read on the internet or in the original text, but it will suit my purpose for telling it."

With her legs crossed and hands clasped, she became still. "Okay, are you ready?"

"Sure, ready as I'll ever be!"

"Okay, so there is a group of people in a cave who are chained up to face the back wall of this cave. They are prisoners who have been chained up like this since they were born."

It was an intriguing start. "Why, what did they do?"

She waved her hand to dismiss my question. "This does not matter. It is not a true story, it only serves as an allegory. It is a metaphor."

She resumed. "It is dark in the cave, and the prisoners cannot see each other and cannot turn around to see the cave opening behind them, or the outside of the cave beyond the opening. All they can see is the back wall of the cave they are facing. Do you have this picture in your mind?"

I nodded, as it was pretty clear. "Yes, prisoners in a line, chained together in a dark cave; not sure why, but they're staring at the back wall."

She looked a little put out by my brevity, but continued.

"Okay. Behind these people is the cave opening and beyond the opening is everyday life. Normal people walk past to go about their daily business, doing what it is they do, day to day. Talking, working, shopping, playing music, dancing, and moving about. The exact details are not important, but what is important is that there is a lot of movement outside of the cave."

She stretched her fingers out on her right hand, bending them back with her left. "Due to the sunlight shining outside the cave, shadows of the people passing by the cave's entrance are projected onto the back wall of the cave, the same wall the chained-up prisoners are facing. The prisoners see all that is happening behind them as shadows on the wall in front of them. You have this picture?"

"Yes, I have it."

"In addition, all the sounds from outside the cave's entrance also echo off the back wall of the cave, making it sound as though the noises are coming from the shadows on the wall, and not from outside. Does this make sense?"

"No, it doesn't make sense, but I can understand how the prisoners think they are hearing the shadows."

"Okay. As the prisoners have not seen the cave entrance or the people outside it, when they see a shadow moving across their wall, they believe it is because of the shadows' – how you say – volition. When they hear conversations of the same people echoing off the wall, they believe it is from the shadows talking to each other. To the prisoners, the shadows are real beings. To the prisoners, the shadows are their reality, and their only reality. Do you understand?"

The story made sense as a story, even though it didn't make sense in reality. "I think so. The prisoners know no different so have constructed their own version of reality based on what they can see and hear—"

"And smell, feel, and taste; except they themselves have not 'made it up', it is their reality."

"But it isn't reality though, is it?"

"To them it is real, and what is more, it is their one and only true reality."

I wanted to roll my eyes but kept them fixed on her face. "Okay, I can accept it for the sake of this story, and provided it is not the end of the story. It isn't, is it?"

A grin spread across her face, and I got the impression that she was going to enjoy dragging out her point for as long as possible.

"No, it is not the end; it is still only the start. One day, one of the prisoners breaks free. She breaks her shackles and turns around for the first time, but as she does, she is blinded by the bright sunlight from outside. She shields her eyes and turns back to face the wall, fearful of being blinded again. She replaces her chains and focuses on the comfort of the wall in front of her.

"As time passes, her curiosity about the bright light behind her continues to grow, until she can no longer resist the urge to remove her chains and turn around again. And, as before, she is again blinded.

"Except this time, she perseveres with the blindness, and crawls on her hands and knees slowly and carefully towards the entrance of the cave.

"As her eyes adjust to the sunlight outside, she sees people and animals in three dimensions, and in full colour, and not just shadows of black on grey. She sees mouths move and hears the voices and sounds coming directly from those mouths. And as she becomes braver, she moves outside the cave. For the first time in her life, she feels the warmth of the sun and the wetness of water. She hears music and learns to dance. She eats new foods and drinks new drinks, and she learns how the light from fire creates shadows, just like the shadows projected onto her cave wall.

"It does not take long before she realises the shadows she had known for her whole life, were just shadows, and not the actual reality she now experiences. She realises that true reality was happening outside of the cave and not inside the cave as she had believed; that the reality of her fellow prisoners was not real at all."

Aha! So, this is where you are going with this!

I began to understand why she was telling me this story, and opened my mouth to confirm my understanding, but she cut me off with another one of her pushing motions: *wait.*

"Amazed by everything she learns and experiences, she returns to the cave to tell the others and to set them free from their chains, so they too can experience the true reality for themselves. But as she re-enters the cave, she is blinded by the darkness and cannot see. She stumbles around, and bumps into things, and falls over, cutting and bruising herself.

"The other prisoners see her blindness and injury as punishment from the shadows for escaping the cave, but the more she tries to explain that the shadows are not real, the more they shout her down. They call her crazy and do all they can to prevent her from speaking. As she continues to argue with them and plead for them to believe her, one of the other prisoners grabs her and breaks her neck to silence her."

As she spoke, the Dutch counsellor held out her hands and abruptly turned them in opposite directions, mimicking the breaking of a neck. "Crickkk!"

I sat back in my seat, shocked by the violent twist in her tale.

"Wow, I didn't see that coming! Plot holes aside, that's quite a dark turn of events! Those prisoners were the crazy ones considering she was telling the truth!"

"Crazy is in the eye of the beholder I am afraid, and the things called crazy by the loudest voices, are the things perceived in society as crazy. People's belief systems, especially about themselves and the reality in which they exist, are very powerful; and people do not like their realities being questioned, especially when they believe they are right. There are very few people in this world who will change their view of themselves when presented with new information."

I now knew for sure why she'd told me this story. A good story, well told, and a great metaphor.

"I hope I can be one of those few people," I said, slowly. "Sure, I don't like being wrong, but at the same time, I don't mind if it's an opportunity to learn something new."

She pulled at the hem of her emerald-green blouse and straightened its edges with her palms, an unconscious soothing gesture. I wondered what, if anything, I should take from that. She continued, with another question.

"So, how powerful are your belief systems about you and what you think you know about yourself and others?"

I pursed my lips to answer, but she didn't wait for me to muddle my way through, instead, uncharacteristically taking the lead for what she hoped I'd say.

"You need to work out if you are the prisoner who escaped, or the prisoner still chained to the wall. You came to see me because your wife left you, and so you could learn new ways to process problems and information."

Actually, I wasn't sure why I came here! But it – sort of – makes sense.

"Your ex-wife unshackled you almost a year ago, and during this time, you have dared to turn around a few times to see what is behind you; but each time you have been blinded by the light and have turned back around to the comfort of your shadows and chains, and to what you think you know to be your truth and reality."

Actually, I'm not sure that's true either!

"The question for you is: are you prepared to deal with temporary blindness in order to let your eyes adjust to a different reality and truth? Are you prepared to crawl out of the cave into the unknown of the unknown and not retreat again? Will you venture out to see what is there, even if you do not understand it, or cannot make sense of it? Even if it forces you to question everything you think you know about yourself? Are you willing to know the causes of your shadows? Are you prepared to find out what could be real for you, even if it is not real for others?"

I wanted to scream 'YES!' to her questions, like affirmative hallelujahs, but there was something about her cave story that wasn't quite gelling for me in the way she hoped it would.

With all her talk of shadows, realities, and temporary blindness, a contrary question was stirring into existence; a provocative line of enquiry that was now shining brightly at the entrance to my own cave; a question that could not wait for me to answer hers.

My brain was spinning. I swallowed away my inhibition and asked the questions I wanted answers to.

"Tell me, if we are all prisoners in caves of our own perceived realities, then surely it means that *none* of us really know what is true and what isn't, or what is real and what isn't. How, then, do we know if any of this is real? How do we know what is genuine and authentic and what is not? You speak of empaths and psychopaths and narcissists as true and real, but how do you know they are not just shadows of another reality being projected onto your own cave wall?"

She remained silent, so I kept going.

"For example, how do you know I'm not sitting in this armchair in your living room acting as an imposter? How can you know with any certainty that I'm not a narcissist pretending not to be, or that I'm not a psychopath posing as an empath? How can you be sure that what you're saying is true? How can you be sure that I'm an empath and not the opposite of an empath?"

Chapter 2

This time it was me eyeballing her with an intensity she couldn't escape. If she was going to ask me to question my reality, then I figured it was ok if I also questioned hers.

She straightened herself up in her armchair and reclasped her hands in her lap. *Listen*, her gesture implied: *this is important.*

"Do you remember earlier when I mentioned that empaths typically align with the Myers–Briggs INFJ preferences and traits, but that not all INFJs are empaths, and likewise, not all empaths are INFJs?"

Um … not really the rebuttal answer I was hoping for! Just another question …

"Yes, I recall."

"Well, it is widely believed by many psychologists that about half of INFJs exist on the psychopath side of the psychopath-empath spectrum."

Again, not the firm rebuttal I was hoping for!

"And as a psychologist, what do *you* believe?"

She laughed to herself. "I believe that INFJs are *the* spectrum!"

Huh? My brain was melting.

"You are familiar with the protagonists in World War II and the holocaust, and the events on September 11, and the mass loss of life in Waco, Texas, yes?"

"Yes."

"And with the leaders who fought for independence in India, civil rights in America, and the dismantling of apartheid in South Africa?"

"Yes, I know who you are talking about."

"And the prophets who gave birth to Christianity and Islam?"

"Yes."

"Well, each of these people have been typed with INFJ preferences and traits, and as such, each belongs to the same one percent of the population you and I belong.

"Do you understand what I am saying?"

I absolutely do not!

"No, I don't think I do, but out of curiosity, why haven't you used their names?"

"Names are just labels, and the events are far more important. We can talk about this another time, but the idea I want you to understand, is that people with INFJ traits are passionate, insightful, and persuasive. We are idealists who get caught up in the way things could be, and have many ideas on how to improve people, situations, and how to make the world a better place. Does this sound true for you?"

"Yes, it does!"

I was an idealist, but I was also a realist, which is why I rarely felt the impulse to share my thoughts with others. I enjoyed critical thinking and trying to see through the noise to a better end, or at least a better outcome, but frequently found that others didn't, which is why I kept my thoughts and ideas to myself. Did this explain why?

"Our idealistic nature manifests in many different ways, and our idealism can exist at either end of the psychopath-empath spectrum, and sometimes both. We are the best people in history, and are the worst, and can be seen as both at the same time, depending which side of the fence you are on."

What was she saying? That perhaps I am a psychopath?!

"INFJs are described as misanthropic philanthropists and philanthropic misanthropes."

Huh?

"Aren't they opposites? Aren't philanthropists, people who help and serve other people; and misanthropes, people who don't like people? Aren't they contradictory terms?"

"They are opposites, and they are contradictory, but this does not make the descriptions any less true. All people are contradictory, and the sooner you accept that, the better!"

No way was I going there. I disliked contradictions and hated hypocrisy.

She must have clocked the look of scepticism on my face, but chose to disregard it, continuing her explanation.

"If left unchecked, our idealism can be extremely powerful and can lift people up and tear them down. We can unite people behind a cause, and equally, we are capable of destroying anyone who is not behind it. Every war ever waged has been because of some perceived injustice: in a nutshell, because of 'what your father did to my father', and it *is* usually men who figure in these scenarios, but that is not the point. If we put all that to one side for a moment so I can answer your earlier question, there is a fine line between the two ends of the psychopath–empath spectrum, and I do not know with any certainty that you are not a psychopath pretending not to be. And in the end, I do not have to know. It is not for me to judge."

But it is for you to judge, that's why I'm here!

I tried not to let my impatience show in my voice. "I'd still like your opinion though."

"I have given you my opinion, but I think you do not like it, or at least, you do not understand it, which is why you continue to be resistant."

Was I being resistant?

"My opinion is based on the reality I currently know, and I know my reality may change at any time; however, for the moment, I can feel your feelings as my own, and I can feel you struggling with the idea of empaths, just as I did many years ago when I first heard about it."

Struggling indeed!

"Are you familiar with the law of parsimony; that the simplest answer is likely correct?"

"Yes, I think I have heard that before."

"Your life as an 'unknowing' empath may be the simplest answer for why you are here. Feeling the feelings of others and believing they are your own, may be the simplest explanation for why you are the way you are, even if you do not yet know how or why."

At last, she'd provided me an opening to learn more.

"Can you help explain the how and why?"

"Remember back to our last session when I described the different dimensional consciousnesses and realities? Where 3D is based in ego and judgement and thinking you know everything you need to know; and 4D is about questioning everything you think you know, and about deconstructing your realities, and where 5D is about acceptance and knowing all things are interconnected?"

"Yes, I remember."

"And last time you were here, you thought you were most likely in 4D."

"Yes, that's right, or at least I think that's right."

"Well, yes, that was right, and it is still right! This is a time for you to question everything you think you know about yourself, and for you to start exploring the reality outside your cave. The question you asked me about being an imposter is evidence you are already doing this. You must be willing to keep asking questions like this, but you must uncover your own answers within yourself, rather than continue to ask other people for theirs. You must uncover your own truth and must uncover your own programming."

So, remind me why I'm here again?

"The escaped prisoner I described earlier is like a philosopher. They are not afraid of the unknown, and do not accept what is in front of them as real or true. They keep questioning and questioning and questioning, without end. Each time you think you have an answer, you need to ask another question. Philosophy is not about obtaining truth; it is the endless search for truth. There is no end to this path, and if you start, you must accept it will never finish. This path is not for the faint hearted as it is vague and ambiguous. Is this something you can accept?"

Never finish? Perpetual ambiguity? Sounds foolish!

But I found myself nodding my head up and down even though I wanted to shake it from side to side.

"Think of the cave as your operating system, and your shadows as your programming. You need to uncover your own programming and your own operating system in your own time. And you are the only one who can do it."

Her use of the word 'programming' prompted a memory of a resolution I'd made a few months ago whilst lying in Parc des Buttes-Chaumont in Paris. It was under a conifer's billions of inky-green needle leaves that I'd resolved to keep vigilant to my programming and my habitual mistakes, and to make changes where I needed to.

I'd vowed not to take anything for granted and to question everything I thought I knew.

However, no sooner than I'd made the resolution, I'd forgotten it.

Since strolling out of the park, I hadn't given it a second thought, at least, not until now.

Was it even possible for me to discover my programming, if my discoveries would be limited by my programming?

My head started to spin.

We were drifting too far away from my core questions, and in particular my wish to better understand my life as an unknowing empath.

"I'm not sure I completely understand what you mean, but I'm willing to give it a go, one step at a time, and yes; to answer your earlier questions, I'm prepared to be blinded by the light and to turn more of my unknowns into knowns. So, please drag me outside the cave and help blind me. Tell me more about what it means to be an empath, and how not to cross the fine line into becoming a psychopath. If I haven't already!"

She smiled and clapped. "Oh good! You are familiar with the concept of known knowns, unknown knowns, and unknown unknowns!"

This time it was my turn to double-bounce, distracting her with a tangent I didn't want us to go on.

"Yes … and I'm also familiar with the idea of unconscious incompetence, conscious incompetence, conscious competence, and unconscious competence. But based on our discussion today, I now know that I have many more unknown unknowns than I knew I had!"

My tongue was as tied as my thoughts.

Had I said that right? And now I know I have many more unknown unknowns than I knew I had…

"Yes, I think I said that correctly."

She ignored me and continued her own train of thought. "The principles of the different dimensional consciousnesses and realities apply equally to the allegory of the cave. They cannot be taught, and likewise, the reality outside the cave cannot be taught. It is something you must experience in your own time, and when you are ready."

But I'm ready now!

"Ech hu gesot, mäi Wee wäert Iech kee Sënn maachen, well ech wäert sinn wéi wann ech mat Iech an enger anerer Sprooch schwätzen."

Her words had become gibberish, or was it my hearing?

I leant forward. "Sorry, what was that?"

"I said that my path will not make sense to you, as I may as well be speaking to you in a different language."

She laughed at my look of incomprehension. "It is my native Luxembourgish."

Luxembourgish?

"Think of me as the returning prisoner, and you are still in the cave."

I certainly am in the cave! I thought you were Dutch!

"You will not be able to understand my version of my reality, and you must find your own path, and your own way out. When you make your uncoveries, you will understand why it is difficult to share them with others, and why a person cannot simply be told such things. The understanding of the uncovery comes from the experience of the uncovery."

She was being duplicitous again, but I had a more pressing question.

"Why are you using the word uncovery instead of discovery?"

"Uncovery is about what is in here." She pointed towards her chest. "Discovery is about what is out there." She waved her hands over her head as if shooing flies.

"I saw you resisting the idea or existence of empaths earlier, but I see your curiosity now. You need to make your own uncoveries in your own time, or they will mean nothing; and if you stay wedded to the person you think you are, you will not be able to ask the questions you need to ask to peel back the layers of yourself to reveal the truth about your nature and who you really are. Can you embrace the fact that you may know nothing and that you may need to learn everything from scratch, from tabula rasa?"

"Blank slate? I hope so!"

"I hope so too. Everything you need to know is already in you; you just need to uncover it, in your own time and in your own way.

"You must respect the process."

"Funny story, I used to use that phrase at work all the time! I'd ask my team to respect the learning processes of others, and not to rush them."

"Exactly! So why can you not do it for yourself, if you ask others to?"

She had a point, but as I'd told her earlier, patience was my weakest link; and that wasn't something I felt I needed to uncover. I *liked* getting to my destination as fast and efficiently as possible, and I hated dithering and dawdling.

She picked up the teapot and used its spout to gesture towards my cup.

How long has that been sitting there? Surely, it's cold by now!

But I didn't want to appear rude. "Yes please."

She filled our teacups with the honey-coloured liquid of over-steeped chamomile flowers. Face-puckering astringency awaited.

As the fluid reached the rim of her cup, she whispered to herself, "Tao called Tao is not Tao. The path called the path is not the path. As soon as you are on the path, it is no longer the path. The path you seek is the pathless path."

Huh?

"I'm sorry, but what does that mean?! I'm barely on the path, but now you're saying I'm on the wrong path! And what on earth is a pathless path?"

"Never mind. This is also for another day, but you will know what this means in your own time."

I was beginning to wonder!

"Maybe you can treat this process like you would learning to ride a bicycle. Did you know balance cannot be taught; it can only be experienced through practice?"

"I've not thought about it. I learnt to ride a bike when I was five; one minute I couldn't do it, and the next minute I could."

"Exactly! No one can tell you how to do it, or show you

how to do it, and when you do it, you cannot explain how you did it. You cannot learn balance; you can only practice balance and you must trust your balance for balance to happen. I am sorry to say this, but the more you try and force yourself to balance, the less you will."

Was she being contradictory again, and had she forgotten I was here for counselling help, and not a philosophy lesson?

I was here for answers, not more questions. For the quickest way from A to Z, not the long way around via L, M, N, O, P.

Respect the process …

No!

I wasn't ready to concede. She'd been outside the cave, and I wanted to hear more about what she'd seen.

Could a change of tack work?

"Yes, I think I understand you; no one can teach you balance but there are some principles that can be taught, so I'd like to know more about the principles; about what I should look out for; and about how I can take more notice to learn my programming, and to know if my feelings are mine and not someone else's. Can you provide me with some stabilisers?"

She ignored me and continued with her previous train of thought. "Also, please be careful with who you talk to this about. Every narcissist and psychopath on this planet thinks they are an empath, and that they know other people better than they know themselves, and maybe some of them do, but they do it to take advantage of others, and not to help them.

It is the fine line I mentioned to you earlier, and I am only sharing this information with you because I know it will be helpful for you."

What information was she talking about? So far, she'd given me nothing!

I felt my tension rising as my patience was tested.

An eruption was imminent.

I steeled myself to be as forthright and as straightforward as possible.

"I just want to know what you know so I can take it away and think more about it!"

She looked faintly appalled, but quickly hid it with a wry smile.

"Know what I know?! Did you not hear what I explained earlier? You did not understand a simple word in my native Luxembourgish, did you? So how can you expect to understand *this* so quickly?"

If only you knew I'd thought you were from the Netherlands!

"Have you ever learnt another language?" she asked.

Another tangent!

"Yes, I learnt a little Italian through primary school, and some at high school; about five years all up."

"And can you speak Italian? Fluently?"

"No, not really. I can understand some words and I was able to get by with the basics when I travelled there."

She leaned forward to pick up her cup, pausing for me to catch up and follow her lead, but I didn't want to acknowledge the point she was making.

She sipped her tea, her face scrunching at the taste, before placing the teacup back onto the table between us. "Ugh! Terrible! Sorry about this. Too strong and too cold. I will make another pot soon."

Another pot? I'd lost track of time but if she thought we had time for another pot of tea then I wasn't going to complain.

"So, you studied a language for five years and you are not competent in it?"

"Yes, that's about right, but I can get by."

She paused again for me to put the pieces together, but I resisted making it easy for her.

"Okay, so rather than riding a bicycle, how about you think of our sessions as learning a new language. It is not possible to learn everything you need to know in just one or two hours. You must learn the basics, then you must learn to conjugate your verbs, then you can construct sentences, and then you must learn context and intricacies and jargon before you can be competent to have a conversation. Capisci?"

Italian too?!

"Ho capito … I understand, but how do I best start?"

"Like this: Tell me why you and your wife— I mean ex-wife got together."

Argh!

I couldn't hide my frustration or sense of deflation at her change of topic and let out an audible sigh. She was the teacher, and I was the student, and I wasn't going to get the responses I was seeking, at least not at the pace I wanted.

Rispetta il processo …

I had to trust she knew what she was doing, and also trust that learning more about empaths was probably going to have to wait for another time, but I had one last shot in me before giving up.

"Do you mean, *how* we got together? Because it feels like we've already been through that multiple times. I really don't want to spend more time on the past, as I want to know more about the empath stuff."

She seemed to be tiring of my persistent questioning of her questions, and the illusion of benevolent wisdom had faded from its earlier golden glow. Her voice took on a stern, matter-of-fact tone. "Not how. I meant *why*. You were single, and then you were not; so, I would like to know your reasons for why this happened."

Whilst not her intention, she'd succeeded in baffling me further. "I'm still not sure I fully understand your question, or how it relates to what we've just been talking about. Why does anyone do anything?"

"Exactly!"

"Exactly?" I gave her my best inquisitive look, but she stayed silent, unwilling to elaborate.

Her quiet resistance beat down my persistence. It was time for me to answer.

"I guess I'd been single for about three years by that time and probably had one eye open for a relationship for about half that."

"Yes, but why then, and more importantly why her?

You were in the UK working as an expat, and seeing the world, or at least seeing Europe, and she was in Australia in another relationship … or just coming out of one. Clearly, you had not needed to be with someone to enjoy yourself, or to be content, and if you did, then surely there would have been someone more … how do I say this … convenient?"

I'm sure you're right!

I smiled at her use of the word 'convenient' as it was a humorous truth.

"I don't think attraction works like that, or at least it doesn't work that way for me. I'd met her a few years before we got together, and yes, she was with her boyfriend at that time, so I left her alone, but there was something about her though … I can't tell you what it was because I don't know what it was, or at least don't know how to describe it. It was an invisible connection, something intangible and other-worldly. I guess that is what attraction is, something that can't really be explained.

"As I recently discovered, she was in a terrible headspace at that time due to her bipolar disorder, most likely somewhere between depression and mania, and although I didn't know it, and contrary to what my previous counsellor told me, I still don't think I suspected it."

"That was your discovery, but what was your uncovery?"

"What's the difference again?"

"Discovery is about her. Uncovery is about you."

I paused to take a breath and better connect my thoughts,

increasingly aware that there might be an answer to her questions in here somewhere.

"As I mentioned earlier, he hypothesised that I may be subconsciously attracted to people who need help, or who might need an escape from their current situation, and she fit the bill perfectly. Abusive relationship, unresolved family issues, bad financial position, career on the rocks, and diagnosed with a mental illness."

Winner, winner, chicken dinner!

She leant forward slightly and clasped her right wrist with her left hand. She spied me examining her gesture and dropped her eyes to my legs, smiling. "Did you know these things before or after your attraction to her had started?"

I was doing it again! I uncrossed my legs and clamped my now unclenched hands between my knees.

"I was attracted to her before I knew any of that, I think it was as soon as we met, but not in a love-at-first-sight kind of way. She had this vibe I liked being around, but because she was already in a relationship, I didn't pay any attention to the attraction. I didn't think we'd get to be together, so I put it out of my mind, but when the opportunity came up a few years later, I guess I jumped at it, or at least the memory of it. It felt like something I should do or should pursue."

She sat back and raised both her index fingers to her lips, tapping them gently. "The memory of it ... this is an interesting phrase, as is your use of the word vibe, as some may call this energy, but we will come back to that.

Energy? Was I absorbing her energy and projecting it as my own?

"Were you holding a flame for her during that time?"

"I don't think so, but I do remember thinking after meeting her, that if she ever showed interest in me, then I'd drop what I was doing to see where it took me, or where it could take us."

"This is another interesting phrase; however, I do not think you have answered my question. I would like to know why you wanted to drop everything for her. You told me how happy you were when you were overseas; and that you were quite content doing what you were doing. Why did you want to give that up?"

Her question seemed unfair, and I couldn't resist my compulsion to object.

"I don't think I *did* want to give that up. I guess at that time I wanted more; I must have wanted someone to share it with, but I honestly can't remember. It may have been because I'd recently turned thirty and I'd thought I should grow up and settle down with someone."

"And now? You are forty and have been single for almost one year, and you have started travelling again. Do you want someone to share this with? Do you want to settle down?"

Fuck no!

The thought echoed in my head so loudly I thought I must have verbalised it. But she made no response. I stared at the floor shaking my head slowly, wincing in imaginary pain at the thought of getting into another relationship. Eventually I pulled my thoughts into an answer of sorts.

"Much has changed between then and now, including me.

That period of time in my life seems surreal, and even though I've replayed it a thousand times in my head, I still can't explain why things happened the way they did, nor why I made the choices I made then—"

"This is exactly my point."

What point?!

Her nonsensical interjections were starting to irritate me, and I wished she'd just say what she needed to say.

Respect the process …

I took a deep breath and continued.

"Without hypnosis or better still a time machine, I'm not sure I will ever be able to go back to that time and remember what I was thinking and what I was feeling to cause me to do the things I did. That whole period, start to end is a blur, like a dream within a dream, and the more I try to remember it, the more it seems to elude me.

"The one thing I do remember quite vividly is that my feelings and emotions back then were incredibly intense, almost primitive, and so physical, and I guess, at that time when she sent me her flirty text to start our relationship, I had no reason not to give it a go and to see where it took us."

"Had you felt this way before?"

"I think so, at the inception of each of my other failed relationships; and before you ask, my feelings at those times definitely felt like they were mine, even if they felt foreign."

She shuffled in her chair.

"If you had felt their feelings as your own, would this be an explanation?"

I still wasn't buying what she was selling. "I guess so, but only if I was able to validate that their feelings at the time were as intense as mine, and I have no way of doing that or knowing for sure."

A sudden weariness overtook me, and I wanted to rub my eyes but refrained.

"That being said, I was all-in from the very start. From 4:44am that morning, my ex's text turned me upside down and inside out. It was like she flicked a switch in me I didn't know I had, and after it was on, I had no sense of what 'off' looked like."

"4:44am, you said?"

"Yes, I remember the symmetry of the timestamp on the text. I guess it would have been 3:44pm her time. Why, is that important?"

"This is only important if you believe in numerology or angel numbers. Four four four is a signal to pay attention to your intuition and inner wisdom."

I couldn't restrain a guttural scoffing sound from escaping my throat.

Numerology? Angel numbers? I don't think so!

She ignored my noises and continued.

"Do you remember what your intuition was telling you at the time?"

"I can't, but if I was to guess, I suspect it was telling me to run a mile in the opposite direction!"

She smiled and nodded and gave me a thumbs up.

"It's as though I have no normal speed in relationships; I

have one thousand miles per hour or complete standstill, and there's no in-between, and I think I've always been that way, through all of my relationships. Perhaps it's the esteem thing you mentioned earlier. Perhaps, when people show interest in me, and when they boost my ego, I give them everything, and when they do the opposite, I slam the door shut on them."

I was getting tired. None of this was new information.

"Or perhaps, the simplest answer to all of this is yours; that we were simply two polar opposites attracted to each other with an invisible magnetism; her psychopath to my empath. It may have been all we were, a bunch of protons and electrons, lining up and doing their thing. And maybe this is true for all my relationships. Me just loving them for loving me, like a magnet would a piece of iron, guided by its molecules, unable to do anything different."

I'd run out of sensible things to say and found myself passive-aggressively poking fun at her earlier theories.

She didn't answer, seemingly unfazed, and her expression seemed to brighten. I wondered if she might actually be *encouraged* by me repeating her earlier words.

I paused to take another slow three-four-five breath and ran my fingers through my hair. A shudder emanated from the base of my neck and travelled upwards past my ears.

My hair was thinning, and I didn't like it.

"Have I told you what I did as soon as I got back to Bristol after our first few weeks together in Brisbane?"

She shook her head and looped her necklace around her left index finger. "No, you have not. What did you do?

I closed my eyes and squirmed for bringing it up.

Idiot!

I took a deep breath and exhaled. "I resigned and started packing my things to return to Melbourne."

Her widening eyes revealed her surprise. "From your job? From the UK, to come back to Australia? Why?"

"Yep, after a fortnight with her, I resigned from my job, and from the whole life I'd been creating to that point. I was earning more money than I knew what to do with and I had everything paid for me by my employer, and yet, after just fourteen days, I was fully committed and prepared to throw it all in and give it all away for her."

"I am not sure I understand. You were on a contract, yes? How long had you been there?"

"About eighteen months, and I had eighteen months to go, although I could have probably stayed indefinitely or possibly moved to another country after that. Actually, come to think of it, I'd already been asked to move to Sweden, or perhaps that offer came later, I can't remember—"

"And you resigned, to give it all up for someone you had been with for two weeks?"

I rolled my head from shoulder to shoulder to loosen the tension that was rebuilding in my neck and jaw. "Yep, and yep."

"Did you not just tell me that you wanted someone to share your travels within Europe? How was resigning from a job in the UK, which is a great place to travel from, going to achieve that?"

I shrugged like a three-year-old caught out in a lie, except I wasn't lying.

"When I left her at the airport in Brisbane, she'd told me that she didn't want to move to the UK as she wasn't ready, but that she'd been thinking of moving to Melbourne for some time before we met, and that we could arrange to meet there for us to be together.

"In the end, I guess it didn't really matter. She changed her mind, and I was able to change mine. I stayed with the company, but in a different job, and she joined me; and we travelled, and we got engaged, we came home, we got married, so, I guess it all worked out in the end."

She shook her head and clenched her jaw, apparently trying to prevent herself from saying what she wanted to say. Regardless, she was making her point anyway.

"We shall talk more on this later, but as you mentioned it, tell me the story of why you went to the UK in the first place."

Another why?! What's with all the whys? Didn't I say I need a how, not a why?

I needed to do something with my hands to stop them clenching into fists. I scooped the teacup off the table between us and tipped half its cold and acrid contents into my mouth, restraining an almost unstoppable urge to spit it out across the table and all over her.

She looked horrified that I hadn't learnt from her earlier tea-sipping mistake but again stopped herself from saying anything. Slightly ashamed of the violence within me, I continued my story.

"Well, this is interesting, in a way. You see, the truth of it was that I didn't initially want to move to the UK—"

"Sorry?"

"When I was asked by my manager, I said no, then she asked again and again, and I kept saying no and no. That went on for a few months, but in the end, it was a night out at dinner with friends that changed my mind, even though I'd believed no one could."

She looked confused. "How did they change your mind?"

Based on her reactions to the past few minutes of conversation, I was pretty sure she wasn't going to like my answer.

"My friends convinced me that I didn't have a reason not to go."

Her stare became more intense.

"No reason not to go? And before, you said you had no reason *not* to be with your ex-wife. Too many double negatives in what you are saying."

I raised my eyes to meet hers in rueful acknowledgement. My previous counsellor had called me out for the same thing. "Seems I do that a lot."

"So, you went to the UK because you did not have a reason not to?" She tapped her right index finger on her left.

One.

"Yep, I had reasons I wanted to stay in Melbourne, but no reasons not to go to Bristol, and with no reasons not to go, it seemed like an opportunity I should take up."

"And you had no reasons you can remember as to why you got together with your ex-wife, other than some invisible something?" She tapped her finger again.

Two.

"I'm not sure that's fair, but yes, it seems I have no good reasons for anything." She was wearing me down, and I was battling to curtail my flippancy.

"And if I asked you why you stayed with your ex-wife, what would be your reason for this?"

Tap.

Three.

"Oh, I have a reason for that! It was out of obligation and trying to do the right thing—"

"The right thing for who … or is it whom? I can never remember."

"The right thing for her, and for us. I promised I'd stick with her, and I wasn't going to break that promise."

"Why not?"

"Because she was sick, and she needed me, and that's not who I am. If I commit, I commit, and I don't abandon things when they get difficult. If I make a promise, I keep it. If I pledge to be with someone through sickness and health, then I will see that through."

"That sounds very noble of —"

"I wasn't trying to be noble; I just think people give up too easily and that they should sometimes stick with things beyond the shiny new phase."

"So, there were no reasons for you to stay, just reasons for you to stay *for her?*

Not fair!

"And if I ask you why you got together with your previous partners, or why you chose the career you did, or the university courses you studied, or the friends you have, do you think your answers will be similar?"

Tap, tap, tap, tap.

Four, five, six, seven.

My energy was waning, and I didn't have enough in my tank to interrogate my memories of each situation individually, so I gave her the answer she was angling for.

"I guess so. I guess I've always done what I thought was right at the time, or what I thought I should do in any given circumstance."

"There is this word again."

"What word?!"

"'Should'. You use the word 'should' a lot. Did you know this?"

"No, not really."

"There is an unconscious substitution happening when you describe your actions. Each time you use the word 'should', you use it in the place of the word 'want', so in a way, saying 'should' conceals your fundamental desire, by covering it with the *opposite* of what you wanted to do at that time."

Neurolinguistic programming again?

"Is that right? I think my whole life is full of shoulds!"

"I think you are quite right about that!"

She smiled with an attempt to comfort me as my life felt

as though it was being shredded into ribbons onto her living room floor.

I couldn't ignore the truth of her observation. All-too-often I felt I was living my life to the expectations of others, as a witness rather than a participant. It was as though I was watching myself as a character in a play, following a script that was being written for me in real time, based on the reactions of the other characters, as well as the audience's expectations.

"You know, I think I tend to live my life by going with the flow."

She looked towards the window and opened her mouth to reply, but suddenly made a choking sound, before slumping forward in her chair, and coughing uncontrollably.

I set my teacup down and jumped out of my seat to help. "Are you okay?"

It was as though an insect had flown into her throat. She gestured with a wave of her hand for me to sit back down. As she struggled to breathe, I cleared my own throat in reflex.

"Actually … this is not true for you and may be the opposite of the truth." *Cough!* "Going with the flow is a mindful intention of acceptance, to maximise your life's experiences." *Cough!* "It is something done with purpose so you can live your life to the fullest." *Cough!* "Flow is about embracing things not in your control and letting go of your shoulds." *Cough! Cough!*

She took a moment to rub her throat and to catch her breath before continuing with her admonishment. "You do not have flow. Your life is about force and resistance, about cause and effect. You have no intentions for yourself, and you seem to be holding on and waiting for some better future."

Well, fuck!

Why don't you tell me what you really think?!

Chapter 3

I brought my hand to my throat, unconsciously mimicking her, or possibly, to restrain the defensive retorts crowding my throat.

"Actually, let be more clear. Your life at this moment, is about your lack of intentions for yourself. You have intentions for others, but not for you. You are full to the brim with intentions, aims, and purposes for other people, but very few, if any, for you." She pointed her right finger aggressively at me. "Such a caring person. You are happy to maximise the experiences for others, but not yourself. Why do you think this is?"

Her follow-up assessment again knocked the wind out of me, so I shrugged my shoulders to buy time to see where this was going.

"I do not say this to criticise you, as my purpose is to increase your awareness to yourself, so you can consider new ideas as they apply to you. Remember my Taoist farmer story;

there is no good or bad, or right or wrong, there just is what is; but beyond this, there is what we choose to do with it."

I released the grip on my throat and blinked away the tears welling in my eyes from her choking incident.

"If there is no good or bad, or right or wrong, then why is it beginning to feel like I've been living my life all wrong up until now?"

For the third time this session, our eyes were again locked to each other's in silence; mine pleading for a small sliver of hope that I hadn't fucked up *everything* in my life, and hers blank as she formulated a response I could better comprehend.

During our two sessions together, she'd injected me with a serum of new information and awareness, of hypersensitivity and hyper-perception, and of dimensional consciousnesses and varied realities.

She'd told me stories about narcissists and psychopaths, empaths and philosophers, and shadows and caves, but little of it was coming together as an antidote to the poisons of what I believed to be real and true.

She cleared her throat to respond, that discreet sound snapping me out of my head. "You asked me earlier to tell you more about empaths; about some of the principles, and what you can do to learn more about your programming."

My eyes widened, and I bolted upright in my seat.

"Yes, yes, I did!"

My relief was overwhelming: she *had* been listening, after all. Was she finally throwing me a bone? Had my persistence finally beaten her resistance? Was my little pity party going to get me some of the answers I was craving?

How much time did we have left?

Our session had to be in its second or even its third hour, but as she didn't seem concerned or hurried, neither would I.

I returned to the edge of my chair, feet planted firmly on the ground, elbows on knees, and hands clasped together. She had my full attention, and I wasn't going to miss a word of what she was going to say next.

Ready! Go!

"Let me start with a most basic question. Do you know the most significant difference between a psychopath, and an empath?"

My cheeks contracted with the irony of her question. "I still don't know what an empath is, so I think my answer is a safe no!"

She shook her finger at me. "You know more than you think you know; it is all within you."

I shook my finger back at her. "I wish that were true, but – so to speak – I'm still chained up in the cave, I'm afraid!"

She shuffled back and crossed her legs to resume her earlier storytelling pose, our cold half-full teacups still on the table between us.

"You will notice that I use the words psychopath and narcissist interchangeably, but they are not the same thing."

"I did want to ask you about that earlier."

"They are different personality disorders; however, both exist at the opposite end of the empath spectrum, and for this purpose, this is all that matters.

"I do not want to dwell too much on the descriptions of psychopaths or narcissists as we are not here to learn about them, but it is important for you to recognise their traits, so you can better recognise yours.

"I will show you some of the people outside your cave so you can start making more active decisions for yourself rather than passive decisions for everyone else."

She stopped abruptly to draw breath.

"Okay, that sounds like a plan."

It was time for another drumroll.

"The single most significant difference between psychopaths and empaths is this: psychopaths have no conscience for other people; but unknowing and unaware empaths have no conscience for themselves. Psychopaths destroy other people for themselves, but an unknowing empath will destroy themselves for other people. It is very important you understand this because it is central to everything else."

It was an interesting point, and one I hadn't previously considered.

"Do you think you have a conscience for yourself?"

"I'm not sure how to answer that. I'll need to come back to you."

The intensity of her stare suggested I already knew the answer, and that I was kidding myself if I thought it was anything other than a 'no'.

"A psychopath has many victims, but an unknowing empath usually has only one."

"Let me guess … themselves?"

She nodded. "A psychopath has no limit for how much they will take from other people, and an unknowing empath has no limit for how much they will give, so in a way, they are a perfect match for each other; a perfect, yet destructive match. Do you see yourself as a giver or a taker?"

"A giver, I suppose. But I do it subconsciously, as to me it's normal, and I can't say I give it much attention."

"Yes, and this is a big problem for these types of relationships as the unknowing empath does not know they are giving, not until the moment they have no more to give. Have you ever reached this point?"

A thousand times!

"I have. There were several times during the last year of my marriage where I'd felt the final drops of energy drip out of my body and I'm kind of feeling it again now. It's a primitive feeling of emptiness and hollowness, even helplessness."

I pressed my hand into my stomach, and into the void that was opening within it.

"You need to recognise this before it happens, so you can stop it from happening."

"Your colleague who referred me here didn't mention anything about psychopaths or empaths, but he did mention that narcissistic personality disorder can sometimes be misdiagnosed as mania in bipolar, and we both know who was diagnosed with that!"

"Yes; this can be true, and sometimes the two will

coexist together, with symptoms of one presenting as the other. Antisocial personality disorders are very difficult to diagnose because the people with them do not see their traits as problems." She drew a quiet breath, before proceeding: "Narcissists and psychopaths have exaggerated self-importance and an excessive need for admiration."

Aren't they the traits of most politicians?

"They both value power and control, and they will take advantage of most people around them to get it and exert it."

Yep, I think you're still describing most politicians …

"Keep alert for signs of arrogance, contempt, and a distorted sense of self. Narcissists and psychopaths value themselves over all others and disregard the wishes and feelings of everyone else. They expect to be treated as superior, regardless of their achievements or status."

And now you're talking about most Presidents and CEOs …

As she continued to speak, I rewound through my memories of me as a manager, assessing my own values and behaviours for examples of the traits she was describing.

"Narcissists cannot tolerate criticism and will aggressively turn the tables when they are criticised. A person with this disorder cannot have meaningful relationships or friendships.

"It is rare to encounter anyone who identifies as having one of these antisocial personality disorders, because they view all others as inferior, including the professionals who are able to make the diagnosis."

She fell silent for a moment, before finishing with:

"Anyway, you can read more about this online, but for someone to be diagnosed, they need to frequently meet at least five of nine diagnostic criteria."

I must have looked as though I'd zoned out because she seemed to cut her descriptions short.

I needed to apologise for letting her down with my inattention.

"I'm sorry. I was listening, but at the same time I was trying to work out if I've exhibited any of the behaviours you were describing. Some of the things you mentioned, I find myself constantly worried about. Like coming across as contemptuous or arrogant. I know I have no right to be. Or being seen by colleagues as patronising or condescending. That's not my intention, ever. Worst of all, I'm petrified of making someone feel like I'm gaslighting them."

"Ah, so you are familiar with this term, gaslighting?"

"Yes, I know it and I think it's a horrible thing to do to a person. Making someone doubt their own mental state or sanity is an awful thing to do."

"It is an awful thing, so I must ask you, why do you do it to yourself?"

Huh?!

Her question pinned me back in my seat.

"Gaslighting is a tool used by narcissists and psychopaths to obtain psychological advantage over someone else. You know that. But what you might not know is that it is also used by empaths to doubt themselves, and their own psychology, and you seem to be doing it right now."

I am not! Am I …?

"Try not to criticise yourself for past mistakes if there is nothing you can do about it, and do not distrust your positive intentions. If you need to take action to change, then take action, but if you cannot, let it go. Anything else you do to yourself is not helpful and is a form of self-harm.

"Earlier you asked me if you were a narcissist or a psychopath pretending not to be, and if you were the opposite of an empath."

"Yes, and I was worried about your lack of direct response!"

"Can you now see the fine line of similarities and differences between the two? Can you see that you are not a psychopath, but that your attitudes, behaviours, and beliefs towards yourself may be similar to how a psychopath views others?"

Her evaluation was confronting and made me writhe in my chair.

"I don't think I am gaslighting myself; it's just that I'm overly introspective and like to think about things until I can be completely sure of myself … or at least more sure than unsure; but I do constantly worry about how my words and behaviours affect other people, and I fear being perceived as gaslighting when I'm trying my hardest not to."

She seemed sympathetic to my explanation, or was it empathetic, or even empathic?

"I spent my entire marriage being hyper-vigilant with my words and my actions as I never wanted to undermine my wife, and never wanted to blame her condition for her behaviour, or blame her for having the condition, but at the same time, I'm not sure I was always successful with that aim. This must be one of the reasons I find it difficult to participate in conversations and to communicate my views freely. I am forever worried that I will come across in an unintended way."

"You live your life through the eyes of others, yes?"

"Yes, I think I do."

"You will benefit from reading about the psychoanalytical constructs of ego, the id, ego and superego, and also about the theories on the competing selves, the ideal, social, perceived, and actual." Her words rang bells from my past life as a psychology student, but none of them produced any revelatory insight. "This can be your homework."

Homework?! It really was like being a student again.

I nodded. "I will, thank you."

I knew I needed to take her advice as all of my strongest memories over the years were of interactions I wished I could change; wrong words, wrong tone, wrong expression, and wrong body language. They weren't even of interactions where things had gone egregiously badly because they rarely did; they were simply interactions where things could have gone *better*, or where I would have felt better for them happening differently.

The memories would pop up from nowhere, without warning, reason, or purpose, and they'd play over and over, like broken records. Sometimes, they'd strike in times of silence, and other times during unrelated activities or conversations. They were like mosquitos, annoyingly in my face, and capable of inflicting real pain. I summoned up one of them – twenty years old, but still stinging, so I could tell her about it.

"There's this one memory that just won't leave me alone. It's small and almost irrelevant, but I can't get rid of it.

"I was about twenty-eight and I'd just been promoted at work, so the people I'd considered to be peers were going to start reporting to me, as their manager. Titles and hierarchies were, and still are unimportant to me, and I didn't want anything to change."

"So, what happened?"

"Rather than leave things the way they were, I spoke with each of my colleagues to let them know that I wanted our working relationship to stay as it was."

"Sounds like a positive thing to do."

"It wasn't. Whilst two of the meetings went well, the third meeting did not, and ended with me being called condescending and patronising. Those words were like a spear through my chest, and if I'd overanalysed myself up to that point, I've overanalysed my overanalyses ever since."

I grabbed at my heart as if the spear was being twisted for the millionth time.

"The crazy thing about it is that we'd been great friends before that meeting, and we're still great friends today."

"Have you asked them about it?"

"Yes, I recently built the courage to ask her what I could

have done differently, and long story short is that she has no memory of it happening.

"Whilst I continue to carry it around, she has no recollection of it; and not only that, she can't believe my version of it had. Regardless, it hasn't changed the way I feel. I still wish I'd not said anything at all."

"So, who has been suffering all this time, you or her?"

"Me."

"And to what end? She told you she does not remember, so why are you still holding onto it? This is the self-harm I mentioned earlier. You are gaslighting yourself, doubting yourself, and you need to stop doing this."

"I'll try."

"Not try, do!"

"Okay, I will dooo!"

But I had my doubts. It was a logical way to approach it, but for whatever reason, logic played no part in the way my memories made me feel.

"Anyway, enough talk about gaslighting, and back to the principles, and what you can do to learn more about your programming."

"Oh yes! I'd almost forgotten!"

How could I have almost forgotten?

"I can offer you three pieces of advice to help guide you on your path, to help you balance on the bicycle, or learn this new language."

I leant forward again, this time like a slips-fielder in the first overs of a cricket match, fired up and ready to catch whatever information she sent my way.

"Firstly, and I think this will come as no surprise to you, you must pay more attention to your own wants and needs, and to what it is you want from your own life and experiences. You need to become a proactive participant in your life rather than a reactive bystander.

"Empath or not, you cannot keep living your life for others, within the realm of ideals and shoulds. It is unsustainable, and I am surprised you have not broken yet."

I grinned at the thought. "That's quite an assumption! What makes you think I've not broken yet? I am here, aren't I?!"

She ignored my light-hearted quip and continued. "Develop clear reasons for the decisions you make. In other words, the *why*. You do – and have probably always done – things by reflex, or because you think you should, or because it is a part of some grand plan or scheme you set for yourself many years ago, or more recently, because you said, 'I do' at an altar. These are not good reasons, or at least, not *sufficient* reasons, even if you think they are."

I thought there was no such thing as good or bad …

"You went to the UK because your manager and friends thought you should go. You started a relationship with your ex-wife because she sent you a text message, and your other relationships may have started because you reciprocated their feelings towards you. It seems you did not seek any of these things for yourself with any specific intention for you.

"I am sorry to say this, but your ex-wife may have been looking for a quick and easy exit out of her existing relationship and into a new life. Maybe she manipulated the situation to get what she wanted. Maybe she found a giver and knew there was no limit to how much she could take."

You may be right!

Her appraisal wasn't as revolutionary as the tone of her voice indicated she thought it was; rather, it was a partial confirmation. The idea had crossed my mind many times both at the start of our relationship and again at the end, but I wasn't sure I agreed that I *only* did things because other people wanted me to do them. Sometimes I did things because I had no excuses not to.

"Doing something because you do not have a reason not to, is also not a reason to do something, even if it feels that way."

She smiled at me, knowing she'd just read my mind.

"You told me last week that you can feel other people's intentions more than their words, but what are yours, for you?"

"That's the million-dollar question!"

"So, find the million-dollar answer! Knowing your intentions will help you make decisions more consciously and purposefully. Your version of 'going with the flow' is to let others make your decisions for you, either directly or indirectly. My advice to you is, do not let them. Do not make decisions because you have made them that way in the past. Pay more attention to what is going on around you and within you. Be conscious of what you are doing, what you are thinking, what you are feeling, and then make your decisions accordingly.

"You must be prepared to say no."

A novel idea.

"Try to think back to the way you lived your life when you were travelling in Hong Kong or New York, consciously and purposefully, deliberately experiencing new things. As it stands now, you are on autopilot and living your life to a predetermined plan."

Sheesh! What are you talking about lady?

I thought I'd lived my entire life with my eyes wide open and I was present each time I'd made a decision. I was conscious after all, and I made my decisions on purpose, and I was quite sure I made the best decisions for me at the time I made them, based on what I knew and what I wanted—

You're ranting again. Respect the process ...

She leant forward and tilted her teacup to look into it to see if it had magically filled with fresh tea, which it had not. "Speaking of Hong Kong and New York, I would like to ask you another question. Tell me, where was your *first* overseas trip, and what is your best memory of that time?"

Another tangent!

"Paris."

"Such a beautiful city."

"Actually, it wasn't Paris, it was Llanelli, or Cardiff if I was to split hairs; however, Paris was the second, or third overseas city I visited during that trip, but it was the first city I visited as a tourist."

"Wales to get to Paris? Why did you not fly direct or via London?"

"I'd flown to Wales from Melbourne to visit my mum's side of the family—"

"Are you Welsh?"

"No, not Welsh, but my mum's side of the family emigrated there before I was born, so I hadn't met most of them before that trip. Going over to see them was something I thought I *should* do." I gave her a wink to let her know I was half joking.

"How was it meeting them for the first time in adulthood? Was it a good trip?"

How am I going to get off this tangent, and back to her advice? Better just play along.

"It was a great trip, and knowing how wonderful they all were, played no small part in my final decision to move to Bristol nine months later, even if spending more time with them wasn't my overriding *reason* or *intention* for doing so."

She interrupted. "At some point in the near future, we will talk more about families and about how all the answers about your programming exist in your nature and nurture."

"I thought the debate was nature versus nurture?"

"This is what many people believe, and want you to believe, but my position is this; why not focus on both for a holistic view?"

"Why not indeed?!"

"We get too caught up in dichotomies, and lose focus on the full spectrum, and by concentrating on the two ends, we lose our focus on the bigger picture. Anyway, before we get too far off track, how does this trip connect to Paris and your best memory of that time?"

"Paris is Paris! What's not to love?!"

As it was my first time on the other side of the world, I'd asked my travel agent to arrange a twenty-four-hour stopover for me on the way home. I'd asked him to book Rome but as there were no direct flights from Cardiff Airport, Paris became my more-than-adequate consolation.

I had no map and no plan for what I wanted to see or do there. I was just happy to spend the time in a new city and to see what I saw, when I saw it, and was confident I'd bump into the Eiffel Tower at some point during the day.

I set myself two rules for my stay; the first was to remain on foot the whole time, and the second was to stay out and about until I needed to be back at the airport for my return flight to Melbourne.

At that time, I was blissfully unaware that I was going to be offered an expat assignment four or five months later, so twenty-four hours in Paris felt like a once in a lifetime opportunity and I didn't want to waste a second of it inside a hotel.

From my starting position in the 15th arrondissement, my first stop was the Eiffel Tower, as I could see its spire from just about every street corner; however, it was by dumb luck that my random zigzagging of lefts and rights teleported me into the middle of the Champ de Mars.

I'd been busy staring at the meticulously cut straight edges of the plane trees on Avenue Charles Risler, when I reached a clearing, and the top-to-bottom view of the iron monument in all its autumnal glory.

After taking dozens of photos, I climbed the seven-hundred-odd stairs to the middle platform to stop and take in the view, and I remember thinking three things as I walked over the nord, est, sud, and ouest corners of the tower.

The first was that I wished I hadn't climbed the stairs as my knees were already starting to hurt; the second was that Sacré Coeur looked too far away to walk to; and the third was that Paris' most quintessential landmark was nowhere to be seen; because I was standing on it.

After descending the stairs back to ground, I meandered across Pont de Bir Hakeim before doubling back on the other side of the Seine, crossing again at Pont de l'Alma, and again at Pont des Invalides to enjoy differing perspectives and views.

I walked down Avenue Franklin Delano Roosevelt, and with more dumb luck, arrived smack bang in the middle of the Champs-Élysées.

From there it was an easy stroll to the Arc de Triomphe and back again towards Place de la Concorde, but without a map, I hadn't realised that Jardin des Tuileries was just beyond the obelisk, instead turning right to recross the river, and eventually finding myself in Saint-Germain-des-Prés, sipping on the worst coffee I'd ever tasted. How it was made to taste like soap, I still don't understand.

During that most wonderful day, I walked ugly areas, beautiful areas, through gardens, and past architectural marvels. I got rained on, dried off, deafened by police sirens, and almost broke both my shin bones on Paris' many low-lying stone bollards.

I missed seeing Notre-Dame, the Tuileries, Montmartre, Le Marais, Place Vendôme, and Palais Garnier, and even though I broke both my rules, I still felt as though I'd seen more of the Parisian streets and side streets than many Parisians.

I'd made it to about 1:00am before I stopped at a picture-perfect café with a red awning and red window frames, and no customers inside. I needed a chocolat chaud recharge to keep me going for the next four hours before I'd need to pick up my suitcase from my unused hotel room and head to the airport; but by the time I was ready to leave the café, I couldn't.

The cold night air had gripped my legs, and both seized with debilitating cramps. I stretched and I massaged, but they refused to carry my weight any further. They were done and my Parisian adventure had come to a premature close, and whilst I wished I'd kept moving rather than stopping, I also felt I'd experienced enough.

I *'monsieur s'il vous plaît'ed'* a taxi back to my hotel and lay down for a few hours before making my way home.

There were many highlights during my first visit to Paris, but which memory was the best?

"One of my favourite memories was my first sight of the Eiffel Tower from Champ de Mars as I couldn't have planned it better, but the memory I still get the biggest kick out of was crossing Pont des Arts, and sitting cross-legged on a stone bench in Cour Carrée, having no idea I was in a courtyard of the Louvre. I sat there for about thirty minutes, oblivious to the fact that the glass pyramids were less than one hundred metres to my right; and when I did get up, I walked towards them by complete accident. Had I walked in any other direction, through any of the other three archways, I would have missed them and the Louvre forecourt entirely."

She smiled, glassy-eyed, with her own memories of Paris.

"Cour Carrée is very beautiful."

"It sure is. I still revisit that stone bench each time I go back to Paris, just to relive the surprise of the pyramids, even though I now know they're there.

"However, to answer your question, I think my most favourite memory of my first overseas trip to Paris was ending it with a hot chocolate at a typical Parisian café after walking myself to injury. The bartender was so rude, probably because it was late and I didn't know much French; and the hot chocolate itself was terrible; likely made that way on purpose for the ignorant tourist walking the streets at midnight, but regardless of those things, I had the entire café and the whole of Paris to myself, and it felt wonderful. I was on my own on the other side of the world and my day had been the opposite to any other day I'd had up to that point in my life. I still get a little shiver thinking about it. I felt like a child experiencing the world for the first time."

"This is shoshin."

"Sho-what?"

"Shoshin is Japanese Zen Buddhism and translates to beginner's mind. It is about being open and having a lack of preconceptions—" She put her hand on her chest to stop herself from talking. "Sorry, I did not mean to interrupt you. Please continue."

"There's not much more to tell. I was half a world away from all that was familiar, and I'd used the opportunity to do something different, be someone different. It had felt a bit frivolous not to plan an itinerary to see all the attractions, particularly within such a short timeframe, but I found the feeling freeing and exhilarating."

Her smile spread wide across her face, irradiating it in the familiar golden glow from earlier. "You have the best memories of this day because it was what you wanted to do, and because you did it on purpose, and with intention."

Aha! So, this is where you're going with this …

"You had no one to worry about except yourself, so you chose to do what you wanted to do. From the outside, your day may have seemed unplanned as you moved from place to place in a seemingly random manner, but actually, you made decisions consciously and purposefully and with intent, and your intention was to experience Paris on foot and by surprise. You did not know what was around the corner, so you were mindful in the moment, and alert to your experiences, and you took nothing for granted. You had not seen the city or the streets before, and you had not sat in Cour Carrée before, so you also did not take them for granted. You were consciously wide awake during that experience, and I think since then, you have been subconsciously asleep, but maybe this advice will help you wake up again."

Awake? Asleep? Now, who is gaslighting who?

"I suspect you travelled in a similar way to other places when you were living over there, yes?"

"Yes, absolutely! That first time in Paris became a template for me and I did the same thing in just about every other city I visited.

"You know, I've been to Paris seven or eight times since, and still have no idea where that café is, or what it is called. Beyond the surprise of the Louvre, I can't retrace my steps, or remember what else I saw. The café could have been in any of the arrondissements, and I'm almost pleased I don't know where it is, or how to find it, because now, it is allowed to live in my memory just as I remember it."

Her face scrunched as if she'd taken another sip of the acrid tea.

"This is a good segue to my second piece of advice for you, as it relates to what you have just said."

What did I just say?

"That I need to travel more?"

"Yes, sure, travel more, but this is not my second piece of advice for you. I do not know how to say this in another way, so I am going to say it, and I am sorry to say this, but to better discover your programming, you need to find a way to drop your storylines."

Why did she keep apologising for saying things?

"My storylines?"

It was an odd thing to say, and I wasn't sure what she meant.

"Like, I need to write my stories down? Drop them onto paper?"

"Oh, no, no, sorry, I think I have used the wrong words."

She rubbed her finger on her lips, as if scrolling through synonyms for the right ones.

"What I meant to say is that you need to stop telling stories to explain your experiences, or at least become conscious they are stories and not the truth."

And now, she'd lost me.

She'd asked me for my story about my first overseas trip, and my best memory of that time, but now she was asking me to stop telling stories. How was I supposed to do one without the other?

She leant forward again, this time putting her hand under the table between us and pulling it back to reveal a little drawer.

Tricky!

She extracted a yellow notepad and a silver fountain pen with guilloché-type engraving on its barrel. She unscrewed its lid and licked the nib before using it to divide the top page into three vertical segments.

With her eyes focussed on the pad of paper, she began her explanation: "There are three parts to an experience; first, there is the experience itself or your awareness of the experience; then there is the memory of the experience which happens any time after, and thirdly, there is the storyline of your experience or memory, or both.

"You will benefit from becoming more aware of what is in this third column. Recognise the storylines you tell yourself about your experiences, so the stories do not change your memory of the experience, or the experience itself."

As she spoke, she wrote the word experience across the top of the page, and the words, awareness, memory, and story into each of the segments, putting a big X through the word story. She tore the page out of the notebook and handed it to me.

Something to throw away later.

I received it and stared at it blankly as I still didn't understand what she was talking about. I needed her to spell it out more clearly.

"So how does this relate to my story of my favourite memory of Paris?"

"Well, to repeat your story, your favourite memory was your time in a café you can no longer find, with a bad hot chocolate and a rude waiter?"

"Well, no. My favourite memory was of having all of Paris to myself. Yes, those other things happened, but they're not important, and neither detract from the experience, or my memory of it."

"Yes, but these things are not your experience in column one. The actual experience was— how many years ago now?"

"About twelve."

"Okay, so your experience was twelve years ago, this goes into column one; and now you have a memory of this experience, which goes into column two."

She pointed her pen towards the sheet of paper still hanging loosely in my hand.

"Yes, so where does the story bit come in?"

"Well, there are at least three stories you tell yourself about the experience and memory which may or may not be true."

Three?!

"Story one is about the bartender's rudeness because it was late or because you did not speak French. Story two is about him making you a bad hot chocolate on purpose because you were a tourist, and story three is about you being happy you do not know the name of the café or where it is, so it can live in your memory."

Her attempt to clear things up, muddied them further.

"How are these three things stories, when they were my experiences?"

"They are stories because they may not be true and may not be a part of your experience. They are the storylines you have made to fill in the blanks."

"But—"

"It is something we all do, so this is not specific to you, but if these stories get out of hand, they can alter the memory of the experience to something it was not, which may then confirm your programming, rather than have you question it."

"But—"

"You are familiar with Gestalt psychology, yes?"

"Yes, that the whole is greater than the sum of its parts, and that our brains fill in blanks to construct whole pictures."

The Kanizsa triangle was one of my favourite optical illusions; a picture of two triangles, neither of which existed.

"Yes, well, storylines follow a similar theory, with your brain filling in the blanks to make an experience whole."

She'd piqued my interest. "How is this similar?"

"Stories like yours make people think all Parisians or French people are rude and do not like foreigners."

"I don't think that, but that's what happened to me. Sure, the bartender may have just been tired or having a bad day and it could have been that he was just crap at making hot chocolates, but I am still happy I was there and that I had the experience—"

"Having a bad day and being crap at making hot chocolates are two more stories you are making up to explain the experience. They are not true unless you asked him, and he told you.

"Did you ask him?"

"I could barely ask him for a chocolat chaud, let alone strike up a conversation with him in French!"

"It is more likely that the truth of your experience was that you did not enjoy the way he treated you, and that you did not like the taste of the hot chocolate he served you. I suspect these were your actual experiences at the time, the experiences without the storylines."

I took a moment to process her explanation, and felt my memory of that time in Paris, separate itself into the three components listed on the page still hanging in my hand.

She was probably right. "I think I understand what you're saying now."

"In many cases, like this one we are talking about,

people's storylines are not a problem, and will have little or no impact on their lives, or the lives of others, but in other situations, when the story becomes stronger than the experience, and when it starts to become an alternative to the truth, then these storylines can become very dangerous indeed. When storylines are viewed as the experience, rather than being *about* the experience, they can cause many problems."

She'd reduced my defences enough for me to probe further. "So, how does this advice apply to my programming, and how do I put it into action?"

She smiled. "If I may bring up your ex-wife again—"

I rolled my head in feigned annoyance. "If you must!"

"You have many storylines about her and her mental health; about her bipolar disorder and the way she was; about the way she treated you and how she surprised you in Tokyo about wanting to leave you; and you have many more stories about your role in your marriage and about what she expected from you, and what you did for her."

"Indeed, I do, except none of these are stories, they are all my actual experiences in column one and are etched into my memory in column two. They are all true and factually correct."

I held up the page and pointed to the first two columns for emphasis.

"And whose truth are you talking about? Yours or hers?"

Huh?

"Isn't truth just the truth? I mean, those things *happened.*"

"Have you forgotten my cave story already?"

"No—"

"Well then, you should know that truth is never *just* the truth."

"But—"

"During your years together, especially the last few years when things were not good, did you ever ask her what she needed from you, or what she wanted from you, or did you just go ahead and do what you thought needed to be done?"

Blood surged into my face, and the hair on the back of my neck bristled.

"I don't think that's a fair question. She was mentally ill: I did what needed to be done and gave her the support she needed to be better. I gave her everything I had to give to my own detriment."

"I am sure you did, and I do not want to take anything away from what you did, but my question is, did you ever ask her what she needed from you, or what she wanted you to give?"

"I'm sure we spoke about it all the time—"

"You know, speaking and asking are different things—"

"She wasn't in the right headspace to be able to answer the questions, so no, I don't think I asked the questions as directly as you have put them."

"Who said she was not in the right headspace to answer your questions?"

My surging blood was now pulsing through my face. "Her doctors, her disorder, her illness, the way she was, and she probably said it herself."

"Did you ever talk to her doctors, or did they talk to you?"

"No, of course not! She was an adult, so all her consultations were private. What difference would it have made anyway? She was my wife, and she needed my help and support."

That was, until she didn't ...

The pulsing stopped, and a cooling sensation took over.

"Think of storylines as a filter on your glasses."

Another glasses analogy!

"If you have a red filter on your lenses, you will see red. Red objects will appear redder, but objects that are not red, will also appear red; and just because they appear red, does not mean they *are* red."

So much red!

"Storylines are the same. If we view people and situations through our storylined lenses, then all we see will be through our storylines, and our experiences of those situations may become something they are not."

It was another simple analogy that made sense.

"Is this like confirmation bias? Like thinking that all white cars always drive together because we only notice when they do?"

"It is much stronger than this. You accepted things in your marriage you did not like, and you constantly put yourself second because of the storylines you told yourself about your ex-wife and your relationship. This is a part of your programming, and it is not healthy."

"But—"

"Please do not beat yourself up for this; everyone has their own storylines. We subconsciously tell ourselves hundreds of stories every day to make sense of our experiences, and sometimes we do it consciously too.

"If people are rude to us, we may think they are rude people, rather than them having a bad day. If someone cuts in front of us, we may think they are selfish, when they simply may not have seen us."

"If they are so pervasive, how do I make the storylines stop?"

"Easy: awareness. Become aware of your storylines, so you know when you are telling them. Feel what you are feeling without needing to explain it, or to explain the other person. Each one of us have our own version of the story, so it is impossible to know which one is true. Truth is therefore subjective, and not objective as you believe."

"But—"

"If you continue to live your life through your storylines, they will prevent you from having fulfilling experiences. You will not order another hot chocolate in Paris, and you will not get into another relationship for fear of mental illness."

Theirs or mine?!

She may as well have been speaking Luxembourgish again, as to me, all my experiences and memories were just stories I told myself, and dropping my storylines would be dropping the memories they sprang from, and I was not okay with that. However, I wasn't going to debate the issue any further. I was tired and wanted to go home.

"Okay, I will try to become more aware."

"Good, because my third piece of advice follows directly on from this."

I folded the piece of yellow paper into half and then half again and levered it into the back pocket of my jeans. I'd almost forgotten there was a third piece of advice.

"Boundaries, boundaries, boundaries. Boundaries are crucial for highly sensitive people and for empaths. Unconditional love does not mean unconditional acceptance, and you must must must create some healthy boundaries for yourself! Empaths without boundaries will self-destruct!"

Boundaries by three, and musts by three! She was serious about this one!

"You must know what is your business and what is not. Identify what is your business, what is someone else's business, and what is the universe's business, and make your decisions accordingly."

I literally have no idea what you're talking about right now.

"I think I have quite good boundaries."

She stabbed the nib of her pen into the centre of the pad she was still holding, slowly but forcefully twisting it, whispering under her breath, "Du geifs net wessen wat eng limit ass wa se dech an den aarsch bäissen."

I didn't ask her to translate her wessens, aarsches, or bäissens as the stabbing motion inferred it wasn't anything complimentary.

"Remember my example earlier, about me scalding my hand with hot water?"

"I do. I still don't quite understand it, but I remember it."

"And remember when I said an empath will feel the scalding of the hot water on their own hand, and their empathic reaction will be to jump in to alleviate the pain in the other, so it alleviates the pain in themselves—"

"Yes, or the other way around—"

"Yes, or the other way around; and that the empath will react by doing what needs to be done to fix the situation?"

"Yes, I remember."

"Okay, to give you a practical example on boundaries, let me ask you another question: why is fixing the situation the empath's job? Why is it their business?"

What the fuckkk?

"I'm not sure I understand your question, because if there is someone in pain and if that pain is being felt by the empath, why wouldn't they jump in to act?"

"But my question to you is why, why is it the empath's *business* in the first place? Why do they need to fix the situation if it may not be theirs to fix? Is the other person not capable?"

I still didn't grasp the line of her questioning.

"Perhaps they are, or perhaps they're not, but I don't think it has anything to do with capability; it has to do with needs—"

"Whose needs are you talking about? Your previous counsellor hypothesised you are attracted to people who need saving, yes?"

"Yes, that's the gist of it."

"Well, my question for you is, why do you think this is your job? Why is it your business?"

I sat back and crossed my arms with a physical demonstration of protest.

"What do you mean? First of all, I don't know if I agree with him, but second of all, if someone needs help, you help; if someone is in pain, you support them and help lessen it—"

"But why? And why you?"

What do you mean, why me?!

"Ask yourself, did they ask you for help, or were you just giving it— how you say, unsolicited?"

I wasn't enjoying her cross-examination.

"Why does it matter if I hadn't been *asked* for help before jumping in? Surely it was enough to see the need, and fix it?"

She shook her head. "Each time you are attracted to a problem, or a situation, or to a person in need, you must try to take a moment to ask yourself whose business it is? If it is yours, theirs or the universe's; and then you must ask yourself whether you should get involved, or better still if you combine this with my first piece of advice, ask yourself whether you *want* to be involved; and if you do, then ask the person if they want you to be involved. This is a simple method you can use to create boundaries."

Simple?!

"That sounds like a long process and I'm not sure I have the time for it. If I'm there, then surely, it's my business.

Wouldn't I be a psychopath if I stood by watching someone die, waiting for them to respond to me about whether they wanted my help or not?"

I could almost hear the sound of her gritting her cement-coloured teeth, whilst her lips forced a smile that informed me of her mounting exasperation. "You are taking this literally and are still being too black and white. Of course, if someone is in imminent danger of dying, you help, but if someone is depressed, is that for you to cure them? What if you are depressed too? Then whose responsibility is it then?"

Still mine!

"Are you familiar with the word equanimity?"

"I heard it a lot at the meditation studio in New York and remember looking it up at the time, but no, I can't remember what it means."

"Equanimity is about being calm and undisturbed in challenging situations. It does not mean you do not *care* about what is going on, it means you do not destroy yourself with your caring. Equanimity is important for empaths.

"Creating boundaries is not building brick walls around yourself and not letting anyone in. Creating healthy boundaries is about you taking care of yourself. It is about your right to have your own feelings, your own opinions, and your own wants and needs, and not only to have them, but to value them and protect them. It is about you having the right to say no."

"That's a novel idea … taking care of myself, and saying no."

It made logical sense that other people's business was first and foremost theirs, but waiting to be asked for help, especially from friends, family, or partners was something I'd never done. Jumping in and helping was what made me, me. It was my *raison d'etre*.

"I'll tell you right now that I understand this on an abstract level, but I don't really believe I can live a life doing what you're saying. I am human, I have humanity, and I'm hardwired to help, and have always been this way. It is my programming, and I'm not sure I can change that—"

She twisted her pen further into the pad of paper. "Please understand I am not asking you to change. My advice to you is to take a moment and ask the questions before you make other people's problems your own. What you do after is still up to you."

She closed her eyes looking a little irritated, an expression mirrored in my own face, I was sure. But she wasn't finished.

"In my earlier analogy, the way forward is to consciously transform your empathic response into an empathetic response by asking if you can help, or how you can help, rather than jumping in and helping. My earlier point about empaths is that because we feel other people's feelings as our own; the question for us must be, 'is this really ours, or is it someone else's'? Is another person's emotional state causing our emotional state, and is our instinct to alleviate this for them, or for us? Do we do what we do for our own good, and not necessarily only for the good of the other as we may believe?"

Her last sentence lit a fuse in my mind.

Could this be true for me?

"Do I do what I do for my own benefit, and not necessarily for the good of others as I believe?"

"Yes, this is the question. This is the question for all empaths. My advice to you is to know what is yours and what is not, and then make a conscious, rather than subconscious decision about what you want to do next."

The fuse continued to burn.

Had I got into each one of my relationships because I'd misappropriated the angst and turmoil of my partners as my own; and could it be that I wasn't rescuing them, but rescuing myself from my own feelings?

No, none of that makes any sense!

"By creating boundaries, questioning your storylines, and focusing on what you want for your own life, you will uncover your programming. Peel back your storylines to find your truthful reasons for your choices, or at least give yourself time to think about your reasons why."

Her three pieces of advice seemed impossible to achieve, but I needed to at least let them sit and percolate before discarding them. Until this moment, I'd thought I'd lived my entire adult life with an intentional plan of action for where I wanted to be and how I was going to get there, and for the most part I thought it was working out quite well, but obviously, it wasn't.

I was a prisoner chained up in a cave believing the shadows were real.

"Thank you for your advice. I will keep these things in mind."

I hoped that my gratitude would hide my turmoil, but her expression suggested it didn't.

Regardless she played along. "You are welcome. So, if we play the analogy again of me burning my hand, what will you do?"

"I will ask you if you need help, or how you would like me to help?"

"Yes. And if I was to ask you what you would do if you end up in another relationship with someone with a mental illness or personality disorder?"

"Well, that is not going to happen, but, hypothetically, if it does, then I will ask them what they need from me."

"Good, and if they ask you to do something you really do not want to do, even though you think you should do it, what will you do?

I paused for a second.

"That one I can't answer, not if I'm being honest."

She smiled and I wondered whether I spotted a look of faint relief on her face as she put the pen and pad of paper back into the secret drawer. "Okay, two out of three is a good start."

I hoisted myself up off my seat, ready to leave, but she still wasn't finished with me just yet.

"Before you go, I would like to give you three extra pieces of advice to help support what I have just told you. These are the training wheels for how you can learn balance to ride your bike, or a phrase book for learning your new language."

She smiled again, causing me to return the same.

"One, be mindful, and present in the present. You live in the future whilst being tormented by the past. Let go of both as you cannot do anything about either. You started something in New York with the mindfulness studio and you can continue this into your everyday life. Do classes like you did there, or not, but try to keep a mindful practice whenever you can. Remember, mindfulness is a practice for always, and not just for the meditation cushion. You can be mindful anywhere and everywhere; when you are walking your dog, eating your breakfast, watching TV, or listening to music. It is about being in the moment and paying attention to the *present*, and letting things be as they are. Feel your feelings without making up storylines for them, and let them go."

Sounds easy enough.

"I think mindfulness will also help you to stop and take a moment to know your intentions before you react, and to know your business; and a moment is all it takes for you to alter your decisions and direction."

Her smile widened as she made connections from our past few minutes of conversation.

"Two, become more aware of your energy. Feel what fills you up and what empties you out. Energy is not static, it is constantly moving through you, and within you, and I do not mean this in the traditional sense of eating food, drinking water, exercising, and getting a good sleep at night. You mentioned earlier you feel drained of energy by people and situations. Whether you realised it or not, you were talking about your energy reserves. You give all you have, and others take it, but how do you top yourself up?"

"I guess I don't, which is why I ran out, and still feel like I'm recovering."

"Exactly. You cannot pour from an empty jug."

It was the same sentence used by the support person who'd introduced me to the word 'carer', the same person who quite possibly kicked off this whole mess.

"Extroverts get energy from other people, but introverts get energy from being alone. Extroverts deplete their energy when they are alone, and introverts deplete theirs by being with other people. Did you know this?"

"No, not really, but I guess it depends on the people you're with—"

"Know where your boundaries are and keep them. You currently have no boundaries, and it is not good for you."

You've said that already!

I raised my hand to object, but she continued. "Three, pay more attention to your intuition. I think you will not like this one, but all your answers, past, present, and future are already within you. To live life as a knowing empath is to tune in to what your gut is already telling you."

My gut? How did we get to my gut?

"We use three parts of ourselves to think; our head, our heart, and our gut, but you only think with one part of yourself."

I thought men only thought with their—

"My head?"

"Yes, and you will benefit from balancing this with the other two. Trust your gut to process information from your senses and from other places you are not consciously aware of."

I'd received similar advice from my previous counsellor. He too, had told me to think with my gut, rather than my head. I hadn't fully understood what he meant, and I wasn't sure I understood it any better now.

"Pay attention to what you see, hear, smell, feel, taste, and pay more attention to what lies beyond those senses. Use your hypersensitivity to your advantage. Know there is no right or wrong, but the key is knowing. To understand how to live peacefully as an empath is to tune into your intuition and to know why it is there. You must be conscious. You must be awake."

Again with the awake!

Had I been sleepwalking through my whole life?

Her three pieces of advice and three bonus training wheels were the blinding bright lights at the entrance to the cave I'd asked for, and whilst they weren't the Gestaltian answers I was hoping for, they were better than nothing. A step forward if I wanted to take it.

I recapped the list: *know my intentions, drop my storylines, know my business, create boundaries, be mindful, feel my energy, and tap into my intuition.* Got it.

I wanted more from this session, but I also wanted less. Less introspection, more action.

I wanted her to tell me that the problem wasn't with me, and that other people needed to change; but something told me that if she had, I wouldn't have believed her anyway.

I was already an overthinking overthinker, and now I needed to overthink my overthinker's overthinking.

Applying her advice was going to keep me stuck in my head for the rest of my days. I tried not to feel profound despair at the thought.

I was exhausted.

She looked concerned and stood up. "We have run over time! I am sorry to overwhelm you. I am getting ahead of myself and of you, but to finish this conversation, the best thing you can do for yourself right now is to get out into some wide-open space. Get into nature, into the quiet, where the sky is big and where there are no people; where you can see the horizon and where you are surrounded by big trees, or the ocean, or mountains, or fields. Space is where things will make sense, it is where the answers are. It is where it is easier to be mindful, to notice your energy, and where your senses and intuition will thrive. Space is where new thoughts and ideas will come, and where your storylines will disappear and where your decisions will become purposeful. Nature is where you will discover what it truly means to experience life as an empath."

If only it was that easy …

Chapter 4

Space. It was the only piece of the counsellor's advice I could easily understand and effortlessly follow. I enjoyed being in the wide-open space of nature and especially liked being near the water, escaping whenever I could to the infinity of the ocean and the hypnotic sound of its crashing waves.

Between work commitments, counselling sessions, overseas travel, catching up with family and friends, and navel-gazing, I'd been escaping the city to my little holiday shack by the sea.

My windswept home-away-from-home was a four-hour drive from Melbourne, and was surrounded by hills, farmland, and a high-energy beach.

Whilst the sky was big, and the horizon was visible in all directions, my time at the property during the past year had not generated any new thoughts, ideas, or answers; at least none I could remember or make clear sense of.

I wanted to be more mindful, conscious, awake, and more aware of my energy and intuition, but as to *how* I was going to do it on a daily basis, I wasn't yet sure.

It was within the realm of possibility that the not-Dutch counsellor's advice was all philosophical supposition rather than psychological practice and that none of it had functional application beyond sparring in a counselling room.

Regardless, there were things I could do immediately; the first of which was to interrogate my memories of past experiences to search for other – better – reasons for why I did the things I did.

It had been two weeks since the not-Dutch counsellor had walked me to her front door, leaving me parched from the lack of fresh tea and thirsty for more specific information on empaths.

Until a fortnight ago, I'd believed I'd consciously made all my big life decisions with intention and because I'd wanted to, but her words had eroded my confidence in that view, and I was now doubting myself. My inability to satisfactorily explain my reasons for why I went to the UK and why I'd got together with my ex-wife may have been more revealing than I wanted to admit.

The not-Dutch counsellor was adept at using words and phrases to engrave into my brain, similar to the etched guilloché on her pen. She'd told me I was on some sort of cruise control or auto pilot, but if I was, how could I switch them off and snap myself out of it?

By my optimistic calculations, I'd already lived half my

life, and I didn't want to live the second half in the same way as the first; not if it was going to lead to the same mistakes and failures.

I needed to wake up, and I needed to become more conscious, but how?

How was I going to learn my programming?

How was I going to get out of the cave to see outside, when the cave itself may not be real to begin with?

Now, that would have been a good question to ask her!

The time had come for another road trip to the rugged southwest coast of Victoria, not because I *should*, but because I *wanted* to. It would be the perfect spot to contemplate, ruminate, and be still, although contemplation, rumination, and being still hadn't always been the property's purpose, at least, not for me.

After packing my car with supplies for the week ahead and securing my dog into her passenger seat harness, I set off with extra caution; conscious that my mind was full and that the first part of the drive was usually the most perilous. Living near the industrial heartland of Melbourne meant navigating B-double trucks, multi-lane intersections, and impatient drivers trying to knock a few minutes off their journeys.

Within fifteen minutes, I was on the freeway, engaging the car's cruise control and disengaging my own. The remainder of this drive would be spent on better answering the counsellor's question about why I'd wanted a relationship with my now ex-wife, and why I'd jumped into asking her to marry me so quickly, when I'd wanted neither prior to knowing her.

At the time she'd sent me her flirty text, I'd been in Bristol for about a year and a half and was enjoying my new life as an expat and world traveller.

After a bumpy first few months in the UK, and sixteen-hour workdays and six-day working weeks, my manager told me I was burning out and needed to slow down.

It was unsurprising feedback, as I hadn't been enjoying my time there and had subconsciously slipped into my normal pattern of trying to get everything done at once, working towards completing three years' worth of work within a framework of three months.

I took his advice and forced myself into better balance by reducing my workdays to five, and with both Saturdays and Sundays free, I was able to start booking my monthly weekenders to Europe.

By the time she sent me her flirty text, I'd completed nine hops across the Channel and enjoyed between twenty-four and forty-eight hours in Amsterdam, Florence, Venice, Rome, Madrid, Brussels, Berlin, Barcelona, and Prague; and had four more planned to Toulouse, Nice, Bern, and a longer stay in New York City to round out that year.

Whilst I hadn't travelled anywhere during my first twenty-nine years on earth, I was now making up for lost time.

I was living a dream, and I knew it.

Prior to booking NYC, I'd made the decision to stay in the UK for Christmas that year, to spend it with my mum's family in Wales. A white Christmas with my maternal relations was something I was keen to experience before my expat assignment came to an end, and as I'd returned to Melbourne the year before, it had become a choice between that year or the year after before my time in Bristol came to an end.

It was a significant decision as I'd spent each of my previous thirty-one Christmases with my mum, dad, sister, and extended paternal clan, but to alleviate some of my guilt about breaking the tradition, I'd arranged to visit Australia in mid-January instead.

During my first few months in Bristol, and before I started to take full advantage of my proximity to Europe, I'd started emailing regular updates to a small group of family and friends back home.

They were short descriptions of my experiences of work and life in southwest England, and I'd share my favourite photos of people and places from the past week or fortnight. I'd write about my misunderstandings of their colloquialisms; of thinking I was being called Paulie when asked if I was sick; about how 'cheers drive' was their form of 'thank you' to a bus driver, and about how I didn't feel right using the phrase 'gurt lush' to describe something 'really good'.

As I began to travel, I wrote more about the joys and challenges of my short stays in great cities; about the enjoyment of learning new languages, transport systems, local etiquette, and locating accommodation when street numbering was based on the year a building was built, rather than in any logical sequential order.

I enjoyed writing the emails, and the recipients seemed to enjoy reading them, but in hindsight, I think my underlying *intention* was less about storytelling, and more about keeping connected with those back home.

As my weekends away increased, so did the volume of my emails, as well as my distribution list for them. Friends and colleagues were forwarding my stories and photos to others, and it didn't take long before those others asked to be added as primary recipients.

It was whilst adding new names to my list that my ex-wife's came up as an auto-complete in the 'To': field and with no reason not to, I clicked to add her, sending her editions of my stories from then on.

No reason not to, eh?

She'd known I was over there as we'd spoken about it prior to me leaving, but we hadn't spoken since. During those first discussions, she'd made herself out to be envious of the opportunity and of all the adventures I was going to have, whereas I'd played it down, telling her it would be all work, and no fun at all.

It seems we were both right …

She'd told me she had a UK passport due to her father's ancestry and joked that she wanted me to pack her in my bag and take her with me. She'd told me that she'd wanted to live and work in London, and that she and her best friend had planned to do so before life got in the way, and before they'd settled down into adulthood. I didn't read into her comments as we barely knew each other, and I didn't consider what she said to me, to be any more than harmless banter between work acquaintances.

My travel emails reconnected us, and it didn't take long before we became each other's pen pals, emailing each other about our days, weeks, and our lives.

So, it was me who reconnected us, not her!

Fucking storylines!

She told me about her business ideas and her love for shoes, and she kept me up to date with her life in Brisbane, writing her own tales about her everyday experiences. She wrote to me about her relationship and its trials and tribulations, and she kept me up to date with 'ring watch' as she waited with bated breath for her boyfriend's marriage proposal.

How did I not remember this?

There was nothing improper in any of our emails, and we kept it all above-board. There was no flirting, no hidden messages, and nothing untoward said by either of us, and I'd simply been happy to have a new friend who I'd had no history with, and who had no preconceived ideas about who I was, or who I should be.

Her first text message came through to my UK number in the early hours of the eleventh of November, and it knocked me off my axis. Whilst we'd emailed regularly during the preceding nine or ten months, we'd not seen or spoken to each other for more than double that and had not used text messages or phone calls to contact each other.

'You know I'm just crazy about you. I was the first time I met you and am more so now'.

It was early on a Friday morning in Bristol and late on a Friday afternoon in Brisbane, and she'd been out with friends, getting an early start on the weekend.

I was awake, sleepless in anticipation for my flight to Toulouse later that evening and was wondering whether I'd have time to visit Carcassonne or not.

My heart skipped a beat as I read the text, but diffidence quickly followed, and I reassured myself by thinking it was most likely alcohol induced, and probably not meant for me, anyway.

In our dozens of emails, she'd not mentioned breaking up with her boyfriend, nor that she was prowling for a replacement.

I took a few minutes to respond, and when I did, I did so with trepidation, not wanting to embarrass her for sending it to me by mistake, but also not wanting to shut it down, in case there was a chance she hadn't sent it in error.

Our subsequent text exchange during the next few minutes confirmed it was indeed for me, and that she'd become 'a bit tiddly' and had used her cocktail-inspired courage to free the secret she'd been holding on to since we'd first met, more than two years earlier.

Had I known?

No, absolutely not!

Had I wished?

Maybe …

But why?

That she could have a crush on me for two years whilst waiting for her boyfriend to ask her to marry him should have told me all I needed to know about her headspace, but for some reason it didn't.

It was a red flag I paid no attention to.

Again, why?

At that time, I wasn't looking for reasons not to be with her, or for us not to work out, I was only looking for reasons for why it could. I didn't want reasons to keep my guard up, I only wanted reasons to take it down.

Still … why?

I spent the rest of that November day pinballing between states of cynicism and optimism, realising that I didn't know her well enough to recognise whether she was joking or being serious. She had a dark sense of humour, and there was a real possibility that she'd texted me as an experiment, just to see how I'd react.

And if that's what she did, I will now never know.

During my moments of optimism, her messages turned me inside-out and upside-down and had me completely smitten, hook, line, sinker, and rod. I hadn't felt that way in years, if at all, and until 4:44am that morning, I certainly hadn't felt that way about her either.

So, what changed, and why did it change so quickly?

Was this the empath thing at play?

Had I absorbed her feelings as my own?

Was I just reciprocating her feelings towards me?

Or did I have buried feelings for her?

We got on like a house on fire and I found her attractive, so why does there need to be a better explanation?

Because there does …

The not-Dutch counsellor's first seed of advice was beginning to take root. It seemed that I wouldn't be letting myself out of this investigation so easily, after all.

I couldn't just park my thoughts anymore. I needed to know my intentions and needed to know why I wanted to start a relationship with someone so inconveniently located on the other side of the world, when I was already living my best life without her in it.

Why, why, why?!

During the following few days, she emailed me to tell me her relationship with her boyfriend was all but over and had been for some time, but that she hadn't previously mentioned it because she didn't want to burden me with the detail. She told me she'd become fed up with waiting for his proposal and that she'd stopped wanting it months ago.

She told me he'd wanted children and she didn't, and although she'd told him years earlier she'd have them for him, he hadn't been convinced. It seemed he was right.

She'd been with him since she was nineteen and he was her comfort zone, but she'd come to the realisation she didn't love him anymore.

She told me she'd been making the decision to leave him for months, and felt she'd finally reached a point where a decision no longer needed to be made. They were sleeping in different bedrooms and were living their own lives, apart but together … but the thought of splitting their possessions and moving out of their apartment was still too great a prospect to get her head around. All too hard.

It was over, she said. She just hadn't told him yet.

It was another red flag, and in hindsight, the comparison between what she did to him in Brisbane, and what she did to me nine years later in Tokyo was becoming blindingly obvious.

Was this another bright light behind me at the cave entrance?

She'd arranged to spend Christmas in Perth that year, with her mum and the boyfriend, and didn't want to go alone, or have to spend her entire holiday explaining to her family why he wasn't there. She hoped that they could play happy couples through the holiday and return to Brisbane in the new year to start her new life. She said she wanted me to meet her in Queensland during my holiday back to Australia.

The tone and content of our emails changed significantly from that Remembrance Day, and once we'd shared and reciprocated our feelings, it was as though we'd started dating, and getting to know each other on a more intimate level.

It was during those following weeks that she shared her struggle with bipolar disorder, her job hunting to find something new, and her intention to move to Melbourne to get away from her ex and to start a new life.

She described her unhappiness, in work, family, love, and life, and told me she was going to overhaul it all, making it crystal clear that she wanted me to be a part of those plans. She told me I was the cure to it all. She told me I was loved and *needed*.

She cut her hair short, stopped taking her bipolar medication, interviewed for jobs too senior for her, and started house hunting for rentals in both Brisbane and Melbourne; and as the days and emails passed, I slipped into a role of of confidant, coach, counsellor, and support worker, all without any conscious thought or decision.

As if by osmosis, her plans became my plans, and her life's mission became my own, and I'd been happy to become whomever she wanted me to be.

But why?

Had I been an emotional sponge?! Absorbing her feelings as my own and making her business my business?!

As these revelations whizzed through my head, so did the countryside outside my windows. Flat plains, ancient lava flows, and extinct volcanos dotted all the way to the horizon, the expanse of country between Inverleigh and Lismore never failed to disappoint.

It was greener here than it had been for months, greener because of the recent rain feeding the canola crops guarding both sides of the highway; crops ready to burst into colour in a few weeks' time, to transform the landscape into a vibrant sea of acid yellow and fluorescent gold, before completing their life cycle and dying off as vacant silver stalks in summer.

This was a big open space, domed by a big open sky, and I was the only one on this black potholed ribbon of highway. This was a place where things could make sense, and where new thoughts and ideas could appear, but as much as I wanted to force them into existence all at once, they were content to slowly appear to me one by one, in their own good time. I would have to be patient.

Within a few weeks, we'd set the day for our first date, and our now daily emails to each other had become a countdown timer to that day. The subject line was a number, and she decreased the number by one each day, a not-too-complicated cypher to let us know how many sleeps we had left before we'd see each other again.

We were acting like thirteen-year-olds.

I'd taken three weeks leave for my Australian holiday, and my plan was to fly to Brisbane three days after landing in Melbourne. A few days in Queensland wasn't going to affect my holiday, nor my ability to catch up with friends and family back home, but as the countdown counted down, I became less and less concerned with spending time on my past, and more obsessed with pursuing my future.

By email '40', it was clear that we were already in a romantic relationship. We wrote to each other as though we were together and had been for years. She showered me with words of love and affection and made me feel like I was the only person on earth. She called me her soulmate, and the cure to all her ailments, and she told me she didn't know how she'd lived without me in her life.

She'd love bombed me from afar, although at the time, I didn't know what love bombing was.

With Luxembourg's descriptions of narcissists pinging about in my mind, I could now imagine her, and her psychopath friends huddled around her phone, shouting out suggestions for what she should write next to keep me on the hook.

I enjoyed the insanity of how we started out but was equally afraid it would all fizzle before we hit 'Day 0'. She was still living in her apartment in Brisbane with her ex-boyfriend, and the two of them still planned to proceed with their holiday together to Perth.

I didn't like either situation, but from sixteen thousand kilometres away, there was very little I could do about it. She had a plan, and I had to respect her right to do what she needed to do, whether I liked it or not.

Did I have to, though? I could have walked away …

As much as I didn't want to admit it to myself at the time, her Christmas trip was going to be a litmus test for our fledgling relationship. It was going to be a time of opportunity for her and her man to reconcile, and for them to rediscover the spark of why they'd got together in the first place. Breaking out of the comfort of a five-year relationship was going to be tough for them, but I hoped it wasn't going to be too tough for her to see through to the end.

It was as though I was her boyfriend and that she was about to visit her family with another man, when the fact of the matter was that the exact opposite was true; I was the other man, and he had no idea I existed.

She was an excellent liar.

It must have been a tricky time for her living a double-life, and she made no secret of her brain feeling scrambled and her trouble focusing, not helped by her withdrawal from lithium making her feel 'high' and affecting her in more ways than one.

She hadn't trusted her bipolar diagnosis and had told me she'd never taken it seriously. She told me she felt well enough and that she didn't like the numbing feeling of the drugs.

I tried not to judge her for her diagnosis or for not taking her medication, as her mind and body were her *business*, but the fact that she experienced a numbing feeling when taking them, should have indicated to both of us that they were probably doing their job.

I did what I could to support her from afar whilst doing my best to shelve my theoretical understanding of how her disorder was affecting her and affecting us. I kept my mind open, and my thoughts and opinions to myself and accepted her for who she was, something she told me was a welcome and refreshing difference between me and so many others around her.

Our communication felt free and unencumbered from expectation. We didn't play games and there were no mandatory waiting periods between texts and emails, and if we had something to say, we said it, or at least that's what we made each other believe. We emailed or texted each other when we wanted to and knew that if the other took a while to respond, it was because they were busy, or because they were sleeping.

We were clear about what we wanted from each other and from a relationship together and we were clear with our intentions. Our time in Brisbane wasn't going to be a holiday romance, or a three-day hook-up; it was going to be the start of something more. We wanted to progress things with each other at the exclusion of all others but knew that the distance between us was going to be problematic. We told each other to take it one step at a time and that step one was going to be our very first date.

After three years single, I could barely remember the highs associated with my previous relationships but knew that none before were comparable to what I had felt with her. It felt like first love all over again.

I enjoyed the novelty of the feelings, and the uniqueness of our honesty had felt both uplifting and invigorating. I liked that she liked me for me and that neither of us seemed to be holding back from the truth, but now I wasn't sure that any of it was real.

As we learnt more about each other, we felt more connected, like we'd found our long-lost other halves, as though we were two becoming one.

If only I'd known about the vesica pisces back then, I would have known to keep my circle whole and to simply share my radius with her.

We seemed to know each other's thoughts and feelings and knew what to say and when to say it. We claimed to be synchronised in an other-worldly way and whilst we emailed and texted almost every day, we told each other we didn't need to. We believed we had a telepathic connection and that we knew what the other was thinking and feeling without needing to be told.

She appeared to understand me better than I understood myself, or at the very least, she knew how to make me feel that way.

Or was that just her psycho'ness to my empath'ness?!

The build up to our first date in Brisbane was epic and our emails and texts continued at an increased volume. No longer was it just one email per day, it was now eight or nine. From the interesting to mundane, she narrated her life for me, choosing which aspects to include and which to leave out. She spoke about work and about life outside of work, but mostly she spoke about what she was going to do to me once we were together.

As her texts and emails became faster and more furious, so did her disinhibition and promiscuity. She continually pushed the envelope of what she'd say, her language and descriptions leaving little to my imagination.

I'd not met anyone as candid and unrestrained as her, but tried to take it with a grain of salt, as none of it really mattered. We had a lifetime ahead of us, but I was equally happy to let her take the lead and set the pace.

Note to self: this is not going with the flow …

Amongst all our communication, the daily ritual of sending each other a numbered email remained. The countdown continued and we'd not missed a day since '55', but as soon as we hit '25', the emails, along with all her texts simply stopped.

And stop I would too, as I'd just driven into Derrinallum and the halfway point of my journey; and a good a place as any for a stretch and a pee break.

I'd driven through this town scores of times but knew little about it beyond its visible landmarks: a half kilometre of bitumen, a tree-lined avenue of honour, an old red-brick toilet block, and Mount Elephant in the near distance.

The mount was a dormant volcano that looked like three connected hills, the highest of which soared hundreds of metres into the sky. Its scoria cone and steep green sides looked smooth like felt, and disused quarries scarred its northern and western flanks; each carved out during a time when cultural and environmental significance wasn't given the attention it deserved. The excavations caused the hillside above to appear unsupported, and as though it could slip down or fold into itself at any moment, but during the six years I'd been driving through here, neither had happened yet.

Metaphor or not, my memories of how and why I'd got together with my ex-wife also appeared unsupported, and there was a burgeoning risk I was going to slip and fold into myself if I didn't uncover some better explanations soon.

Day '25' was Christmas Eve. She was in Perth with her *ex*-boyfriend and mum's family, and I was in Wales, excited for my first Welsh Christmas; twice as excited for my upcoming trip to Manhattan, and thrice as excited for our first date in Brisbane.

Since her first text a month and a half earlier, we hadn't gone for more than twelve hours without contact, and whilst she'd told me she would be preoccupied in Perth and that communicating was going to be more challenging than usual, she assured me she'd always find a way, each and every day.

By Boxing Day morning, a silent forty-eight hours had passed, and I'd become cloaked in misery. I'd lost my appetite and wasn't sleeping; partly because of the anxiety riddling my system, but mostly because I needed to stay awake to check my phone every three minutes for notifications that weren't there.

By Boxing Day afternoon, I'd boarded my flight to New York City, clueless about what was happening with her and with us. It was a seven- or eight-hour journey of hell, as I couldn't stop my mind from rinsing and repeating catastrophic scenarios.

It was my first time to the Big Apple, and my friends and I had billed it as a once in a lifetime opportunity to experience the cliché of New Year's Eve in Times Square; however, if I hadn't made the commitment to meet them there, I probably would have cancelled the whole trip without a second thought.

I was gripped with unreasonable and uncontrollable grief; unlike anything I'd encountered previously. There were no tears, just an indescribable hollowness I couldn't comprehend. I didn't know if she was okay, or if she wasn't, or if she was reconciling with her boyfriend or not, or if she simply had another rational explanation for the radio silence.

I didn't know what she was doing, and why she wasn't replying, and I didn't know what I was supposed to do whilst I was waiting. Our daily texts and emails had consumed me, and the void their absence left behind felt larger than the space they had inhabited in the first place.

My friends consoled me and my anguish and tried to convince me that she wasn't replying because she'd lost her phone or was out of range, but I wasn't able to believe their logical excuses.

I'd arrived at the conclusion that she'd find a way to contact me if it was something she really wanted to do.

They must have thought I was out of my mind.

I'd thought I was out of my mind.

My logic and rationality deserted me when I needed them most, and the tools I'd used to survive heartbreak in the past were as non-existent as she was.

Our *relationship* was a mere six weeks old, but I'd lost the capability to treat it that way. She'd become the primary focus of my energy, and I was already unsure how I was going to carry on without her in my life.

None of it made any sense, and whilst I was inside my body feeling my innards being minced out, I was also on the outside trying to pull myself out of the mincer.

She'd changed me into someone I was not, and amongst everything else, I couldn't reconcile how she'd transformed me so quickly from a thinker into a feeler. She'd opened me up to a full spectrum of emotions, and for the first time in a long time I was feeling raw and exposed.

I'd prophesised that her Christmas trip to Perth was going to provide fertile grounds for her and her ex to rekindle their broken relationship; and that with his back to the wall, he would finally pluck up the courage to pop the big question and give her the engagement ring she'd patiently been waiting for, for the past five years.

The newness and excitement of what we'd had during the past forty-five days had no way of stacking up next to the safety and security of what she'd been building with him during the past one thousand, eight hundred.

I'd been burnt in similar situations before and had already started mentally self-flagellating for not learning my lesson the first few times around. I'd previously fallen for friends who had fallen for me, and as with her, only after they'd made the first move. They too had been unhappy with their situations, using me as a confidant, comforter, and potential escape route, only to retreat to the safety and security of what they knew best when it all became too difficult.

My relationship patterns were becoming obvious.

I was annoyed with myself for letting it happen again, but I was even more annoyed that I was wasting my time in NYC thinking about the situation when there was little I could do about it. I knew it couldn't get worse than it already was, and I knew that whatever I was feeling would soon subside, but I still wasn't able to shake it off.

I'd wanted to know for certain that it was all over, so I could extinguish the last flame of hope that refused to go out.

I wanted to hear her say the words and hear her excuses.

I wanted to know what was hiding in her silence.

New Year's Eve in Times Square didn't eventuate; but not because I was pining and moping. It was because my friends and I had quickly worked out that New Year's Eve in Times Square was an elaborate trap.

Unbeknown to us when we'd booked our accommodation on West 42nd Street, the roads in and around the Times Square district transformed into pedestrian one-way routes from 12:00pm on the thirty-first of December, and once you were in, you were locked in.

Police used fluorescent batons to guide people into the

maze, and walking against the flow was met with whistle blowing, shouting, and a berating in the most New Yorker of ways.

From early that morning, hundreds of thousands of people corralled themselves into Broadway and 7th Avenue with no exit or escape until after the countdown and the ball had dropped.

Spending twelve hours crammed into the same place was not for us, so with the crowds moving in, we decided to move out. We spent the day trudging the streets of Chelsea, Union Square, and the Flatiron District, before finding a jazz bar in NoMad for dinner, drinks, and an ill-timed 'happy new year'.

It felt like that year was not going to start in the lifechanging way I'd expected it to, but I still had Australia and more of Europe to look forward to, as well as another year and a half in Bristol.

The first day of January brought about some solace and resolution. A new year meant a new start and whilst I felt I'd lost something, I reconciled that it wasn't mine to lose to begin with. My logic and rationality had come back online, and my head had regained supremacy over my heart.

I wonder what my gut was saying about it?

My friends departed for London that day, but I had a further thirty-six hours on my own to explore Manhattan, and as I'd done with the other cities I'd visited, I did it without a map or a plan, walking around to simply see what I saw, when I saw it.

As I strolled down 5th Avenue, my pocket vibrated with an incoming message. My assumption was that it would be more friends and family wishing me all the best for the new year, but after a few minutes, my 'what if it's her' got the better of me.

I found a quiet place in a doorway of one of the many luxury boutiques and extracted my phone with restrained optimism, like I was about to open a bar of chocolate hoping for the last golden ticket.

After eight days of silence, her initials once again graced my screen.

'Sorry I've been out of touch. I'll explain everything as soon as I can.'

I didn't take pause, and clicked reply to type as fast as my frozen thumbs would let me.

'Are you okay? Is everything okay? Are we still good for Brisbane?'

She replied immediately. 'Of course! Nothing has changed and I can't wait to see you!'

Her twelve-word text erased the past week like it never happened, and the euphoria it induced filled the voids, and inflated my heart back to beyond its normal size.

A new flight of butterflies invaded my stomach and limbs, hatched fresh from cocoons of my decaying logic and rationality.

None of it makes sense!

Later that evening, she emailed me to explain that her ex-boyfriend had hacked into her computer and had found a copy of our most recent numbered email; and because our emails were always replies to the previous one, what he'd actually found was all of them; all sixty chapters, thirty of which, were written by her.

What he'd found were our private and uncensored messages of new love, messages that were not meant for anyone else's eyes, let alone his.

He'd read them all and she'd been forced into crisis management and damage control; not only for her, but for him, and her family. Her laundry was out in the open, but they were stuck together, him jilted, and her doing the jilting, three and a half thousand kilometres from their home.

She'd spent her past week doing whatever she needed to do to make her own life easier, and one of those things was putting her phone and laptop away, so they could talk.

Her story didn't make complete sense at the time, and it didn't make sense recounting it now, but it didn't need to.

She returned to Brisbane a single woman, and I returned to Bristol, eager to change that for her again in a few weeks' time. Things between us had gone back to normal, and our texts and emails were back in full swing.

At the end of each of my previous three trips, I'd sent her a package of trinkets and mementos I'd gathered along the way, and even though we'd been out of contact during my time in New York, I'd still collected a mishmash of things to give to her. My entry medallion for The Met, a swizzle stick from the jazz bar, a matchbox from the hotel, napkins from diners, and other paraphernalia were all stuffed into an envelope, except rather than posting it, I'd be able to deliver it to her in person.

In addition to the anticipation of our first date, I was also excited to be returning to Australia for a real holiday. I'd completed half my assignment in the UK, and whilst Bristol was beginning to feel like home, I was going to be happy to feel the warmth of family, friends, and the summer sun.

I hadn't told my parents about her as yet, as I hadn't seen them for over a year, and wanted to tell them in person. I knew I'd need to explain why I'd be leaving them after only a few days to head to Brisbane, but I wanted them to hear it from me, face to face.

Day '0' finally arrived without any further hiccups, and I'd flown from Melbourne to Brisbane with the excitement of a schoolboy going on a first date. My anticipation and expectation were about to crescendo, and my two months of overactive imaginations were about to be relegated to the past.

We hadn't seen each other for more than two years, and I'd done my best to keep a lid on my doubts and reservations. Everything had felt right, and it was going to be a good day.

It was a normal working Wednesday for her, but she'd taken the rest of the week off, trusting we'd fall into each other's arms and wouldn't want to let go.

I'd booked an apartment in the central business district

of Brisbane, a few minutes' walk from her office, and we'd decided to meet there.

Beyond 5:00pm, we'd had no other plans.

It was a few minutes past five when she gently knocked on the door.

My heart raced, and my body felt electrified. Adrenaline shot through my veins, and my senses felt heightened like never before. The moment of truth was upon us. My time for thinking was up, and the time for action had arrived.

I'd opened the door tentatively, peering out to ensure it was who I'd hoped it would be, and not the cleaner.

She brushed past it with her shoulder and took a step towards me, dropping her bag on the floor. I said, 'hi', but she didn't reply, instead throwing her arms around my neck, and kissing me so passionately that I lost all sense of time and space.

The kiss had been worth every second of the two-month build up, but I could see now, that it was at that precise moment, that I lost all conscious control over my life's direction and decision making.

She'd inhaled it right out of me there and then.

If I'd thought my rationality and logic had been thin on the ground during the preceding two months, they now ceased to exist.

Her kiss had been a portal to another world and another way of being.

There was nothing normal about the way our relationship started, and nothing normal about how it progressed. That we could construct a meaningful bond from different sides of the globe beggared belief, and that we were both able to get through the turmoil between Christmas and New Year, meant that our relationship passed the test.

The truth of it though, was that there was nothing normal about her, and none of our tests had been passed.

She was fantasy fiction, falling in love with me without knowing me, pushing me out of my comfort zone to do the same.

She had an inflated sense of self and had no inhibitions. She made her choices without fear or favour, and was willing to try new things to see how they felt. She was forward-facing and wasn't concerned with repercussions, imagined, real, or otherwise. She had a zest for life and wasn't an overthinker like me; she was a doer, and she got things done.

I was full of inhibitions, careful and considered and used the past to determine my future. I was an analyst who predicted the consequences and ramifications of my actions and decisions, before doing anything and everything, and I'd never, not once, done anything – outside of getting into the relationships I'd got into – without overthinking it first.

She was my opposite.

To the age of thirty-one, I'd lived my life to fulfil what others wanted from me, and who they expected me to be. Their expectations became my own, and empath or not, I lived my life to satisfy the image of how others saw me.

I was careful, calculated, planned, controlled, diligent, and had always aimed to do the right thing.

I was her opposite.

Perhaps that was the real me, and perhaps it still is, but at the time she popped into my life, I must have wanted a break from it all, and she seemed the perfect person to break me out.

She didn't know me and didn't expect those things from me. She didn't expect me to be anyone other than myself, whomever or whatever that was.

At that time, I must have been bored with me, and my planning, and my stiffness about life, and the way I was living it; and she represented an opposing and invigorating way to do it all differently.

Perhaps, moving to an antipodal city had turned me upside down in more ways than one, creating a craving for more things that were at the opposite end of my spectrum.

To be my opposite and do the opposite.

My ex-wife and I didn't connect all those years ago because we were similar, or the same, we connected because we were different.

She was spontaneous, and reckless; hedonistic and self-serving, careless and carefree, and if she wanted something, she went after it, regardless of the consequences.

She didn't care about what anyone else thought, or what anyone else wanted her to do, and if she wanted to do something, she did it.

She'd broken the shackles of her relationship, her mental illness, her home, and her job. Her actions seemed brave and courageous, and she exhibited a joy and excitement to be alive.

She had an infectious energy I couldn't help but absorb.

It hadn't occurred to me that her behaviour during that time could have been indicative of a bipolar hypomanic episode. It hadn't occurred to me that her elevated levels of happiness and energy may have been abnormal and unsustainable, and that her increased levels of self-indulgence, promiscuity, and risk-taking could have just been symptoms of her mental illness. And it certainly hadn't occurred to me that her behaviour during that time was ruining others and could have been characteristics of narcissistic personality disorder, sociopathy, or even psychopathy.

If anything, I'd found all the ways she was, alluring and attractive.

The only thing that did occur to me at that time, was that I thought she loved me and that I thought I loved her and that we were both feeling the ecstasy of new love and feeling the elation of finally finding 'the one'.

What was becoming more apparent now, was that it may not have been love at all. I wanted to be more like her; and if I wasn't capable of being so, then the next best thing was to be with her.

I wanted to be with her because she was different.

I wanted to be with her, so I could be different.

I wanted to be with her, because the truth of it was, I was sick of myself and my ways of living my life, and I didn't want to be the person I was anymore.

Woah. Intention solved!

Ms. Luxembourg would be most impressed.

Chapter 5

My quiet drive through the wide-open space of nature had uncovered a new reason for why I'd pursued a relationship with my ex-wife.

It was plausible that my intention back then was straightforward: I was in search of something different, something *new*. I wanted to do something different, and therefore, *become* someone different.

Had I been trying to turn myself inside out to be more like her, to connect with her? Was my attraction to her simply a case of the old cliché: that opposites attract? Or had I just spent the past three hours replacing one set of storylines with another?

How was I going to know for sure?

How could I know *anything* for sure?

How was I going to know what constituted my experience, my memory, and my storyline?

What a mind fuck!

Her text had been the starter's pistol to a nine-year race to nowhere; but was it her fault for pulling the trigger, or mine for starting to run?

So … back to basics then. My third-dimensional answer would be that the fault lay with me, and that I should have been more conscious of my intentions, and that I should not have reacted to her in the way I did. But with my new fourth-dimension lenses on, it seemed I was now less concerned with answering the question of blame, and far more interested in learning *why* it happened the way it did. Why would I want to become my opposite, when being me had been working out perfectly okay?

The westerly winds were whipping up and the sky was transforming overhead as I continued my drive through the countryside. The bright blue in the city, had converted to silvery grey and was now a darker charcoal as I approached the coast.

It was still dry outside, but the sky over the horizon looked like it could burst into tears at any moment. If it did rain, I hoped the downpour would be short lived as I was desperate for a walk on the beach once I arrived. I needed to loosen up my tensing muscles, and escape from this hellish contemplation, if only temporarily.

New knots were forming in my hips and hands, and whilst I could release them by breathing in and relaxing, I couldn't prevent them from reoccurring every few seconds. Like my autonomous leg crossing, my hips and hands were being controlled by my subconscious, but my consciousness was now aware of my physical self, and paying more attention to when these involuntary tensions arose. The not-Dutch counsellor's words came to my mind once more.

'Tension in your body is a sign of tension in your mind. You are tying yourself in knots trying to make sense of something that does not yet make sense'.

She was right.

None of this was making sense.

I had an hour left of this drive, and ten towns to pass through before arriving at my destination with some better clarity. Woodford, Yangery, Tower Hill, Killarney, Rosebrook, Port Fairy, Yambuk, Codrington, Tyrendarra, and Narrawong before my final stop in Allestree; ten more towns to pass through, to find ten more reasons for doing the things I did, as my first new reason didn't seem to be real or complete. I needed more.

Our first three days together had extended to nine and then to fourteen, with the last five spent in Melbourne for a change of scenery. We'd been optimistic that three days would have been enough to sate our appetites for each other and were soon telling each other that three lifetimes wouldn't be enough. Or had pessimism guided us? With neither of us being able to truly believe that the reality could live up to the romantic hype? Either way it didn't matter. Flights and accommodation were effortlessly changed and arranged, and our time together was easily extended.

Our fortnight was spent doing the ordinary and mundane; sleep–ins, breakfasts out, picnics in parks, and walks around the city's tourist sites hand in hand. They were the simple things we'd missed out on by courting via email, and we were keen to wind the clock back and to gain some semblance of normality after two months of craziness.

What we did, we did slowly, immersing ourselves in each other, both conscious of the end date approaching, and neither of us wanting our time together to pass any more quickly than it had to.

She tried not to dwell on life after my return to Bristol; but I knew she was building a house of cards that was sure to collapse as soon as my last day in Australia rolled around.

I'd broached the subject in humour a few times, with comments like, 'we won't be able to do this soon', or, 'this is going to be challenging when we're ten thousand miles apart', but she refused to bite, waiting until the last hour in the departure lounge at Melbourne Airport before saying what she needed to say.

We'd arrived early and had sat in silence, neither of us knowing how to start the conversation, or how it was going to end.

I didn't want to scare her off by asking her to join me in Bristol and again waited for her to take the lead at a pace she was comfortable with.

When that didn't happen, I decided it was up to me to act. How did she want our relationship to continue, I asked, and how were we going to manage it?

For a split second, I wondered if I'd blown it by being too assertive. Between her indrawn breath and her subsequent words, I thought she was going to thank me for a great holiday and wish me all the very best in life; in short, bye bye. But she didn't.

Instead, she told me without hesitation two things that split me in half: she wanted us to be together, but that she wasn't going to move to Bristol to make it happen.

As a whole, it was hardly a statement of commitment, but I didn't hear it that way. "We'll work it out!" I'd said, with absolute certainty, when what I'd actually meant was, "*I'll* work it out!"

As much as she'd pretended to be envious of my overseas move, it wasn't something she was ready to do. She'd already told me she needed to make her mark as a professional marketer and that the last thing she wanted to do was to take a backwards step in a smaller city with less opportunity. If I'd been in London, it would have been a different story, she'd said. Was there any chance I could do my job from there?

She'd told me she'd had enough of Brisbane and was ready for a fresh start in somewhere new like Melbourne, and that she'd move there if I wanted her to.

At the time, I felt conflicted, as I was finally getting into the groove of Bristol and wasn't yet finished with it, but I knew that if I wanted to be with her, then I had no option but to leave it all behind.

It was a clear sign that she wasn't prepared to sacrifice her wants or needs; or her career for mine, even though I was happy to sacrifice mine for hers; but at the same time, I hadn't been paying attention and hadn't seen it that way.

I'd seen what I wanted to see and heard what I wanted to hear; that she wanted to be with me, and I'd responded without thinking, telling her I'd organise to return home to Melbourne as soon as I could.

Looking back, I wonder if she ever expected me to say yes, or was her proposal another test to see how much I'd be prepared to give, and how much she was able to take?

But it wasn't her first test though, was it?

She'd already pushed me to travel to Brisbane for our first date and had somehow persuaded me to organise and pay for all our travel and accommodation for our two weeks together.

It wouldn't have made any difference anyway, and it didn't make any difference now, as the fact remained that I had been prepared to give up my entire life for her; all in the pursuit of creating a new one.

All of my life plans, up in smoke, just like that.

Boundaries, boundaries, boundaries!

Prior to her flirty text message, I'd focussed my life towards a singular goal: to be financially independent and to retire early from corporate work and to live an easier and freer life, doing the things I wanted to do, when I wanted to do them. I didn't need ostentatious wealth, but simply to have enough to live on day to day without being uncomfortable or stressed.

Since receiving my first pay cheque at the age of

fourteen, my life plan was straightforward: work hard, invest harder, sacrifice unnecessary luxuries and extravagances, and make *sensible* choices that would lead me closer to my goal.

My expat assignment in the UK had provided an unexpected boost to my finances, with the company paying for my rent, utilities, and car expenses, and with those major outgoings covered, my savings and borrowing capacity had been supercharged.

By the time we were sitting together in Melbourne Airport's departure lounge, I was close to achieving my goal, calculating that I had just eighteen months to go before I could quit my corporate job and do something different.

By good planning or good fortune, it was the exact amount of time I'd had left on my contract. To the day.

It wasn't just Bristol I was choosing to leave behind for her. By the time I kissed her goodbye at the gate and boarded my flight, I'd handed her full power and control over me and my life.

Looking back, I'm still amazed at the enormity of my decision that day. After eighteen years of sensible choices, I spent less than eighteen seconds making an unsensible one. From that day forward, she took charge of me and my decision making; or more accurately, I gave it to her.

Boundaries, boundaries, boundaries!

As soon as I'd returned to Bristol, I met with my manager to tell him the good news about my personal life and the not-so-good news about my professional.

I'd had no idea how he'd react, or if he'd be willing to transfer me back home to Melbourne considering I was only halfway through doing what I was contracted to do for him.

Privately, I'd already talked myself into unemployment as a viable option if it was going to be the only way for us to be reunited in Melbourne.

He'd listened to me without interrupting, and seemed genuinely happy for me, and my new situation, and apart from hopefully asking whether she would move to Bristol, he didn't try to change my mind or negotiate a different outcome.

My request to end my assignment early was accepted, albeit without a firm date, or details for what it would mean for me and my future employment. Neither of us knew if I'd have a job when I returned to Melbourne, and we both agreed not to worry about it until we got closer to finding my replacement in Bristol.

He knew the local employment market better than I and had estimated it would take us a minimum of three months to find the right candidate. I remember being horrified at the thought. How was I going to manage for *three whole months* without her when I'd barely survived two in the lead up to our first date?

Without considering the consequences, I'd asked him whether I'd be able to work from our Melbourne office for a week at about the halfway mark, and remarkably, he agreed without pause.

I remember feeling uncomfortably selfish for putting

myself first and for asking for such a thing, but in hindsight I wondered if it wasn't as simple as me being selfish; what if it was me being selfish on her behalf?

My storyline at the time was that he was rewarding my sixteen-hour days and six-day work weeks, but thinking back, it was equally plausible that he'd seen the desperation in my eyes and didn't want me doing something stupid like leaving my job behind before I'd handed it over to someone else. Either way, I was going to be back in Melbourne in six weeks' time.

By the end of that day, I'd booked my return flights and had sent her the details with the hope she too could organise a 'business trip' to our Melbourne office for the same week.

I hadn't done anything as impulsive as that before, and that I'd 'hoped' she could arrange a trip without asking her first, was evidence that I was already adopting her way of being.

A preorganised weekend jaunt to Venice was my halfway point to the halfway mark, but I'd developed a severe case of the CBFs, and had no interest in going. I'd booked the flights and accommodation six months earlier, at a time when it was cheapest to do so, and when she'd been nothing more than a pen pal.

My colleagues in Bristol encouraged me to see it through, telling me it was a once-in-a-lifetime opportunity to experience Carnevale, and worth doing before I returned to Melbourne. They didn't get it: I didn't want a once-in-a-lifetime experience if it wasn't with her.

Their encouragement didn't quite win me over, but after three weeks away from her, I needed to do something different to eliminate a few days before we met again.

I'd thoroughly enjoyed my first exploration of La Serenissima and trusted that a second visit would provide me with a decent distraction.

It didn't.

One hundred thousand people were crushed into St. Mark's Square, and I was the only one not wearing a mask, costume, or gown. Music blared from a stage near Museo Correr, and light projections beamed from unknown locations onto the Campanile and perimeter buildings.

The colourful chaos overloaded my senses, and instead of elevating my mood and disrupting my pining, it had the opposite effect. The energy in the Square had drained my own, and I wished I wasn't there.

Wishing to not be in Venice was a feeling I was no longer familiar with, and whilst I would have given just about anything to have gotten myself out of there back then, I'd give just about anything to be back there right now.

Rather than sitting, paralysed into inaction by emotion, I tried to outrun my feelings by getting out of the city and visiting somewhere new.

I caught a train to Verona and mindlessly raced around the two-thousand-year-old city like a child jacked up on red cordial. From Porta Nuova to the Verona Arena, to Piazza delle Erbe and Torre dei Lamberti, to Piazza dei Signori, to Casa di Giulietta and the world's most famous balcony; I'd seen and photographed them all in less time than it took me to get there, and I took none of it in.

If I'd taken a moment to pay attention to where I was and where I'd been, I might have noticed that I'd stood in the courtyard location of the greatest love story ever written; a story that might have reminded me of the fine line between love and obsession; and of new lovers destroying themselves for each other based on false facts and false realities.

It was a metaphor hiding in plain sight, but I was too busy documenting my visit to *see* it for what it *was*.

With more time to kill, I power-walked back to the train station and bought a return ticket to Milan. On arrival, I quickstepped down Via Vittor Pisani and Alessandro Manzoni to see the inside of Galleria Vittorio Emanuele II, and the outside of the Duomo, leaving just enough time to jog back to Milano Centrale to catch the very last train back to Venice before services ceased for the night.

I woke early the next morning without noticeable change to my depressed mood, but rather than trying to outrun my feelings again, I'd chosen to stay with them.

My fifty euro per night pensione hadn't afforded me my own bathroom, but oddly, the bedroom did come with a pink enamel pedestal sink. I washed my face, brushed my teeth, and had a quick birdbath, before checking out and heading around the corner back towards Piazza San Marco.

Despite the sub-zero temperature, the crowds were already heaving en masse, and I'd been unable to get past Piazzetta dei Leoncini. Without an obvious path through to the Bacino and Riva degli Schiavoni, I hoisted myself without too much effort onto the marble plinth under the granite lion statuary to get a better look at what was possible and what wasn't. There were tens of thousands of revellers packed into the square facing the stage, and they weren't going anywhere.

It was a brutal contrast to when I'd been there thirteen months earlier, when at that same hour, I'd had the entirety of St. Mark's Square to myself.

Rather than battling my way forwards or backwards, I stayed on my plinth and surveyed the area, before finding an escape in the most unexpected of places.

St. Mark's Basilica was surprisingly quiet, and I'd initially thought it was closed, or at least closed for Sunday mass. There was no line of people to get in, and no one milling about its central doors, but it was the people exiting near to where I was, that alerted me to its open state.

After poking my head through the door to make sure I wasn't trespassing, I stepped into the nave, paid the entry fee, and climbed the tight internal stairway to the loggia dei cavalli.

The interior decoration of the basilica was mind-blowing, and the artistry and workmanship seemed beyond human capability. What I'd thought were paintings, were mosaics, and what I'd thought was gold paint, were actually gold tiles. The opulence was overwhelming, and no sooner than I was in, I wanted to be out again.

It made the loggia the perfect place to do both.

I took a seat on the eroded marble bench high above the costumed revellers, and breathed in the spectacular views of the Piazza and Piazzetta, Campanile and Colonne, and the Church of San Giorgio Maggiore ... and it left me unmoved.

I'd been in one of the greatest cities on the planet, at possibly the best time of year, and was surrounded by pure energy and joy, but I'd had none of my own.

Sitting there, freezing on the icy marble of the seat, I noticed a familiar inability to snap myself out of the wretched state I was in; the same state I'd been in, whilst in New York City, seven or eight weeks earlier. What was *wrong* with me?

I realised that thoughts of her had consumed me since her first text, and there was nothing I could do to snap myself out of it. I didn't know how to stop my feelings; how to pause them so I could get through the next three weeks, and the six weeks after that, without simply wishing the time away.

It was as though she was both the cause and the cure for my mental and emotional states, and none of it had made sense.

I'd reached a place of grateful contentment just three months earlier and all of it had simply evaporated.

I was no longer me.

I'd known then, that something wasn't quite right with me, and I knew it again now whilst whizzing through the town of Rosebrook, but I still didn't understand why it had happened – nor *how* – to a sensible, focussed person like me.

I'd once been skilled at compartmentalising my thoughts and feelings, and at getting on with whatever I needed to get on with, but she'd infiltrated all my compartments, and had fused them together, so that thoughts and feelings were one.

It had been in those moments on the loggia, staring at Colonna di San Todaro that I'd felt a deep-seated dread and despair; as though I was homeless and hopeless, that I had no prospects for the future, and nothing to look forward to, even though the opposite was true.

If I'd known about empaths back then, I might have considered the possibility that those feelings weren't mine; but if they weren't mine, then whose would they have been? Certainly not the joyous revellers partying and celebrating in front of me.

It was as though I'd been possessed by the devil of despondency, by an entity I wasn't familiar with; and that I was powerless to do anything about it.

I'd wanted to exorcise it, and her, or at least the thought of her, just for the time I had left in Bristol, so I could enjoy my travels like I did prior to knowing her.

I compared my happy and contented state when lying under the flowering chestnut trees in Parque de El Retiro, to that time in Venice, sitting with the replica horses on the balcony atop St. Mark's Basilica.

They were stark opposites.

Whilst I was in Venice, she'd packed her clothes and belongings into her car and left her apartment. She'd told me she could no longer be in the same space as her ex and had no other option but to leave as soon as she could; but with nowhere to go, her temporary solution was to start couch surfing at various friends' houses until she found something more permanent.

It didn't sound much of a plan to me, as I still had a minimum of nine weeks left in the UK before I could get home for us to start building our new life together.

I could tell that she hated the feeling of not having a stable base, and I would have too.

From half a world away, I felt her dislocation and committed to helping her solve it as soon as possible.

I offered to find her a fully furnished short-stay rental, or a serviced apartment to tide her over, but she'd not been interested in replacing a short-term plan with another short-term plan.

Even though I had my own living arrangements to deal with, I'd made her business my business, and had made her living arrangements my problem to solve,

Yes, but that's what people do in relationships; they help each other!

If that's the case, then why wasn't she helping me?

About a week later, she informed me that she was going to start applying for a rental houses in Brisbane, and that she'd break the lease when we knew what we were doing.

Her decision confused me, as it made no sense that she'd sign a twelve-month lease when I was only eight weeks away from returning home, but it was becoming blatantly obvious, that nothing at that time made sense. But naturally, I didn't tell her that.

The story I told myself was that she was giving up far more for me than I was for her, and that for the past four weeks, she'd been doing it far tougher than I had.

Whilst I'd been swanning around Northern Italy, she'd been living out of a bag on a friend's loungeroom floor.

She was obviously unhappy with her peripatetic life, and I'd felt it was unfair to do anything but support her choices.

More than anything, I didn't want her to change her mind about our plans to meet in Melbourne. My larger worry was that she'd change her mind about us, and end things before they'd started.

Not only would that leave me stranded without a job, it would leave me alone in Australia to start my life from scratch. I'd have nothing.

'A narcissist has no conscience for other people; but an empath has no conscience for themselves'.

Fifteen, love, Luxembourg.

She hadn't lived on her own before, moving directly from her mum's house to her boyfriend's, so I'd felt it wise to encourage her to give it a go, and get it out of her system before we inevitably shacked up together.

She had sounded reluctant from the outset, unsure whether she'd be able to afford to live somewhere decent, and whilst I offered to help with the rent, she was one step ahead of me, having already found someone to share with.

The 'someone' was a colleague of hers in Brisbane, and the two of them spent several weeknights and weekends house hunting and applying for several properties before finding her dream house in her dream location, a warehouse-conversion in Woolloongabba.

They signed a twelve-month lease; and when I'd asked if her housemate was okay with her not seeing it through, she told me she hadn't told him about it yet. She must have noticed my faintly shocked tone of voice because she tried to convince me that there was no reason to tell him anything until she had a firm date on when she'd be heading south.

I didn't challenge her way of thinking or her decision-making rationale. Her decisions were hers to make, and it was my role to encourage her from afar and to keep my opinions to myself. It was my role to support her choices, and to ensure I was in no way similar to the way she'd described her ex-boyfriend.

These were my storylines, and they set the scene for the next nine years.

'A psychopath may have many victims, but an empath has only one'.

Thirty, love, Luxembourg.

I didn't get to see her warehouse, and I only met her housemate once, just prior to her moving out. I was of the opinion that he didn't like me, and that he viewed me as his competition. He clearly had his own not-so-secret crush on her.

I let her know about my suspicion as delicately as I could, but she shut me down and told me not to be stupid. She told me she viewed him as her younger brother, and that I had nothing to worry about.

I hadn't been worried or jealous, as she'd made her choice, and had chosen me. I'd told her that she had no control over how others felt about her, and that it made sense that others might well feel about her in the same way I did, but she'd not wanted to hear it.

My suspicion was proven true a few days later when she'd told him she was moving to Melbourne to be with me. He'd burst into tears and professed his love for her on bended knee and asked her to stay with him in Brisbane.

I didn't react with a 'told you so' to validate my own comment and feelings, and I didn't push her to reveal more than she wanted to tell me. But, I couldn't help feeling that there was more to it than what she was letting on.

He would have been her first affair during our relationship, but he would not have been her last. I created our own system of 'don't ask, don't tell', and if the not-Dutch counsellor's assessment of me was correct, then my intuition knew more than I wanted it to know.

Each time I'd felt something in my gut, I chose to ignore it. I had no interest in my gut being right, but equally, I didn't want her to feel bad if it was.

How was I supposed to tap into my intuition, or trust it, when I'd been at war with it; when not only had I ignored my gut instincts, but deliberately supressed anything they had to tell me? This — *this* — was my essential dilemma.

My intuition was my version of Pandora's Box: the evil of knowledge and foresight. Whether I was conscious of it or not, I'd fought my intuition because I didn't want to trust it. I didn't want the evil of knowing more than I should, or worse, thinking I did.

'A psychopath will destroy other people for themselves, but an unknowing empath will destroy themselves for other people'.

Forty, love, Luxembourg.

Whilst she was sorting out her housing situation, she was also trying to sort out her employment situation, and having had limited success with her job applications for roles beyond her experience and seniority, she'd started throwing her net wider and wider. Not only was she applying for positions in Melbourne, she had started to apply for roles in Sydney, Adelaide, and Perth, telling me she'd negotiate terms if she landed any of them in a city other than Melbourne and that I shouldn't worry about it until she had.

Not long before my halfway trip to visit her, her manager had asked her if she'd like to move to Melbourne to be closer to him and his team. It was an unexpected stroke of luck and was a win-win-win, with him thrilled to have her in his office; her thrilled that she'd get a moving allowance and temporary accommodation to move states, and me thrilled, because she was actually adhering to our plan.

It was all the evidence I'd needed to prove that she was

as committed to our relationship as much as I was. If she'd wanted to stay with her housemate in Brisbane, she could have, but she chose not to.

Like me, she was uprooting her entire life to move cities to start a new relationship and a new life.

It was just another story I was telling myself to get me through.

My memories of the rest of that year remain clouded in a haze of jetlag. I did fly back to Australia at the six-week mark, and again at the twelve-week mark, and then again, each and every six weeks between April and October.

At some point between March and May, she'd changed her mind about me moving to Melbourne to be with her, and instead made the sudden decision to move to Bristol to be with me.

In a split-second, she'd upended all our plans made since January and everything we'd worked towards during that time. It was an extreme about-face, but one I welcomed with open arms.

It hadn't mattered that she'd already moved to Melbourne and had found another share house with another man. It hadn't mattered that I'd resigned from my job in Bristol and had already found my replacement. It hadn't mattered that I'd already packed all my things to move back to Australia, and it hadn't mattered that a job was being created for me to come home to.

All that mattered at that time was that she changed her

mind and that we'd get to be together in the UK, and that I could take her away and show her Venice, Verona, and Milan much sooner than expected.

I'd find out later, that whatever she'd told me at the time, her change of mind had little to do with me and far more to do with her. Her best friend had moved to London, and they'd made the realisation that their childhood dream could soon become a reality. Whilst Bristol wasn't London, it was a short train ride away, and could be a stepping stone to get to where she wanted to be. Her best friend convinced her that she had a once in a lifetime opportunity to make an easy overseas move, without having to worry about where she'd live, how'd she'd get around, or how she'd pay for it all.

All she needed me to do was to reverse my resignation or find another job, keep my expat benefits, my house and car, and find her a marketing job whilst I was at it.

And I did.

With cap in hand, I unwound my plans. My manager in Bristol created a special projects role for me, and a special marketing role for her. There was still a mountain of work to do over there, and we were qualified to help. My manager was happy to keep me in the UK and happy to have her help with all the marketing projects he was yet to get off the ground; however, there'd been one sticking point that required our compromise, and that was her move date.

Her manager in Melbourne wasn't happy she'd decided to move so soon after he'd paid her relocation costs and wanted six-months tenure from her before she moved again. Given everything else had gone our way, we agreed to wait until October.

For the nine months between our first date and her move to Bristol, I travelled back and forward to Melbourne six times, squished into the economic back parts of the plane. It had been nine months of both heaven and hell, with heaven being my time with her, and hell being my perpetual state of jetlag.

I'd given her one hundred percent of me during that time, and by the time October rolled around, I'd designed the blueprint for our relationship until it ended.

I was the giver, and she was the taker.

'A narcissist has no limit for how much they will take, and an empath has no limit for how much they will give. They are a perfect match, a perfect yet destructive match'.

Game, Luxembourg.

Chapter 6

Driving towards the gates of my beach shack usually brought on waves of calm and relief, but today was feeling a little different. Today, I'd arrived tired and worn out, and my little shed-like house wasn't appearing as a haven at the end of my journey; rather, it felt like the start of a new one, a new journey of rewriting another storyline, perhaps one of the greatest storylines of my marriage.

I'd bought the vacant plot of coastal land in haste about seven years ago, a few months after my then-wife had collapsed on our bathroom floor. The severity of her mental breakdown so soon after our wedding threw me into a spin and my idea for acquiring the property was to provide space for her recovery and to prevent it from happening again. My plan was to replicate a place where I'd seen her happiest and most relaxed, and to create an environment and lifestyle for her to escape her demons and release her depression back into the aether from whence it came.

As a child and teenager, she'd spent her weekends at her father's small acreage in the hinterland of Far North Queensland. He was an engineer by trade and had designed and built his own house to exacting specifications and standards. It wasn't a big home, but it provided ample space for him and his partner, their dogs, horses, and both of his children every other weekend. Five metres wide by twenty-five metres long, the rectangular house was divided into five, five-metre modules: a bedroom and ensuite, lounge and living, kitchen and dining, undercover breezeway, and a second bedroom and ensuite.

The home was perched on the edge of a dam and each room had a wall of windows to bring the outside in. He'd planted a landscape of native trees and lush greenery to fill the gaps between earth and sky, and to shield the house and his family from the road, and from the prying eyes in the half a dozen vehicles that would pass by each day.

For years, she'd spent her spare time and school holidays helping her father build their dream house and garden, and when she wasn't cleaning or labouring, she'd spend hours bushwalking or horse riding in the hills surrounding the property.

She'd reluctantly sacrificed her formative years to help bring it to life, but once it was complete, she'd enjoyed the fruits of her labour far more than she anticipated. In short, she loved the place and chose to spend as much time there as she was able.

I visited her father's property three times, and the tranquillity of his oasis appealed to me as much as it did to them. She'd been a different person whilst there, more relaxed and somehow better in tune with herself and with nature. She was able to unwind from the stresses of her job and rebalance the perceived demands of the city with the genuine simplicity of the country.

Her favourite thing to do was doze in one of the four hammocks strung up in the breezeway, drifting in and out of consciousness whilst listening to the wind in the eucalypts, and the croaks of nearby frogs.

It was her place of serenity, and she appeared the best version of herself when we were there. So, it was all the more devastating to her when, in what she'd felt was a blindside, her father sold the property at the behest of his partner, before picking up and moving to Western Australia.

The subtraction of the property from her life and all it represented, affected her more than she cared to admit, and I came to the conclusion that the grief caused by its loss only compounded the depths of her depression at that time.

She'd lost her escape, and I'd made it my business to create her a new one.

My business, her business, the universe's business …
She didn't ask for it, did she?
It wasn't really my business, was it?

At the time I bought the block in Allestree, we'd been together for three and a half years and I was already desperate to rewind the clock back to our happier times.

At the direction of our employer, we'd returned to Australia six months after she'd moved to the UK, and we'd both found it difficult to settle into Melbourne life. We stayed in temporary accommodation for three months before finding a place of our own, but it hadn't been right for us, so we moved again six months later.

Marriage planning had kept us both entertained until our big day, but after that, all our big projects were complete, and we started to settle down into mundane everyday life.

The thrill of our first year together was gone, and I wanted it back. I wanted to see her excitement and exuberance again, but most of all, I wanted her to *be* the person she was back at our start.

It was a foolish pursuit, but I hadn't known it at the time. I'd thought that by buying the property, I'd be able to revive the mental and emotional state she'd experienced at her father's house, helping make life a little better for both of us. I thought that by spending time in our own tranquil oasis, that she'd have a place where she could walk on the beach, hear the ocean, and relax by the fire; a place where she could lay in a hammock, listen to waves, and rediscover her serenity. My view of the world was black and white, and it was becoming clearer to me now, that I had treated her mental state as a mathematical problem I was going to solve.

If … then …

I hadn't anticipated that my dream for our sanctuary wouldn't become a reality for another five years, through no fault of my own. The result was that the stress I'd hoped to alleviate in her, by buying the land and building the house, ended up rebounding onto me, in orders of magnitude I'd never anticipated.

Although I'd known that the planning permission process would be drawn-out and arduous, I didn't know that the local authorities in the area had no intention of allowing me, or anyone else for that matter, to build along this part of the coast. Climate change and coastal erosion were their justification, even though their own expert reports said neither would cause an impact on the area for at least one hundred years.

I made it my mission in life to battle the council and the state government, and my fight for justice became my obsession, consuming most of my time, money, and headspace.

I spent years commissioning reports from oceanographers, environmentalists, geologists, indigenous corporations, and archaeologists to justify sustainable development, and spent months in hearings and tribunals, advocating for myself and my neighbours who found themselves in the same position as me. I hounded the planning minister and the Premier of the State at that time and pioneered new legal agreements regarding risk associated with climate change, and penned contracts with the authorities to reduce their liability.

I'd convinced myself that I'd started the project for her mental health, and that her mental health relied on me completing it, regardless of the toll on my own.

It was a storyline to end all storylines.

It took me four years and hundreds of thousands of dollars to obtain the planning permission I needed, and an extra year and many more hundreds of thousands of dollars to have the house built and ready to use; but the cruel irony of the endeavour was that she'd only visit the house once before she left me.

The project had taken too long and based on what I recently learnt, she may have been on the verge of another manic phase, a phase unsuited to quiet time in the country.

Not all was lost though, as I kept the house after the divorce and used it as a refuge after the tumultuous events of Tokyo and Greece. So, although not in the way I had intended, it had still met its objective of escape and respite, and continued to do so as the months passed.

When I decided, all those years ago, to set out on this project, did my intuition know I'd enjoy it here for my own reasons, fuelling my tenacity and obstinance, or was that too, just a new storyline to better fit my developing narrative?

Regardless of my intentions, storylines, and complete lack of boundaries, I loved this place for everything it was – and wasn't – and so did my dog.

The south-west coast of Victoria has dual personalities, much like my ex-wife, calm and serene in summer, and angry and chaotic in winter, with spring and autumn being hybrids of the two. Summer was a time of cool breezes and a lake-like-ocean lapping gently at the shore. Skies were blue and native animals roamed the land as they had for millennia. Wallabies, echidnas, magpies, black cockatoos, and reptiles traversed the property, wary of predators, but not wary of me.

Winter was the opposite, with winds of over one hundred kilometres per hour whipping up ocean swells of nine metres, sending waves up the beach to reclaim the sand it had deposited there in earlier months. Skies were grey, and rain and hail blew in horizontally, like arrows from the horizon.

The land animals disappeared into their shelters, and sea animals took their place, escaping the turbulent sea to rest and convalesce. Seals, sea lions, and the odd penguin would drag themselves onto the dunes, to sleep and regain their strength for future days of hunting and fishing.

Winter was my favourite time here, with the whitecaps, and south westerlies blowing a gale. The sea spray and the icy winds from Antarctica were like acupuncture needles on my face, a free homeopathic therapy, invigorating and healing.

There was something here for all my senses, the ultra-brightness of the sunlight through clouds, the incessant roaring of the Southern Ocean, the umami smell of seaweed and other vegetation, the taste of salt on my lips, and the feeling of air and moisture on my skin; and hopefully there was something here too, for beyond my senses.

During June, July and August, the land, sea, and sky transformed to something new each day, and no two days were alike. The beach was forever metamorphosing, with new contours and new shapes to explore each sunrise.

Walking the dunes was like walking unexplored terrain, and amongst the constant change and instability, I found calm and consistency.

Allestree wasn't a destination for regular holidayers as it didn't offer clean white beaches nor crystal blue water. The sand here was greige in colour, like ash, with specks of grey, black, and beige, and everything in between. This wasn't a place for sitting, swimming, or sunbathing; rather, it was a space for meandering, thinking, and theorising; three things I was doing more and more of.

During the autumn and winter tides, the foamy green ocean brought in something new to investigate every twelve hours. High tides could bring in tonnes of seaweed, mounds of crushed shell grit, quicksand, and dead sea creatures both big and small. Urchins, periwinkles, pipis, velella, starfish, weedy sea dragons, and blue bottles were just some of the many organisms that made walking barefoot treacherous and navigating a straight line near impossible.

Isolation from other places – and people – was one of Allestree's greatest appeals, but I didn't dare tell anyone that. Friends already thought I was weird for travelling here on my own, so explaining to them that I thoroughly enjoyed it, was going to be too much for them to process.

On the rare occasion when other people did cross my path, they seemed to be of the same ilk, people who were content in their own company and in their own thoughts. Avoiding strangers was de rigueur, and others were easily bypassed with a polite smile or friendly wave from fifty paces.

There was no obligation to stop and chat, and unwanted interactions were avoided by altering trajectories, but every now and then, someone would want to stop to say hi and talk about the weather, the beach, or about how great this place was, and about nine months ago, that someone had been me.

After returning from Japan, I'd noticed on various occasions several people zigzagging along the shoreline with their heads down, walking towards me, only to double back to retrace their steps, repeating the process over and over, oblivious to my existence as I walked by.

They were hunched over staring at the sand as if they'd lost something, kicking and sifting through the grit and seaweed with their booted feet. On the rare occasion they acknowledged my presence, I'd ask them what they were looking for, and whether I could help; however, in all but one of the instances, they offered me a stock standard response of, 'nothing' and 'no'.

It was late one afternoon, that I received a different response from a middle-aged lady I hadn't seen here before.

'The reason for all this stuff on the beach is the reef', she'd said pointing out to sea, 'Just over there behind you. When we get big swells and big tides, bits of the reef break away and wash up here, but it's not the reef that people here are interested in, it's what's in it'.

She went on to tell me that the reef was probably a part of the mainland many years ago and was a treasure trove of prehistoric fossils and petrified remains of ancient species of fauna that died out thousands, or tens of thousands of years ago. She spoke of megafauna, and huge wombats called diprotodon, and hippopotamus-like creatures called zygomaturus, as well as extinct kangaroos called procoptodon.

She'd told me that *my* beach was popular in winter with fossil hunters and beachcombers, but as I'd seen so few people here doing it, it was my assumption that fossil hunting and beachcombing weren't all that popular.

After she'd run through more of the scientific names of other extinct animals, she edged closer to me, as if to share a secret.

'Whilst the people here may find bits and pieces of petrified bone and stuff, what they're really searching for are—' She stopped for a moment and swivelled her head like a meerkat to see if anyone else was eavesdropping on our conversation, before whispering to me, '—shark teeth.' She pulled away from me with her eyes wide open, as if to mimic the surprise I should have been showing.

'Shark teeth?' I'd replied.

'Yes, shark teeth! This is one of the few places you can find them, and in the old days they'd come in by the bucket load. They're not so easy to find now, but it's a local's secret though, so don't go telling anybody else about it, okay? We don't want this place overrun with tourists!'

I wasn't sure if she was joking but I assured her that the secret was safe with me. I told her that I came here to escape the city and that the last thing I wanted was for more people to be here.

After she'd gauged my sincerity, she continued to tell me that the shark teeth had no real value and people only looked for them because of the excitement of finding them. 'One of the reasons the fossickers keep to themselves', she said, 'was to protect their patch, and so that there would be no disputes over discoveries'. She told me the holy grail was to find a tooth from a megalodon, a twenty-metre-long monster of a shark that became extinct millions of years ago. 'Only a few have been found during the past twenty or thirty years, but no one is sure if they're actually from here, and not purchased from the U.S. where they are more common'.

I'd tried to keep my face straight as I wasn't one hundred percent sure if she wasn't having me on. People searching for shark teeth was plausible, but people faking their finds seemed not. She held her thumb and forefinger as far apart as they would go to show me just how big they could be. 'They're massive but I've never seen one in real life'.

Hunting for shark teeth seemed like a specifically odd hobby, and an awful way to ruin a good walk, but it wasn't long before my curiosity took over and my fear of missing out got the better of me.

Within a few days of meeting her, I'd slowed my tempo and started zigzagging the beach; hunched over with poor posture and my eyes locked to the sand, kicking through seaweed and rock fragments, searching for fossils and shark teeth, and hopefully, one from the elusive megalodon.

During the time between my ex-wife leaving me to stay

at her brother's apartment and her calling to end our marriage, I'd walked this beach scores of times to decompress, and to ask the universe for clarity on what was going on with her and with us.

I'd while away five or six hours a day with my head down, scanning the beach for fossils and teeth, and I'd hypothesised that if I found a shark tooth, then everything was going to be okay between us, and we'd make it through.

It was a fabricated superstition with no bearing on reality, a throwback to my childhood when I'd invented many others. I thought I'd grown out of them decades ago, but there I was, a fully-grown adult, not fully believing in the delusion, but not willing to disbelieve it either.

My childhood scenarios had been innocent and ridiculous, and like this new one, had zero connection to reality. A psychologist would probably tell me that it was a form of obsessive-compulsive disorder that I never fully subscribed to, but I'd stopped entertaining them before anyone noticed, or before they became a problem.

They were my personal versions of 'not stepping on the cracks in the pavement', and to this day, I had no idea where they came from, or why. I knew they were scientifically unreliable and invalid, but my action or inaction with these superstitions created empirical validation and informal confirmation.

I'd stopped my superstitions almost entirely, no longer needing them, but every now and then, I'd create a new one, and finding a shark tooth to save my marriage had become one of them.

I never did find a shark tooth, and my relationship wasn't saved, so it was just another superstition empirically confirmed.

Chapter 7

As my dog and I reached the halfway point of today's post-drive walk, a tall lanky man I hadn't seen here before materialised from the sand dunes. He was dressed in dark green overalls and was venturing towards the water's edge, possibly to cast a line out into the choppy ocean. He wore a similar coloured wide-rimmed bucket hat, the front part flipped up, and was holding it in place with alternating hands to prevent it from blowing away in the gusty winds. His eyes were focussed on the shoreline, and as he moved in and out of the water, backwards and forwards, and side to side, he repeatedly bent over to snatch things from the sand.

Shark teeth fossicker!

As I approached him, he ventured further into the ocean, immersing himself to his waist. He had no fishing rod, and I could now see that his overalls were green rubber waders rising to a bib and brace over his chest and shoulders.

He was aware of my existence but seemed to be keeping his distance. Rather than leave him alone, I sped up to reach his position on the beach so I could say hi and ask him what he was doing.

He was a caricature of an old-fashioned seafarer, with a wiry white beard sprouting from his gaunt face and tufts of similarly coloured hair falling from beneath his hat. He looked anywhere between sixty and eighty years old and wore rectangular gold-framed glasses.

He did his best to ignore me, but a surging wave had him hightailing out of the water and straight into my path.

He contrived surprise at my presence. "Sorry about that, didn't see you there. Don't wanna drown today. Once water gets in these, you're a goner. 'Aven't seen you 'ere before, You new?" His voice was gruff, but he seemed friendly enough.

"No, not new. I've been coming 'ere for a little while now, but I'm from Melbourne."

"Oh, one of those, eh?"

I tried not to take offence at his insinuation as he was most likely right, but his waders and lack of fishing rod still had me curious about what exactly he was doing.

I wanted to ask directly about shark teeth but decided to take a more subtle approach, to see if he'd tell me the truth, or want me to move on.

"What you up to?"

He assessed me with his crooked jaw and semi-toothless smile. "Just searchin' for shark teeth."

Gee, that was easy!

The lady I'd met here last year had made a huge song and dance out of it, but this guy was giving away the secret like it was nothing at all.

"I've heard they're around, but I've never found one."

His right eye was squinched closed, and he examined me further with his left. He had an underbite and was chewing on something.

"You won't find 'em up there." He pointed his crooked finger towards the path of seaweed and rock I'd just cut through. "They're usually 'ere in the shallows, washin' in and out, but you gotta be quick, 'cause as soon as they come in, they wash out again."

In the shallows?

"Is that right?"

"And watch out for the sand and grit 'cos it covers them up real quick, and you'll never find 'em after that. You gotta be fast and snatch 'em when you see 'em. There's no second chances."

He seemed to have honed his approach to the task in hand and knew what he was talking about, and his easy-going nature put me at ease about interrogating him further.

"How's your search goin' today? Have you 'ad any success? You wouldn't 'av 'appened to have found one today, would ya? One I could see?"

My speech was reflecting his, but I wasn't consciously doing it. I hoped he wouldn't think I was taking the piss. But no, he responded in the same friendly way.

"Sure 'av. It will be a good day today! We're comin' off a 'igh swell and 'igh tide and there's a bit of grit around. I've just got the one so far, but it's early days."

"Oh great, I've never seen one; can I see it?"

"You never seen one, eh?"

"No, never."

He released the snap-buttons from his bib's breast pocket and extracted a small white plastic chewing gum bottle.

How's it fitting in there?!

He popped the top off the container and tipped its contents into his wet hand. Six or seven things fell out and I scanned them quickly but couldn't see the tooth amongst the shiny black fragments scattered across his open palm.

He held it closer to my face as if to say, 'Seee!'.

I didn't say anything and returned my gaze to his. He pocketed the bottle and used his newly freed hand to move the fragments around. "See 'ere?"

I felt panicked, as if my eyes were failing me. "No, sorry, I don't!"

He was either delusional or poking fun at me, or both.

He picked up one of the black fragments and held it up to the sky.

As he brought it closer to my eyes, I could see that it was like obsidian, but as he moved it, it appeared almost metallic, and both glossy and matte at the same time. It was less than a centimetre long and was a quadrangle, but would have been triangular if one of its tips hadn't been missing.

"This is probably from a bull, but without its gum, it could also be from a tiger."

I was still confused.

I poked my right index finger towards the object. "That thing? That's a shark tooth?"

"Yeah, 'ere, 'av a closer look." He handed me the fragment to examine for myself.

I held it between my finger and thumb and analysed it closely. It was flat on one side and had a slight bulge on the other and was thicker near its top than its bottom. Its colour and opacity were indescribable, and its texture was like polished stone, or porcelain. "I can't believe this is a shark's tooth!"

"Why's that?"

"Because it doesn't look like one!"

"It's thousands of years old and has been battered around a fair bit. They come out of the reef over there." He gestured to the sea behind him, confirming the same place the middle-aged woman had pointed out to me last year. "The darker and more eroded they are, the older they are. Some are millions or even tens of millions of years old!"

His words crashed into one another like the waves behind him, and my jaw dropped open in pure disbelief. I felt a slight wobble in my legs, and the blood drained from my brain.

"What 'av you been looking for? Big great white movie-prop-looking things?" His crooked smile spread wide across his face in gentle mockery of me, the city slicker with no idea.

I handed him back his shark tooth and thanked him for showing me.

He dropped it into its bottle and headed back to the shallows. "No problem, now don't go finding 'em all now, you 'ear?"

I stumbled away, my heart pounding.

Since hearing about shark teeth last year, I'd been searching for white triangles on dry sand. I'd calibrated my eyes to locate white on greige, and had picked up more cuttlefish bone, shell, and pumice rock than I cared to remember.

During the past year, I'd searched for objects that were the wrong colour, wrong size, and wrong texture.

During that time, I'd been searching for all the wrong things in all the wrong places.

No wonder I couldn't find one to save my marriage!

As I continued my beach walk, the thoughts in my head spun to a stop.

The sky became brighter, and the aroma of freshly stranded seaweed became more intense. The drone of the ocean separated into individual sounds of each wave, and the winter air felt cooler on my warming skin.

With the seadog's taunt ringing in my ears, I stepped closer to the water's edge, my eyes trained downward for small-black-matte-gloss-metallic shapes rinsing around in the shallow wash.

The gentle surge of water lapping at the shore was opaque with plumes of sandy smoke, but as the water receded, it became crystal clear.

Within a minute, I spotted a black something, and then another, and another, but they moved too quickly to sieve between my fingers before being drawn back into the sea.

He was right. This was trickier than it looked.

I'd not paid much attention before now to how fast-moving the shallow water was, but now that I wanted it to be slow, it was anything but.

I bent down to get a closer look and to decrease the time I'd need to snatch and grab.

Got one! No, that's a bit of mussel shell.

This one! No … broken glass.

That one? No, a bit of rock.

I stood up straight and took a step back, contemplating my nine months of wasted scanning, and felt conceited for thinking I was going to find one so easily today, when the expert I'd just met had only found one in all the time he'd been here.

I cringed in embarrassment, and dropped my head in shame, but as I opened my eyes, a black triangle materialised by my feet; washed in with the last surge of water, stranded by its retreat.

No fucking way!

I bent over and grabbed it with a fistful of everything that was around it, jarring my fingers as they dug into the sand.

With my other hand, I sifted through the wet grains until a black triangle was revealed.

Could it be?

I rinsed it off in the shallows, holding it tight so not to lose it, and then raised it to the sunlight.

It seemed to reflect in the same way the seadog's had, but it was a much darker black, with a more dimpled surface. It was ten or eleven millimetres long, and between my fingers, felt smooth like onyx. It was isosceles in shape and its two longer sides were eroded, with its third smaller side thicker than the rest of it.

Could it be?

I needed expert confirmation, so quick-stepped back towards the seadog who was again knee deep in the water.

I unfurled my fist and called out to him. "Excuse me, excuse me, is this one by any chance?"

He trudged in from the water, and plucked it from my palm, examining it quickly, before putting it in his mouth and biting it. *Gross.* "Where'd you find that?"

"Just over there." I pointed to the place at the end of my footprints where I'd been thirty seconds ago.

"Beginner's luck. It looks old, a million or more I reckon. I've found a few like that." He handed it back to me, spinning around and huffing, wading back to his earlier position.

I froze, stunned.

I found one!

I'd fucking found one!

I wanted to jump up and punch my fist in the air, and scream it out, but my limbs remained locked in place. I closed my eyes and squeezed it tight in my hand, its sharp points piercing my palm. Euphoria surged through me, and the hair on my arms stood on end.

I opened my eyes and tried to slow my heartbeat with three-four-five breathing, and by focusing on the whitecaps in the distance.

That something so small and insignificant could create such a *physical* intensity within me made no sense, but did it need to?

I turned around to continue walking, my mind exploding with a hundred questions.

Why now?

What was the message in this?

Was I still superstitious?

How many of these had I walked past?

Did I find it, or did it find me?

How had I been exactly where I needed to be at that very moment?

Did I really want to have found one before today?

What were the lessons for me in all of this?

Just thinking.

I breathed the questions in and out, over and over, tossing them around. None of them needed an answer, at least, not right now.

During the remainder of my week, my new-found hobby consumed most of my daylight hours, and many of my nighttime hours were spent thinking about it.

For six hours each day, I'd shuffle along the strandline at a tenth of my normal pace, my newly purchased gumboots keeping my feet dry as I waltzed to and fro with the surf; my head down and shoulders slumped. Keeping my face parallel to the water's surface and my eyes fixed on the shallows, I dared not to blink for too long for fear of missing out on the reward of something special.

I hadn't bumped into anyone else during those days, but that hadn't meant they weren't there.

I'd become the oblivious one, the one in my own world, inadvertently ignoring all others, as I'd previously judged them for ignoring me.

I found another ten shark teeth that week to add to my first. Eleven teeth in five days, when I'd found none during the past nine or ten months.

Knowing what to look for, was the obvious bit of information I'd been missing, but not all of my finds were where the seadog said they'd be.

I'd found half my haul in the water and the other half on dry sand, where the water had been the night before. The hightide mark was as good a place as any for my morning search, but the teeth were more difficult to see there, camouflaged by seaweed, and sometimes half buried.

Finding shark teeth seemed easier when the sun was behind me, and easier again when it was overcast, or when there were fewer black shadows acting as imposters.

It was near impossible to spot them at a distance, and I only ever found them within a step or two of where I was standing.

Patience was key, and I'd picked up more than a hundred bits of black detritus for every real deal.

The truth of it though, was that there was no logical process or method – no set of rules to implement, no special skills to learn – to ensure success. The teeth were either there, or they were not.

Fossicking for shark teeth seemed to amount to just four things: being in the right place, at the right time, with the right amount of attention. Knowing what to look out for was the most critical part of the equation.

I guessed it was probably that the same was true for life and relationships.

The space on my beach and my newfound focus kept my mind calm and my overthinking at bay. I breathed more deeply and found it easier to anchor myself to the present.

I'd found mindfulness in Allestree, and I was soon reciting the words of the beautiful brunette who'd greeted me in the subterranean West 8th Street meditation studio in NYC. She'd told me that 'meditation was only ever *practised*, and that it was not merely done.' She'd told me that 'the aim of meditation wasn't to get good at it, but to just do it'.

Perhaps I wasn't searching for shark to meditate; but meditating by searching for shark teeth.

Perhaps, this beach was my meditation studio.

During my five days picking up rocks that turned out to be shark teeth and picking up shark teeth that turned out to be rocks, new thoughts and ideas materialised and dematerialised just as quickly.

I practised leaving them alone, allowing them to ping around in my head for a few moments before letting them ping out and be replaced with others.

I focussed on my counsellor's advice to pay attention to my wants and to my intentions, finding it easier to start with the small things.

What did I want to eat for breakfast or dinner?

When did I want to walk? Fossick? Relax?

How did I want to spend my evening?

I focused on being mindful with my decisions and attempted to let my gut do the deciding. If it felt right, then I'd do it. I would try not to worry about overthinking the alternatives.

The not-Dutch counsellor's advice had been for me to tune into my intuition and know why it was there, but I still wasn't completely sure how to activate said intuition; nor how I was going to recognise the difference between my intuition, my thinking, and my imagination.

I was in nature, and in the quiet. The sky was big, and I could see the horizon in all directions. There were few people around and I had the vast expanses of the ocean in front of me and farmland behind me. This was the place where my intuition was supposed to thrive, but how could I be more conscious, and more awake to it?

I was being mindful, and present in the present, and I was deliberately processing information from my senses; but what if anything, lay *beyond* my senses?

What, if anything, was this lark of finding shark teeth

telling me about my programming, and being an empath? Was it that the teeth had been here all along without me noticing, and therefore my empath self had been here too? That for all my life, I'd been searching for white enamel-like objects on the sand, when I should have been paying attention to the black onyx-like shapes in the water?

Or was it, that I would have ignored and walked over scores of shark teeth without knowing what they were, just because they hadn't looked like I'd expected them to?

Had I been searching for answers about my life and relationships with my rational thinking, rather than focusing on tuning into my gut and intuition? Had I tuned out my gut for my entire marriage because I didn't like what it was saying? Had I shut my intuition down because it hadn't fit with my storylines for our relationship: how it was supposed to work and how we were supposed to fit within it?

Had I deliberately ignored what I'd thought, felt, and known in Tokyo and beforehand, because none of it fit with my expectations for how my marriage with my ex-wife should have looked?

The short answer was … yes, probably. Certainly, the events in Tokyo nine or ten months ago hadn't fit with my vision for what it should have looked like, nor what should have been happening at that time.

And so, in a response that was habitual, I'd deliberately shut out the experience so I could replace it with a better storyline: one that affirmed my own.

I knew why she'd said what she'd said on the mall

rooftop, and why she didn't want me around her in the café garden, and what it was that she'd likely written on her ema at Meiji Jingu Temple.

I knew what she'd meant during our argument on the walk back to the hotel, and why she'd wanted to leave that night.

I knew she would have told her brother she was leaving me when she visited him in Ebisu, and I knew why she'd spent her last day in Tokyo with me at the Tsukiji Fish Market. It was because it was supposed to be our last day together.

But even further back, there were signs. I had to accept that the beginning of the end of our relationship had started a few years earlier when she'd told me that she wanted to get rid of our dog in the most heartless of ways. I couldn't believe the coldness in her voice, the lack of empathy in her eyes, and so, because it too, hadn't fit with the way *I thought* she was, it was easier to deny what I'd seen, and to remain fixated on the memories of how she was during our first year together.

I remember thinking, that my wish for that holiday to Japan wasn't just to give her something she'd always wanted; but to travel back in time to revisit the happiness we'd shared at the start of our relationship, even if it was only for a few days. I'd thought that by granting her a wish, that she would be happy, and by extension, so would I.

The absurd thing was that I could now see that my wish had literally been granted. There she was, transformed into the person she was when we first met. Except this time, I was thrust into the role of her ex.

She was again spontaneous, reckless, hedonistic self-serving, careless, and carefree, doing what she wanted, when she wanted to do it, regardless of the consequences.

As her 'new' ex, I was an unnecessary drag on her freedom. She didn't care about me, or about us. She was breaking the shackles of her home, her job, her responsibilities, and her relationship, but this time around, she wanted me nowhere near her. I wasn't to be a part of her future plans, as I was no longer the cure to it all. I was no longer loved, and no longer *needed*.

It was now clearer than ever that she couldn't break the shackles of her mental illness; she was her bipolar disorder, and her bipolar disorder was her.

My counsellor's advice for me to interrogate my intentions, storylines, and boundaries was gradually seeping into my consciousness, giving me new sight and insight into my emotional programming and operating system.

I was beginning to see that my life until now was a series of storylines, wholly focussed on my inherent need to make things better for those around me, or at least fit better with the way I thought they *should* be. I hadn't had an accurate image of what I was searching for, but that hadn't stopped me from believing I had.

Believing that my life and relationships should be a certain way, was the same as fossicking for shark teeth based on what I thought they should look like.

I had no clear intention for myself in my relationship

with my ex-wife, and because I hadn't, I had no boundaries for what was acceptable and what wasn't during our time together. I'd never used my happiness as a measure for how it was going; I only ever used hers.

Luxembourg told me that narcissists had exaggerated views of self-importance and excessive needs for admiration. She'd told me they had distorted senses of self and a lack of empathy, and she'd told me that they valued themselves above all others.

But I had another question: had my ex-wife been that way all along, or had I shown her how to be towards me, by the way I treated myself?

Could my storylines be less about psychopaths and narcissists, and more about the relationship I fostered by wrapping her in cotton wool and putting her on a pedestal, no matter the circumstance or behaviour?

Luxembourg was right.

I wholeheartedly believed in the storylines I'd created about her mental illness, and the narrative relegating me to second place in our relationship.

I'd believed I didn't matter, and if I was the one telling the stories, then why wouldn't my ex-wife have believed it too?

Chapter 8

Reliving the past decade of my life was time consuming and exhausting. I was trying to erase my own storylines of the events of Bristol, New York, Brisbane, Venice, Melbourne, Tokyo, Kyoto, Athens, Santorini, and Naxos, so I could remember the experiences as they had happened. But in doing so, I was simply creating new storylines, coloured by my imagining of multiple alternatives for what I may have thought, felt, and known during those times.

I'd arranged to catch up with a friend on my first morning back in Melbourne from Allestree, the work colleague I'd been 'patronising' to all those years ago, the one who'd had no recollection of it ever happening. The poor woman had no idea of the conversation she was in for.

Our meeting place was in Yarraville at our usual haunt, a quaint café, set into the corner of a century-old shopfront.

I'd grown up not far from here and had watched the evolution of this suburb from a ghetto people dreaded walking through for fear of being mugged, to an eclectic village that was now safer than ever for the young families drawn to its parks and lattes.

Long gone were the graffitied shutters protecting windows from being smashed; now replaced with boutiques, artisan butchers, cafés, restaurants, and wine bars.

At its heart, a once derelict art deco building, formerly inhabited by vandals and squatters, now housed a cinema and bookshop, jewels in the crown of this ex-working-class suburb.

Today's café was opposite the cinema, and I'd been a patron here since before I left for Bristol, attracted to its unpretentiousness and consistently good food and coffee.

Caffe lattes were made the way I preferred them, tepid and sweet, and their breakfasts were simple and tasty, a likely result of the knobs of butter that were generously added to many of their dishes.

It was a place of comfort and familiarity, its only downside being the competition to get a table, especially during peak weekend times.

Thankfully, today was a Tuesday, and I'd arrived early to take my pick of the nine or ten tables in the main dining room.

My ideal spot was in the back corner looking outwards. It was my preferred position, regardless of the room or venue I was in, but I'd only recently worked out why.

My counsellor's advice to investigate my programming

had me asking 'why' like a four-year-old on a diet of refined sugar, and I was using the way I felt in environments as impetus for investigation.

Whether sitting or standing, I gravitated to a place where I had line of sight to the entire room, but until a few weeks ago, I hadn't realised I always did this. Sitting or standing anywhere else made me feel uncomfortable and being in a place with my back to an entry door made me feel uneasy and distracted. Today, I had no such worries.

It was an insignificant uncovery in the scheme of things, but it was one more shadow on my cave wall for which I now knew the origin.

I made eye contact with the barista and pointed to where I wanted to sit, and he responded with a gentle nod of permission.

I swung myself onto the upcycled timber bench seat and leant against the rough-rendered wall to relax my body and tangled mind. Scatter cushions would have provided additional comfort, but I wasn't going to give up my position for a plusher seat.

I mouthed the words 'caffe latte please' to the person behind the register, knowing I'd have time to enjoy a sneaky one before my friend arrived.

Whereas I could walk here from home, along jasmine-lined streets, she had no such luck, having to contend with crossing the city in post-peak-hour traffic as well as finding a carpark with enough of an allowance to give us adequate time for our chats.

My two-sip latte arrived at the same time she did, and we gave each other a warm embrace; a hug I hadn't known I'd needed until her arms were around me, squeezing tightly.

She hung her coat on the back of her chair and passed me her bag to perch beside me.

"How are things? You look tired!"

As always, I loved her honesty.

"Gee, thanks for noticing, but yes, I am tired. I am always tired, and I can't seem to get on top of it. It's as though my soul is tired, rather than my body, so sleep isn't helping, not that I'm sleeping all that well either."

"That's no good. Why, what's going on?"

Where do I start?!

I enjoyed our time together because we could get into the deep stuff quickly without the need for small talk. We could discuss whatever was on our minds, and could easily swing between the practical and theoretical, or real and imagined. She was a problem solver and was genuinely interested in discussing solutions, but equally, she was happy to spend time interrogating the merits of the problem.

It was time to jump straight in.

"Have you heard the word empath before?"

She looked at me with an expression of, 'are you being stupid?', and I returned serve with a, 'no I'm not' glare.

"Oh, you're being serious. Yes, of course, I have. You have too, haven't you?"

I have? "Seriously? I've never used that word, and until a few weeks ago, I don't think I'd ever heard it!"

"Of course you have! We've discussed it!"

Her response bowled me over.

"We've known each other for over twenty years; and I can't recall using it once!"

She smiled with uncertainty.

"I'd thought that all of our conversations had something to do with our nature as empaths and about how we go about navigating our lives, about what's real and what isn't."

Our nature as empaths?!

She spun me three hundred and sixty degrees.

"Our nature?"

"Oh, you're just having me on, now!"

"No, no I'm not; um, I mean, well, I don't mean to. As far as I know, I heard the word for the first time a few weeks ago. And I still have no real idea about the meaning of the concept."

Clearly something was making her uncomfortable, the way she kept moving about in her seat. All of a sudden, I needed her to be still.

"Hmmm … the word may be new, I suppose. I really don't like using labels, but surely the idea isn't."

Labels?

She continued. "I'm pretty sure that most of our conversations have been about one of us feeling something that is or isn't ours, and how we go about knowing for sure. We've been talking about this stuff for years!"

We had talked about this stuff for years, but I'd thought we were just talking about empathy.

She tucked her hair behind her ears. "Most of our conversations have been about you and your ex-wife, and about me and my husband and my kids, about untangling what emotions and thoughts spring from us, and what comes from others, haven't they?"

The room was spinning.

I scanned through my memories of our past breakfasts, unable to find any specific evidence to support her claim. Conceivably, the not-Dutch counsellor was right. Perhaps, I had been asleep this whole time.

A million questions gushed forth, but only one could win.

I tried to keep my voice calm. "When did you find out?"

She looked at me, a slightly puzzled expression on her face. "I've told you this already. I was twenty-four and going through some stuff and started reading different books which made my feelings and emotions make more sense, and then I spoke to an aunt of mine who introduced me to the idea. I'm sure we've discussed this. We speak about it all the time, don't we; about energy and emotion and about thinking and feeling things without knowing how we came to know or feel them."

Had we? I thought for a moment and decided to play along.

"I guess we have, but I don't think we ever discussed us being empaths. I remember some of those conversations, but I thought we were just talking about being tuned in to others and to society as a whole."

"It's the same thing, isn't it?"

"Is it?"

Her voice sounded so sane; her nonchalance a soothing

antacid to my reflux. Could this whole concept be as simple as she was making it out to be, and was my overthinking causing problems that weren't there?

A hipster teenager materialised at our table, notepad, and pen at the ready. "Want to order something?"

My friend took responsibility for responding. "I'm sorry, we haven't had a look yet." I didn't need to look as I had the same thing each time I was here. She continued: "We're just catching up. Please give us a few more minutes, but may I have a long black please?"

The teenager gave no sign of affirmation and shuffled off, dragging their feet across the uneven concrete floor. I returned to the point in hand: "Tell me more about what this empath thing means for you."

"We've been through this so many times!"

"I'm sorry, but humour me. I need to hear it all again."

"Okay, but if we're starting at first principles, the most important thing, is for us to remember that we experience the world differently to most. You've heard the term neurodivergent, yeah?"

"Yes, people whose brains work differently."

"Well, I hate that term, because all brains work *differently*, but I guess we fall into that category, with a couple of 'extras'. I'm affect-divergent, and sensing-divergent. It's not only my brain that works differently; it's my senses and emotions. If you believe we process the world in the same way as the majority of others, you're wrong!"

That is becoming abundantly clear!

"Have you ever wondered why you can pick the

perpetrator in a whodunnit movie before the end? Or why TV shows that are supposed to be surprising, aren't? Or why you can predict the outcome of actions – or inactions – of people in various situations before the repercussions actually happen?"

"Not really. I just thought I may be a bit smarter than the average bear." I pulled a comical face to let her know I was kidding.

"It's more than that, and for me, it's far more than just being an empath. You're familiar with the Claires, right?"

"Can't say I am. Who are they?"

She smiled. "Not who, but what. You've heard of clairvoyance, yeah?"

"Yes, as in people who claim to see the future; I don't think I believe in it, but I've definitely heard of it."

"Well, clairvoyance is just one of the clairs, and there are a bunch of others, eight or nine, I think. Clairvoyance is usually associated with fortune tellers, crystal balls, and card reading, but it is so much more."

"You're not going to tell me you're a clairvoyant, are you?"

"No, no, not this week." She smiled again. "Clair means clear, and clairvoyants see things that have already happened, or things that are yet to happen, so I think voyance is just another word for seeing, so clairvoyance translates as clear seeing."

"I did not know that!"

"Well, there you go. You've learnt something new!"

"I'm learning lots of new things lately, but what does this have to do with empaths?"

"Well, apart from clairvoyance; there's, let me see if I can remember them all …" She started counting them out with her fingers. "Clairaudience, clairsentience, clairempathy, claircognisance, clairintellect, and others like clairtangency for touch, clairsalience for smell, and clairgustance for taste. There, that's nine all up, but there may be more."

"That's a lot of clairs, and I think I heard the word clairsentience once before, but I don't know what it means. Actually, I don't know what any of them mean!"

"Sentience is about clear feeling, and feeling a physical sensation that someone else is feeling."

"Interesting! Like feeling scalding heat on your own hand if someone else burns theirs?"

"Yes, I guess so, but to differing degrees."

Luxembourg said it wasn't a literal analogy! Liar!

"I'm not sure if anyone has them all, as that would be a shitty life. Imagine having all five of your senses turned up to eleven, and then also having another nine senses beyond those!"

Senses beyond senses?!

My friend continued: "I guess we all have some of them to some degree, and I think they all appear in a similar way, as some sort of insight, or intuition, or gut instinct, like when a situation just *feels* right or wrong, or when a person gives off good vibes or bad."

"So, you're saying that gut feelings are the clairs?"

"Or the clairs are the gut feelings, but I guess it depends on what you believe."

"And what do you believe?"

"I believe in clairsentience, clairempathy, and a bit of claircognisance as they are all real for me, to some degree. I want to believe in clairvoyance, and I wish I had the gift, but I think that is more to do with me wanting to know what's going to happen."

She'd piqued my interest further, although I had a sneaking feeling of unease about the whole thing.

"I couldn't think of anything worse than *knowing* what's coming up. Is there a clair for feeling someone's mental illness or personality disorder as their own?"

She smiled. "Know someone like that, do we? I don't think there is, but I think it's probably just a mix of cognisance, empathy, and sentience."

"So, what's sentience and what's the difference between it and clairempathy?"

"I think it's as simple as sentience feeling the feeling of an emotion, whereas empaths just sense the emotion."

It was a different description to what Luxembourg had said, but then again, she hadn't mentioned any of the clairs at all.

"One long black." The teenager had returned, plonking the coffee in the middle of the table between us, unable to remember which of us had asked for it. "Are you ready to order now?"

We weren't.

"You order, I'll panic order."

Panic ordering was a system which worked for her, and if she was ever stumped, she was good at asking for recommendations.

As requested, I went first to give her some time to work it out. "Okay, may I have the plain scrambled eggs with some smoked salmon on the side please."

"We don't do smoked salmon on the side."

Argh.

I detested this part of the conversation. Always the same with a newbie: they needed training. I hated that it made me feel like an entitled so and so.

"Please ask the kitchen. They will do it if asked."

The teenager rolled their eyes and begrudgingly made a note, before diverting their attention to the other side of the table to take the next order.

"And you?"

"What's good this week? What are your favourites?"

Bingo!

"It depends on what you like. If you want something sweet, try the granola, and if you prefer something savory, I'd try the smashed avo and fetta, but the halloumi and mushroom is nice for something different."

"Easy, I'll have the something different then."

The teenager scribbled more notes on their notepad and repeated our order back to us. "One halloumi and mushroom, and one scrambled eggs with parmesan and cavolo nero with salmon on the side if the kitchen will do it."

Fuck me! Why was this so hard?

"And any more coffees?"

"I'll have another latte please, but can I please have the *plain* scrambled eggs, the one without the parmesan and other stuff."

The teenager walked away, and my friend and I shook our heads at each other and smiled.

"You'd think they'd know your order by now."

"You'd think!"

"You didn't enjoy that at all, did you?"

"Enjoy what? The eye rolling, the wrong order, or me begging for fish?"

"I know, it's hard work, but you handled it well!" She gave me two thumbs up.

I didn't agree. I felt rude. "I feel nauseous. Maybe I should stop drinking coffee. It only seems to make me feel anxious." I thought for a moment before adding: "I don't know why it's so hard – can't they just add salmon to the sides' menu? It's already a part of another dish, and I can't be the only one who'd choose it as a side if it was listed. I've been stressing about that interaction all morning as I knew it was going to happen today."

My friend nodded, trying not to smile. "Is that your clairvoyance or your claircognisance telling you that?!"

"Ha. Ha. Ha. Very funny. I just wish people cared more. They didn't make eye contact with me once and looked as though they wanted to be anywhere but here. If you take a job in hospitality, then the least you can do is try to be hospitable!"

I straightened my back and corrected my posture to

better align with the wall behind me. "So, back to clairsentience, clairempathy, and claircognisance—"

"Oh yes, so as I said, clairsentience is clear feeling, clairempathy is clear emotion, and claircognisance is clear knowing. Put them together and you have us, card-holding empaths!"

"Is that right?"

"Yes, of course! All the clairs are related to sixth senses and energy and most of us have them somewhere along the spectrum of such things."

"Energy?"

"Yes, it's all energy. Our five senses collect inputs from the world as we directly experience them, but our other senses give us additional information about those direct experiences. They are the intangible, compared with the tangible.

"Everything is energy. Sound is energy, light is energy, taste is energy, smell is energy; everything we sense is just the reception of energy or invisible waves."

She was losing me, and one of her energetic sensors sensed it.

"It's all science, and I know how much you enjoy science! Think of it this way. Every atom in us and around us is constantly moving and vibrating at different frequencies. Everything we see is made up of light waves and everything we hear comes from sound waves. Light waves and sound waves are the transmission of energy, and our five main senses are energy receptors, and I think our sixth, seventh, eighth, etcetera, are also receptors for waves we can't perceive, for other energies, energies that feed our intuition."

"Intuition?"

"Yes, so for me, clairsentience is to do with my clear feeling. It happens when I feel something physical in my body, like a sensation, or an ache, or pain, usually in my gut or chest?"

"Or sternum?"

"Your sternum is in your chest, isn't it? Anyway, I seem to get clear feelings when someone is lying or not quite telling the truth, but I also get them when I see people or animals in distress or pain. Don't you?"

"That is so interesting. I do, but I haven't consciously tuned into it, but I think I know exactly what you mean."

Memories of my experience of the cruelty in the Hong Kong markets flashed back to make me wince.

Her expression changed. "You've just thought of something. I felt an anxious feeling in my chest. What was it?"

She was good at this!

I reminded her of my experiences at the Temple Street Night Markets in Hong Kong, and how I'd needed to flee.

"You see? We have been talking about this for ages!"

Was this another lesson to be learned from my experience with the shark teeth? Had she been talking about black shiny things in the water at all our breakfasts, when I'd been listening out for white things up on the dry sand?

"Clairempathy is the one I still have the most trouble with, because I still find it difficult to distinguish between my sensing of what others are going through, and my own feelings about what other people are feeling. For example, I'm sensing a bunch of feelings from over there, near the window, but I'm trying to tune them out."

"Really?"

"Yes, look around, and tell me what you feel?"

I looked around at the other customers in the café and noticed nothing specific.

"I don't feel anything different to how I always feel."

"And how do you always feel?"

"Anxious, confused, and highly strung!"

She laughed, but it was true.

I thought some more. "I feel a jumble of things and no one feeling is clear. They are like waves on waves on waves, and rips on rips on rips. They seem to be all things, and all at once, like white noise in the foreground and background, and always on."

"Exactly!"

"Exactly?" I shot her my best quizzical expression.

"Okay, look over there." She nodded towards a couple sitting near the window.

They were sitting side by side; him shovelling food into his mouth with one hand, scrolling on his phone with the other, and her holding her coffee and staring wistfully out to the street.

"Yep, what about them?"

"Well, there is something going on there. If they're in a relationship, it's almost the end. He's in an oblivious comfort zone, and she's checked out, longing for something different."

"Wow, judgemental or what! How do you know?"

"Is it judgement? Or is it my clear knowing?" She winked at me with a cheeky smile.

"Okay, how about them?" I discretely pointed to a couple of ladies near us.

She leaned towards me and whispered, "Old friends who have known each other for years, but actually don't like each other very much. Or, they may not like each other's partners, or the fact that their partners are the reason for them drifting apart." She paused and then nodded decisively. "Nope. I was right the first time; they have never really liked each other but pretend to."

"And the two guys behind us?"

"Real estate agents, both at the start of their careers, but one has a bit more experience than the other and is big noting himself about how good he is."

She smiled at me, but I remained unconvinced.

"You're just being critical and judgemental. None of what you said is true and you're just making up stories."

"I don't think it's judgemental if you don't cast judgements, and I'm not doing that. It doesn't matter if any of what I said is true or not, as for me it's not about the truth. It is about me tuning in to what's going on around me, to know whether it's going on within me, I need to know if they are my own feelings, or if my own feelings are being affected by others. Are these feelings mine or someone else's?

"Observation helps me to leave negativity here, and not take it home with me. That's been my biggest learning during all these decades; to tune into a feeling and why I'm having it, and to consciously leave it here if it's not mine. The worst thing I can do is take window-girl's energy home as my own, because it's not. She's longing for something different, and I'm not."

"I can't believe we haven't spoken about this before!"

"Me too!"

I was curious. "How do you make your assessments so quickly and with so much detail?"

"I don't think about it, and I don't think about whether they may be right or wrong. I'm scanning the energies in my body, so I can be clearer about me and what *I'm* feeling. I have to accept that I am the way I am, and that I can't turn it off. Whether I like it or not, I'm a beacon for energy that I can't understand, but not understanding it doesn't make it any less real. There is so much we don't understand. I don't understand how an octopus changes its colours, or how gravity works, but that doesn't change the fact that they do, and it does, does it?'

It was a beautifully simplistic view. "No, I guess not."

"The universe is full of movement and energy, and some of us can perceive this and others may not. And because I'm a parent, I also need to have a good understanding of this so I can notice it in my boys, to help them navigate the world."

"I've always liked your simplified approach to things. I think there's something in that for me."

There was. She wasn't taking any of it too seriously and didn't seem too bothered about understanding how it worked. In fact, it seemed that because she didn't understand it, that she was able to lean into it, and treat it with even greater curiosity and pragmatism.

"I hope so. To me, there is no such thing as 'just feelings'. Feelings come from somewhere, and they come for a reason. I try to learn from others; whether it's things I like or things I don't. For example, those two people near the window; I can feel her quandary. She likes the guy next to her but doesn't know if she loves him anymore. She feels comfortable with him, but wants something extra, maybe some spontaneity, and she's probably comparing him with someone new she's just met."

"Or maybe they're brother and sister!"

"Maybe they are, but it doesn't matter, because regardless of whether I'm right or wrong, I can use these feelings for my own marriage; to avoid a situation where either of us is on our phone or staring out windows longingly. I use my stories about other people to learn for myself and to have conversations with my husband and kids about things before they turn into problems."

It was another interesting method. Perhaps I should sack the not-Dutch counsellor and have breakfast here with my friend more often!

"You used the word stories; well, I recently found out that I'm a great storyteller, and am just full of storylines!"

"Yes, you certainly are! The stories you told to cover for your ex-wife's behaviour could fill a novel or two—"

She stopped abruptly and put her hand on mine. "Sorry, too soon?"

I laughed. "No, not at all! Seems you were tuned in far more than I was!"

"It's much easier to see things when you're on the

outside. We're all storytellers; it's probably one of the most human things we do. Stories are the best form of communication as they create beliefs and behaviours; just look at the Bible, or the Quran. I heard the other day that corporates have started to train their staff to tell better stories as a part of their work. They're actually adopting it as a change management strategy!"

"I wonder if any of them would hire me as their resident expert!"

"Yes, absolutely! That would be a great fit for you!" She grinned, and then said in a more serious voice, "Don't be too hard on yourself. Our stories help us make sense of what is going on around us, because if I was going to try and make sense about what was going on inside me without this frame of reference, I would lose my mind!"

"I know what you mean. I came here today feeling as though I'd already lost mine but am now feeling better I'm not alone."

"I'm sorry we haven't had this conversation before. I was sure you knew all this, especially after you told me about your ex's condition."

I didn't want to get caught up in those storylines again, so I changed the subject back to our earlier one.

"So, what are all the other clairs about?"

"I've got a book I can lend to you if I can find it, or you can search it out online."

It seemed that she too didn't want to get caught up in that discussion again, so she changed the subject to something new.

"Tell me, have you ever had an energy healing before? From a light worker or chakra therapist?"

"Seriously? An energy healing from a light worker?"

"Yes, absolutely! You should definitely give it a go!"

"I don't even know what a light worker is, and I definitely don't know what a chakra is."

"Well then, you are missing out! Imagine having a complete energy reset! It will remove the noise and make everything clearer.

"When are you in Bali next?" She asked.

"In about four weeks. It's been about nine months since my last trip, which feels like way too long."

"Perfect! Promise me you'll have an energy healing over there. Six ley lines pass through Bali, and it is full of good energy. It's why so many people are attracted to the island, and probably why you like it too. Please promise me you'll find someone and go see them?"

"Ley lines? I literally have no idea what you are talking about right now."

"It doesn't matter. Just promise me you'll see a healer, and I promise you it will change your life."

Chapter 9

I was grateful to be back in Seminyak's warm embrace, my home away from home, away from home. Melbourne was wonderful, and so was Allestree, but this place offered something extra. It might have been the ley lines; whatever they were, or perhaps it was nothing more than its comfortable climate and its easy-going nature.

The last time I visited the island, I'd intended to spend each day doing exactly what I wanted to do, when I wanted to do it. I was going to drink coffee in my favourite cafés, eat out at restaurants, try yoga, and drink from fresh coconuts on the beach, and whilst I did some of those things, I'd idiotically spent most of my time worried I'd bump into my ex-wife whilst doing so.

My intentions had been derailed by distractions, both imagined and real: the religious ceremony and the rubbish they left behind, my anxiety about my ex-wife being in my favourite café, and the person who introduced me to the vesica pisces; that little sketch of two overlapping circles sharing a radius which shook my world and redefined my understanding of healthy relationships, of remaining whole, and of two not becoming one.

At that time, I was fresh out of my marriage, and was trying to discover – or was it uncover – what I liked and enjoyed, and what made me happy.

By focusing on the questions, I hadn't realised I was already immersed in the answers. The distractions had diverted my energy to the past, and to my future and had disrupted my enjoyment of the present.

Not this time.

I liked Seminyak and enjoyed the feeling of being here, so my intention for this trip was to do as little thinking as possible, and just be.

I had the opportunity to drop my storylines about what I should do whilst here, and to do what felt good, even if that meant spending whole days lying by the pool without feeling guilty about it.

Apart from sunbathing, the only thing I felt I had to do was find an energy healer. I didn't believe it would change my life, but my friend made me promise, and my gut was telling me I had nothing to lose by giving it a try.

The processes of disembarking the plane, purchasing a visa on arrival, and lining up for passport control were all-too-familiar; as were the feelings of elation and deflation associated with choosing Section C for the final step towards the exit.

I'd chosen to queue in that section because the four attending passport control officers were working with efficiency and had the line moving quickly, but as soon as I'd reached the halfway point in the corral, the line stopped moving at all.

All four passport officers had packed their things and left their posts.

The lack of organisation and non-existent workforce planning of shift start and end times would have infuriated me a year or two ago, but I could now treat it as part and parcel of being where I was. Something in me was changing.

My two options were simple; patiently wait for the next shift to start, or impatiently follow the angering mob into a different section.

I chose to wait and was out into freedom within half an hour.

I'd found my udeng-capped driver within minutes and with hand luggage only, we strode to his car in the multideck carpark to make a hasty exit.

I'd intended to stay in the same villa as last year but after a quick search, found something diagonally across the road that was newer, cheaper, and which served an à la carte breakfast in the villa, rather than a buffet in a common dining room.

It was one of only nine boutique accommodations, each with its own private swimming pool and walled gardens. Whilst the pool was more plunge, than swimming, it would still suit my needs for cooling off, rather than doing any type of exercise. The living and dining areas were indoors, rather than out, and the multizone air conditioning was going to ensure a modicum of comfort on the humid mornings and evenings.

After touring the oversized bedroom, bathroom, and living area, I perched on the edge of the king-size bed and connected my phone to the Wi-Fi.

I'd made the decision to find an energy healer as soon as possible, so I could get it out of the way, tell my friend I'd done it, and get on with enjoying the rest of my time here, promise fulfilled.

My search term, chakra energy healer light worker Bali, was rewarded with more results than I had time to interrogate, and as I scrolled through them, I quickly realised I didn't actually know what I was looking for, or how I was going to know when I'd found the right one.

I was fossicking for shark teeth all over again.

Chakra therapy seemed to be big business over here, and as my friend had predicted, this part of the world was quite focussed on its energy and energetic benefits.

Tour companies offered retreats of various lengths, with ceremonial healings, clean eating, and silent meditations rolled into packages which were priced higher than my entire holiday here.

I wasn't interested in anything more than a quick one-off session, so I kept scrolling, and opening new tabs, learning more about chakras and energies with each hyperlink.

I read that chakras were spinning wheels of concentrated energy located at different points in the body, and that their purpose was to keep us healthy and functioning properly. It was believed that when our chakras were clear, we'd feel good, and when they weren't, we'd be unwell or out of balance.

I read that there were seven primary chakras located along the spine between a person's head and their coccyx, and that each was designated with one of the colours of the rainbow, and responsible for different areas of physical, psychological, emotional, and spiritual health.

I read that the chakra system was invented by the Hindus three thousand years ago, in India, and that Hinduism itself was one of the world's major religions or cultures; and that yoga was also invented by Hindus, with the specific aim of strengthening and aligning the flow of the chakra system.

I read and I read, and I read, but before I lost another three hours down the rabbit hole of internet information on chakras, yoga, and Hinduism, I clicked on the map icon to locate the healer that was closest to where I was staying.

Having decided that proximity was the only parameter I was going to use to make my choice, to my relief and amusement, I found a wellness centre specialising in the service, just ten minutes' walk away from where I was.

After a few text messages back and forth and their unsolicited offer of a thirty percent discount, I booked an appointment for 3:45pm tomorrow.

The single item on my to-do-list was done, and I could

now get on with my plan of doing nothing else for the next week.

I closed the multiple chakra tabs on my phone's browser and headed out for a short walk in the direction of the nearest supermarket, to stock up on snacks and supplies, before I'd have an afternoon by the pool, a sunset dinner, and an early night.

As morning broke, I lay on my back and reverse-engineered my day through to my appointment time to ensure I wouldn't be rushed, and so I could do the things I wanted to do beforehand.

A 3:45pm appointment would mean leaving the villa by 3:30pm, which in turn meant I needed to be showered and ready by 3:15pm. I wanted at least five hours by the pool, so I'd need to be back from a walk by about 10:00am, which in turn meant I'd need to get out of bed now, so I could order breakfast, and be out of here by around 7:30am.

Done!

My day ran like clockwork, and I was out of the villa five minutes early at 3:25pm.

My destination was conveniently located on the same street as my villa complex, and like my villa complex, didn't have a street number. I'd not walked to the northern part of Seminyak before and was looking forward to seeing something new whilst keeping alert for signs of the wellness centre.

With no footpaths in this part of town, I ambled on the road, keeping myself as close to the edge of the open drains as I could, without losing my balance and falling in. It was perilous, but as an experienced visitor to this part of the world, I now knew it was as much the responsibility of others to avoid me, as it was for me to avoid them.

Life here was undertaken with the understanding that it was everyone's job to be respectful and to avoid accidents. It was a system that worked well, but one I couldn't imagine being implemented back home where road users would rather risk injury or death, than give up their right to be where the road rules said they were allowed to be.

After thirteen minutes walking uphill past laundromats, warungs, rice paddies, and small farm plots with a few sacred cows to keep the grass down, I arrived at the wellness centre.

The brown-brick building was fronted by an organic café heaving with patrons in singlets and spandex. Smoothies of unnaturally bright colours were drunk through metal straws, and bowls of granola, yoghurt, and fruit were picked at with forks.

It hadn't occurred to me that the wellness centre might have catered for far more than clients seeking a chakra healing.

The entry door was about fifty metres down a laneway, past a parking garage filled with hundreds of scooters and mopeds, making me guess that the place I was about to enter was already quite full.

My suspicions were confirmed, as ahead of the glass entry

doors was a gigantic gym; full of muscular women and men on treadmills, exercise bikes, steppers, and other equipment I didn't recognise, as well as a floor area blanketed with beautiful active-wear-clad people on yoga mats, following instructions, whilst monitoring themselves in mirrors.

Feelings of 'not belonging' swept over me again, just as they did when I'd first stepped into the New York meditation studio; full of models, actors, and beautiful people. This wellness centre seemed to be another place to see and be seen. Another place I didn't feel like I fitted in.

Patrons streamed through the entry doors and brushed past me on a mission to start their workouts or meet their friends. They swapped plastic medallions for towels at the counter, moving into the grey concrete gym box, or upstairs to whatever was up there.

"Can I help please?"

I looked around to see if the question was being asked of me or another but couldn't locate the origin of the voice, nor where it was being directed.

"Yes, can I help please?"

Behind the shiny white vinyl-wrapped counter was a small Balinese woman who was looking down at a notebook. With her head bowed, she'd been invisible, but with her face raised, I could make out a ponytail.

"Yes, please. I am here for a chakra ... healing, I guess."

"Ah, okay, yes, okay, chakra is on level three. You like to pay for it now or after."

You'd better take my money now because I think I'll be more reluctant to hand it over when it is done ...

"Now, if that's okay."

I handed her my credit card, and she extracted a click-clack machine from under the counter. I hadn't seen one in years, and had thought they were obsolete, or even illegal. She positioned my card in the holder, and placed the carbonised voucher over the top and then clicked and clacked the slider, handing me my card back and the triplicate form to sign.

How many direct debits will I need to change when my card gets hacked?

With an upturned hand, she pointed toward the stairs. "You may go to level three. My friend will meet you there, but please use stairs as the lift is not working today, thank you."

"Thank you, terima kasih."

My legs were still throbbing from the hill climb to get here, so I started on the stairs slowly. Each concrete step seemed taller than it should have been, and I needed to lift my legs higher and higher, so as to not trip and plant my forehead into their sharp edges.

As I reached the top of the first fifteen stairs, the staircase turned on itself to go up again. With my hands pushing down on my knees to assist, I climbed a second flight of stairs hoping I'd skipped level one and landed on level two, or better still, three.

The landing faced an exit door with an outdoor pool and a bar at its far end. Gods and goddesses sunned themselves on lounges and a few others swam parade laps for adoring eyes.

Everyone seemed to be posing for the others, and each kept one eye on what they were doing and the other on who was watching.

It was a mating ritual.

A small sign near the exit door read L1. Argh!

I walked down the hall and up another four flights of stairs to reach level three.

I stopped at the top to catch my breath, and to let the swelling in my legs and the red in my face subside but was pounced upon by two attendants dressed in white rectangular uniforms.

"Please may you take your shoes off and place them there. You can use the slippers if you like."

I replied with a smile rather than breathless words.

There was another reception area up here, smaller but with a massive six-person couch positioned in its middle.

"Please take a seat. Your thrapist will be with you shortly."

I smiled again.

Thrapist.

After a few minutes of mindful resting on the sofa, a lady wearing white pants and a green shirt broke the silence, asking for me to follow her. I didn't see her face as she'd turned around and walked off before I'd looked up.

"This way please."

Wait a second, was that another Dutch accent?

She led me into a dimly lit room with a square table

against its left wall and a massage bed and basin against its right. Between them was a golden buddha on a concrete plinth. Two chairs were placed on either side of the table, and the bed was covered in crisp white linen.

With her back still towards me, she gestured for me to sit in the chair closest to the door and headed to the basin to wash her hands.

"So, why are you here?"

She sounded strangely angry that I was.

"Excuse me for asking, but is that a Dutch or Luxembourgish accent you have?"

"Luxembourgish? I have not heard that before. I am from Holland, but I have lived in Indonesia for thirty years. My husband is from here and my daughter was born here."

If I'd closed my eyes, I would have guessed I was back in the living room of my not-Dutch counsellor in Melbourne. The voice resemblance was uncanny, even if she sounded far curter. I suddenly felt the need to apologise, even though I wasn't sure what for.

"I'm sorry. I have a therapist in Melbourne whom I thought was Dutch, but who turned out to be from Luxembourg."

She wasn't interested in my small talk.

"So, tell me, why are you here?"

She was the opposite of everything I'd imagined an energy healer would be. Rather than being warmly greeted by a holy Hindu woman draped in traditional robes and beads, I'd been ushered in coldly by a small fair woman from Holland dressed in business attire.

Respect the process …

She dried her hands and took her seat opposite me at the table. My heart raced, and a lump grew in my throat. She was a similar height and had the same mousey-brown hair and blue eyes as Luxembourg.

Were they twins separated at birth?

"Um, yes, sorry. I am here because a friend asked me to come. She said it would change my life. I recently found out that I may be an empath, but all of this is new to me—"

"Who told you, you were an empath?"

Her voice maintained its quiet monotone, but still sounded annoyed.

"My therapist in Melbourne introduced me to the term. I'm not sure what it means, or what it means for me, but I'm here to continue that journey of uncovery."

I felt like a fraud, and it felt like she thought I was one too.

"Have you had a chakra clearing before?"

She pronounced the word chakra with a hard 'ch' whereas I'd being using it with a soft 'sh'.

My feelings of unworthiness were escalating.

"No."

"Okay, do you know what it is?"

I wasn't going to recite the internet to this woman or pretend I knew something I didn't.

"No, not really."

"Okay, to start, chakras are energy and when they are clear, they spin, and when they are not clear, they do not spin, and then we have problems in our life. Healthy chakras give good health and blocked chakras give bad health. Today I will clear your chakras. Is that okay?"

I've already paid, so I guess that would be great!

Her words sounded harsher than the message they were conveying, and I couldn't be sure if it was just her accent, or if she believed I was just another westerner coming in for a quick spiritual fix.

Was I just another westerner coming in for a quick spiritual fix?

I wanted to ask her more questions to understand more about what she did and how she did it, but the timing didn't feel right.

It was time to go with the flow.

"Yes, thank you. That would be great!"

That would be great?!

"Do you have any ailments or health problems you would like to tell me."

If we're talking psychological ailments, where do I start?! Better just to talk about the physical.

"There is one problem I have, and it's related to my stomach. I don't feel well after eating. I rarely feel settled, and I feel a heaviness and discomfort in my stomach, regardless of what I eat."

It hadn't always been the case, and I used to be able to eat and drink whatever I wanted, whenever I wanted, but over the years since my wedding, my stomach issues had gradually become worse.

It was about that time, when my newly betrothed had been diagnosed with an intolerance for gluten. We had been sampling the menus at many of Melbourne's fine-dining establishments, trialling each for their suitability as our wedding venue. It was an enjoyable task, and we'd got through six restaurants before she became violently ill after eating at the seventh. We'd both eaten from the same degustation menu, so it had been easy to rule out food poisoning.

She had various blood tests and told me that she had the precursor gene for coeliac disease and that she should lay off gluten.

For ease, we eliminated gluten from both our diets, and became more careful when eating out. She'd initially felt better, but the good feelings didn't last long, and after some internet-based self-diagnosis, she put us both onto a low FODMAP diet.

When that diet also failed, she reintegrated normal foods back into our meals, which in turn, led to me not feeling so good. Taking foods out of our diet may have caused the uncovery of my own intolerances, but it hadn't been enough of a problem for me to stop eating most things.

If my stomach issues were caused by a chakra, then I hoped it could be fixed today. The chakra therapist started to explain. "This could be manipura or solar plexus. This chakra is responsible for sense of self and self-esteem. If out of alignment, you will have digestive issues, constipation, and irritable bowel. You will be quick to anger and have overly rigid behaviour."

I smiled at her. "Well, I think I probably tick most of those boxes!"

She didn't reciprocate my facial expression and was keen to get to work. "I will start you on the bed. Please take off your shirt and lie on your back with your eyes closed." She was all business.

I put my glasses on the table and did as she requested.

Before I closed my eyes, I saw her pick up a small bottle and empty a few drops of liquid into her palms, rubbing them together vigorously.

"This may hurt a little bit or feel a little uncomfortable."

Hurt? I wasn't here for pain!

She pressed down on my stomach, with her fingertips on each side of my navel, and as she did, she hummed.

Oh fuck. Here we go! Straight to the source!

She kept pressing and pressing and moved her fingertips from side to side like she was trying to extract something from my belly button, perhaps an alien or parasite.

As I started getting used to the sensation she stopped.

"You can get up now and sit in the chair."

I wanted to ask what she'd done but again, felt a strange reluctance to question her. My suspicion that this could be a bunch of hocus pocus was strengthening and I was resigning myself to the realisation that I should have spent the time and money on a massage instead.

As I swung my legs off the bed, the two chairs that were on either side of the table were now in the centre of the room facing each other.

How did they get there?!

I sat in the chair as requested and she sat opposite me.

"I am going to put my forehead on your forehead, okay? Please keep your eyes closed."

Righti-o! Just going with the flow …

"Okay."

She put her hands on my knees and leant forward so our foreheads touched, and again she started to hum. She made slight movements up and down and left to right, but our foreheads remained connected throughout the entire process of whatever she was doing.

After a minute or two, she leaned back and I did the same, opening my eyes. My glasses were still on the table, but rather than reach for them for clear sight, I maintained my position, shirtless, and staring at her blurry face.

"Hmmm. You are in transition. You stand in the doorway between realms, between old and new, fiction and fact. What you believed is not true; not about you, not about people in your life, and not about the world. You do not make sense of it yet, but you will."

I hadn't realised I was going to get clairvoyance too.

Was I supposed to respond?

"You have bad relationships. No intentions, no boundaries, no care for yourself."

How did she know?

"You finished something very bad, very toxic, and not good for you, but it has been a pathway to here. You are not in tune with your energy and emotions. You will find a better way and better relationships. You need to make peace. You are a healer, and others can benefit from you, but you do not use your voice. Their feelings are not your feelings. You do not speak up in situations, and you do not participate in conversations or put your views across. You need to stop doing this. You are being disrespectful to yourself and those around you."

What?!

Luxembourg had used those exact words just a couple of months ago. How was it possible they could use the same words?

I could feel the skin on my face heating up from within.

This felt like a setup, even though I couldn't see how it was possible.

"You do not use your voice because you are worried about keeping peace for others, but by doing so, you have no peace in yourself. You must understand why you think you are lesser than others? Why do you put yourself second? Why are you not important?"

Why indeed?!

"I can see you are a very old soul and you have been here for a very long time and have lived many lifetimes. This may be your last life. Your karma is clear, and you have righted your wrongs. You may not need to come back again, as you have learnt what you need to learn. You have done the things you need to do and achieved the things you need to achieve. If this is not your last life, it is close to."

I didn't know how to respond as I hadn't expected to

hear what she'd just told me. I had no thoughts on reincarnation, and certainly didn't feel like my karma was clear or that I'd learned everything I needed to in this life, let alone any others I might have had.

"I am going to do your chakra clearing now and then I will give you new aura, okay?"

So, what exactly have you been doing up until now?!

Her use of the word 'okay' as punctuation was confusing as I wasn't sure if she was telling me what she was going to do, or if she was asking for permission.

Best to hedge my bets. "Okay."

"Please stand, and close your eyes again."

I did as instructed.

I could hear her arms waving around me and felt the breeze they created on my bare torso. I could hear her breath as she bent up and down, and as she fanned my skin at an increasing pace. I could hear a snapping noise from her hands as though she was clicking her fingers around my elbows, knees, and shoulders; it was like she was stripping me of an invisible layer of air that was enveloping my skin.

As her movement became more frantic, the whirring of the air conditioner became louder, and my skin felt colder. I wanted to open my eyes to witness her performance but kept them shut to respect her and her process.

"Think of the colour yellow?"

Yellow?

Again, I didn't ask why, and instead tried to visualise the colour yellow.

Flashes of blue, and red, and purple, and green projected from my mind, through my eyes, and onto the back of my eyelids, and the more I tried to think of yellow, the less I could.

Try thinking of yellow objects!

Taxis, the sun, the buddha; no that was gold, marigolds; no, they're orange, but they can be yellow, but now, all I could see were the colours gold and orange.

Damn it, I was running out of time!

I hope this isn't important because it's just not working!

Canola crops! Think of the canola crops!

I could feel her hands near me again, this time patting me down without touching me. I could feel the pressure of the air pockets between her palms and my skin.

She put her hand on my left shoulder and pushed upwards into my glutes with her other.

Wasn't expecting that!

"Can you please stamp your feet on the floor, hard on your heels."

I did as she requested.

"You can open your eyes now."

"Can I put my shirt back on? I'm feeling a bit cold."

"Yes, of course. This is normal."

Both our chairs had mysteriously returned to their original positions on either side of the table. I stayed standing as I fastened my buttons, before taking my seat, a little bewildered by how she was able to move the furniture without making a sound.

I looked towards the ceiling to see which wall the air conditioner was on, but there was none. There wasn't even a vent.

Curious!

I wanted to ask about her upwards push into my bum but decided to start with an easier question.

"What was the stamping for?"

"It is to ground you, to bring you back into the earth, and back into your body. I am sorry that took so long—"

"It didn't feel that long but thank you."

"I have cleared your chakras and have stripped your aura and have given you a new one with the colour yellow."

Or perhaps it is orange, blue, green, or any other colour that isn't yellow!

"How was my stomach chakra, or solar plexus was it?"

"Your chakras are energised and are spinning better now. Your vishuddha or throat chakra was the most clogged; it was blocked and not spinning at all. It is responsible for finding and speaking your truth. I cleared the blockage, and it is spinning again, freely now, but you need to look after it and take care of it. You should wear blue as this is the colour of the throat chakra. Wear a blue scarf around your neck. Does it get cold where you live?"

"Yes, very cold, especially at this time of year, and yes, I have a blue scarf, actually it's more turquoise, but wearing blue won't be a problem as most of my clothes are that colour."

"Interesting. Vishuddha responds to blue, and you wear

blue clothes to energise it, but it is still not energised. You need to use your voice more. Do you smoke? It is very bad for you and your chakra, and you should not do it."

"No, I don't smoke, but it's interesting you ask. When I was shopping at the supermarket yesterday, I had a craving for two things I've never had a craving for."

"What things?"

"Cola and a clove cigarette. I know both are bad for me, but the craving was so strong that I bought both and had them in my villa as soon as I got back. In the end, I didn't want more than half a cigarette and half a glass of cola, but both felt like something I needed. I'm trying not to question these things whilst I'm here and am just trying to go with it."

She smiled, the first show of emotion since I arrived. "This is also related to your throat chakra as it was trying to loosen. Smoking and sweet drinks or lollies can help loosen it. It will be interesting to see if you have these cravings again, but if you have them, listen to your body, but please do not let it become a habit."

She'd just said that smoking was bad, but now that it was okay in moderation, but I wasn't going to challenge her.

I smiled in return. "I won't."

"Do you have any questions for me?"

Where to start: I have so many!

What was this session all about?

What was an aura?

What did she do to my stomach? What did she do to me?

How did she clear my chakras and what did I need to do to maintain them in good working order?

Why yellow, and why did she touch me up?

And, maybe the most important of all: What was I going to feel next?

"I have so many questions, but I think I'd like to let it all sit first."

"This is a good idea. I hope to see you again before you go."

Unlikely.

"Possibly."

"My advice for you is to go with the flow. Just be. Let things be as they are, and just be. You need to go with the flow and be happy."

"I'm hearing that a lot lately, and until recently, I thought I was good at going with the flow, but now I'm not so sure. I wish I knew how, but don't."

"There is nothing to know, just be happy, just go with the flow."

I suppressed an eyeroll with difficulty. Repeating the same words wasn't going to *make* it happen!

She stood up, walked around the table, and opened the door, leading me out towards reception.

"Take a seat and someone will bring you some tea."

"Thank you."

"After the session, do you feel any differently?"

Without thinking, I heard my voice saying, "no, not really."

A wave of shame washed over me. *How could I be so rude?!*

She smiled. "Take care of yourself and remember to be happy."

"I will." I hung my head to conceal my embarrassment and meekly shuffled to the area where my shoes were. As I picked them up and turned towards the couch to put them on and lace them up, she reappeared at the entrance to the corridor.

"One last thing before you go."

"Yes?"

She gave me a wink. "For sure you are an empath."

Chapter 10

I exited the wellness centre, still feeling shame about my answer to her question. 'No, not really', had been ungrateful and rude, and I should have answered more politely, or at least paused a moment so I could have told her the truth; that I wasn't sure yet.

I used to be better than that!

Kicking myself, I walked past the now empty parking garage, and towards the café at the end of the laneway, also empty, or possibly closed. I extracted my phone from my pocket and opened the maps app to see if I could walk away from the villa, to arrive back at it. The road had felt curved on the way here, and the map confirmed it, showing it as a loop that would eventually get me home. It was a longer way to the villa, but I had nowhere to be, and no curfew.

As I closed the app, I caught sight of the time on my display, 7:05pm.

It had reverted to Melbourne time – why, I didn't know

– but I wasn't going to worry about fiddling around with the settings just yet. It was something that could wait for later.

I re-holstered my phone into my back pocket and started walking towards more of the unfamiliar parts of Seminyak, feeling inexplicably lighter on my feet, as if weights had been lifted from my shoulders. My neck felt straighter too, making me feel a couple of inches taller.

Was this the result of the chakra cleanse, or was it psychosomatic? Either way, I wished I'd noticed earlier so I could have told the chakra lady as much.

Maybe I should go back to tell her.

Or you could stop worrying about it.

What's said is said, and what's done is done.

I was surprised to discover that I was hungry and needed something to eat. Whilst only just after 5:00pm local time, I needed to recharge, but what did I feel like? What did my freshly energised body want in it? What did my new yellow aura desire?

Stop taking the piss …

But I stopped in my tracks and closed my eyes to feel into an answer.

Tune in, tune in, tune in …

What do I feel like?

Doughnuts.

I opened my eyes and continued walking. It wasn't the healthiest of choices, and I'd never seen them sold here, but I wasn't going to overthink it. Doughnuts it would be. Seeking them out could be a part of my long walk home; and if I couldn't find them, then hopefully I'd see something else along the way that might be more nutritious.

I stopped in my tracks again. Something felt off.

If it's only 5:05pm, then why is it dark and why are the streetlights on?

I grabbed my phone, 7:07pm.

I clicked on the settings icon as fast as my fingers would respond and navigated to 'display', but there was nothing there about the time.

I closed 'settings', and tapped on the clock, and then world clock.

Melbourne, two hours in front, 9.07pm.

Seminyak, local time, 7.07pm. So … not Melbourne time after all.

What the hell?!

I looked left and right, and up and down for answers, but the sky was black, and artificial lighting had replaced the sun.

I retraced my memory of the session.

Arrived early, session started at 3.45pm, short chat, five minutes, tummy poking on the table, five minutes, foreheads touching, five minutes, debrief, five minutes, chakra clearing, and aura, ten minutes max.

3:45pm, 3:50pm, 3:55pm, 4:00pm, 4:05pm, 4.15pm.

Add extra time for potentially starting late and drinking tea at the end, five or ten minutes, meaning it should be 4:20pm, or 4:30pm at the latest, not 7:05pm!

I needed verification just in case Bali was in the shadow of a solar eclipse.

I swivelled my head and ran across the road to the first person I saw. "Sorry, excuse me, sorry, but can you please tell me the time?"

The man looked downwards at the phone in my right hand, his expression puzzled, wondering why I couldn't check for myself. *Tourists …*

He rolled his wrist to look at his watch. "A little after seven."

Fuck!

I spun on my heel with a belated 'thank you' and stumbled back to where I'd stopped earlier, swinging myself downward onto a tiled step of the closest shop.

How did this happen?

How had I lost this much time?

Retrace your steps again …

Appointment at 3:45pm. Got there early. Was upstairs by 3:40pm. Was greeted and shown to the room by 3:45pm or 3:50pm at the latest. There was a bit of banter taking us to 3:55pm. On the table; ten or so minutes there, 4:05pm. On the chair, maybe, ten minutes, 4:15pm. Stood up so she could wave her arms around me, another ten minutes, patted me on the arse, 4:25pm. Farewells, tea, and down the stairs, ten minutes.

Therefore, at worst, it should be no later than 4:35pm.

This felt weird.

I was sure I'd been awake during the entire session and had felt her hands on me and around me, as she pressed on my stomach, and put her forehead against mine. I lay down,

I sat in a chair, and I stood up, and each of those things took no more than ten or fifteen minutes.

How had I lost two and a half hours?

My mind was ticking over, but not racing, and I didn't feel panicked. I took a deep breath, and another, and another, my questions dissipating with each additional exhale.

Does it matter?

I could have fallen asleep, but if I had, then I would have remembered coming out of it, wouldn't I?

Does it matter?

I could make another appointment tomorrow to go back and ask her, but what difference would it make?

I needed to accept the lost time for what it was; something I couldn't change. I was still hungry, and the doughnuts weren't going to find themselves.

Time to go with the flow …

I re-started my walk and within minutes, lightning flashed across the sky, and thunder cracked and boomed. The heavens opened and rain poured down in large chunky drops. I had no umbrella or waterproof jacket, and within seconds, I was saturated.

I lifted my face to the sky and let the water hit me square in the face, just as I had done that afternoon in Maruyama Park in Kyoto.

With no awnings or shelter nearby, I continued my long walk home, trusting that the deluge would be quick, and that I'd dry off as soon as it stopped.

As I approached Jalan Kayu Cendana, the storm intensified, giving me good reason to find somewhere indoors for something to eat. A burger joint was closest, making my decision quick and easy.

I made a beeline for its black and white tiled entry and dashed up the steps, stopping just beyond its doorway. I was dripping wet, and my glasses were fogging up. I removed them and wiped them down with my wet shirt, but as soon as I placed them back on my face, they fogged up again, forcing me to repeat the process, again and again until I cooled off.

The shop had a minimalist interior, with a continuous pattern of black and white tiles across every wall. A polished concrete counter fronted a grill and hooked around in a U-shape to create a dining bench along a window facing the street outside. It had seating for five, but thankfully I was the only one here.

"Yes, boss?"

I'd become accustomed to the men here calling other men, boss, or friend, and was no longer surprised that they were talking to me.

"Hi, yes, can I get a basic burger with no onion and no cheese please? Just something simple with tomato, lettuce, pickles, and tomato sauce? I'm not sure if that is on your menu, because I can't see through these," I waved my still-fogged glasses at him, "but is that okay?"

"Yes, sure thing boss. You want to sit here in the dry or take it away in the wet?" He laughed, predicting my answer, before I'd given it.

"Here, in the dry please."
"Chips, drink?"
"No thank you."
"Take a seat, I'll bring it to you."

I sat on the stool nearest the entry door and stared outside at the glistening wetness of everything. Traffic was at a standstill, and vehicle lights cast a red and white glow on the pedestrians crossing between them, sheltering their heads against the rain with their hands or whatever objects they were holding. They *jetéd* across potholes and puddles, and onto the footpath and off it again. It was an unchoreographed dance; a contemporary ballet of weather and movement, and this was my front-row seat.

My burger arrived within minutes, and I savoured it slowly, both to practise some extra mindfulness, and to give the rain more time to ease. It was exactly as I'd requested it and was deliciously tasty.

It wasn't a doughnut, but the sugar content of the brioche bun came pretty close in terms of sweetness.

With half the burger finished, I contemplated ordering a second one, but the not-Dutch counsellor's words rang in my ears like a struck gong.

Be mindful, and present in the present. You currently live in the future!

She was right. Here I was, not yet finished enjoying the experience of my first meal, thinking about the second.

My last bite satisfied my craving for another burger, but my tastebuds were still screaming for something sweeter. The saltiness of the beef and tartness of the pickles had that effect, and it was easy to understand why soft drinks had become part and parcel of a satisfying fast-food experience.

As I stared out past the cars and pedestrians, a shopping centre beyond them slowly came into focus. I'd seen it before but had not paid much attention, but now that I craved something sugary, it seemed a good a place as any to find those doughnuts whilst still keeping dry.

I returned my tray and wrappings to the counter, paid for my meal, and joined the dance across the road, performing my own leaps and bounds over the potholes and puddles.

Before I was permitted to enter the sliding doors of the mall, a security guard waved his metal detector wand over me, front and back before letting me through.

It was another part of the choreography, a meaningless ritual enacted to make tourists feel safer in public spaces.

Once inside, the shopping centre presented like any other in the world; with multiple brightly-lit levels, freezing cold air conditioning, and music piped through invisible speakers.

I scanned the upper and lower floors, disappointed at how empty and deserted it was, but it didn't matter, as my sole objective for being here was about to be fulfilled.

Directly in front of me, was a small pink kiosk with a white gabled roof and the sign I'd been looking for, for the past hour.

Doughnuts.

I walked over to investigate the selection, but there was none. Rather than showcasing a variety of flavours and shapes, this stall specialised in doughnut balls dusted in cinnamon and sugar. The only choice on offer was quantity: I could buy six or twelve.

I only wanted one, or possibly two if they were good, but if the only way to sate my appetite was to buy extras, then so be it.

I thought about asking the attendant to give me two for the price of six, but my previous experiences were that people didn't understand why you'd ask to pay for something you weren't going to get. I didn't want to engage in that type of conversation this evening, and following the path of least resistance seemed the best option.

I placed my order and watched as the six balls were carefully positioned into a pink and white striped cardboard box, with its lock down tab secured by a gold sticker. The box was then placed into a pink and white cardboard bag with pink rope handles, and handed to me with two hands as if its contents were rare and precious. My initial reaction was to extract the box and hand back the bag, as it seemed an extravagant waste, but again, I wasn't going to create an unnecessary interaction.

The packaging was something they were clearly proud of, and I needed to be grateful to receive it, even if it was worth more money than its contents and was soon to be disposed of.

I turned back towards the entrance of the mall and made my way outside. The rain had stopped, but the humidity was rising. It was 8:30pm, and still too early for bed, so I headed in the direction of Kayu Aya Beach.

Without breaking stride, I extracted the box and peeled back the sticker to pick out one of the doughy delights, shoving it into my mouth whole, and squishing it between my tongue and palate before chasing it too quickly with another one.

The dusting wasn't as sweet as expected, and the doughnuts weren't what I'd hoped for. Old, cold, oily, and bready, and not a dessert suited to this climate.

I should have taste tested the first one before committing to a second, but it was too late for that: both masticated balls inching their way inexorably down through my oesophagus.

I closed the box and resecured it with its sticker, torn between throwing it away or carrying it home with me.

Before long, I was sitting on the rock wall facing the sea and horizon, witnessing the end of another religious ceremony, the people wearing traditional clothing in much the same way as they had the last time I was here. The ceremony over, they dusted themselves off and walked off in the direction of their homes or their scooters, again leaving their plastic rubbish behind.

I shook my head in disbelief. I'd thought the last time I'd seen this sort of scene that it may have been a one-off by a rogue group of revellers but was now wondering whether this was an everyday and every-night affair. A thousand bits of plastic by two or three ceremonies per day, multiplied by three hundred and sixty-five days was a lot of plastic to end up in the ocean every year.

I'd burned with anger the first time I'd seen it, but tonight, I felt nothing.

It was their beach and their rules, and if I was going to let it bother me, then I needed to be proactive and do something about it, but even if I wanted to, I couldn't right now, because I could feel my body hitting a wall.

Waves of fatigue were crashing over me, and I needed to get back to the villa and into bed as soon as possible. The tiredness came on unexpectedly, and thankfully, I wasn't too far away from remedying it.

I'd done very little today, but it felt as though I'd done a lot, like I'd read a hundred textbooks and run a marathon. My limbs and brain felt heavy, my head dropping, my feet dragging, and my arms unwilling to swing. I slowed my pace further and kept my focus on placing one foot in front of the other. A walk that was supposed to take me fifteen minutes, would end up taking me longer.

After what felt like an hour, I finally arrived at the laneway of my villa, with just one hundred metres to go to my mattress. I waved to the reception staff as I passed, surprised that the doughnut bag was still looped over my left wrist. Rather than continue to my finish line, I doubled back and opened the glass door to the office.

A young attendant put her phone down in haste and

greeted me at the door. "Hello sir, can I help you please? Would you like to place your order for breakfast?"

Breakfast?

Who can think of food at a time like this?

"No thank you, but I was wondering if you would like these doughnuts? There are four in here you are welcome to, or you can share them with the others if you like?"

She put her hand on her chest, seemingly taken aback. "Doughnuts? For us sir?"

"Yes, if you would like them. I bought them earlier and there are too many for me."

"Are you sure sir? We can keep them in the fridge for you for tomorrow if you like?"

"No, no, please, if you'd like them, please enjoy them."

She received the bag with both hands, as if it contained a billion rupiah.

A smile spread wide across her face. "Thank you, sir, I will share these with my friends."

"You're most welcome. Enjoy and have a good night."

"You too, sir."

Who knew that doughnuts could provide so much joy? Perhaps I could buy them every night …

It was joy in her voice, wasn't it?

She didn't think I was just handing off my leftovers, did she?

It's what you were doing, wasn't it?

I felt heavier than before, but I had to sneak back to check.

Would I see her enjoying them, or throwing them out, or would they be sitting on her desk as she decided what she was going to do with them?

None of the above.

As I peered through the glass from the shadow of a banana palm, I spied four uniformed staff huddled around an empty box, each with half a doughnut ball in their hand, smiling and laughing.

Success.

I shuffled the final few metres and unlocked and opened the unnecessarily large wooden door to my private garden, locking it behind me with both key and chain, doing the same with the door to the villa as I stepped inside.

I flopped onto the sofa and reached for the TV remote to switch it on, something I'd not done before on any of my previous trips to Bali. A superhero movie was on, but I wasn't sure if I'd seen it before, or if I had, where it was up to. I slouched deeper into the sofa; my clothes still damp in places from the earlier deluge.

I needed to get into bed.

The doughnuts and burger weren't sitting right.

Oh no! I think I'm going to be sick.

I rolled off the couch and plodded to the bathroom, leaning over the toilet bowl, careful not to get too close.

I dry retched a few times, but no eruption.

Ah, shit!

I hoped it wasn't the doughnuts, and I hoped I hadn't poisoned the staff!

Argh, here we go again.

My stomach and chest contracted with an attempt to expel the toxins, but nothing came out, leaving me with a vague feeling that my body wasn't quite *right.*

I rarely vomited, so wasn't overly familiar with the sensations, but something about this felt different, an unfamiliar nausea, not like the usual obvious reaction when the food I'd eaten wasn't agreeing with me. I knew *that* feeling, but this was different, as if my body wanted to be rid of something; but if not the food, then what?

I lowered myself onto the floor tiles to wait it out.

This situation had to move on, one way or another.

For the following hour, I did burpee exercises with the toilet bowl, lifting myself off the floor to bend over it, stretching upwards when nothing came out, before lowering myself back onto the tiles, riding alternate waves of rising sickness and subsiding relief.

Eventually, my position looking unlikely to yield a result, I picked myself up, and shuffled to the bed. My teeth were not getting done tonight.

I lay on my back; too hot under the covers, and too cold above them. I increased the temperature on the air conditioner to try and even it out, but within moments, I was sweating, so lowered it again.

My compromise was to lay half in, half out; my left side under the bedspread, and my right side out in the open.

Time to sleep.

Had I drifted off?

How long had I been out for?

I think I'm going to be sick again!

I disentangled myself from the doona and was back in my hunched position over the toilet.

More burpees, but still no result.

Back to bed.

My discomfort was getting worse with dull aches gripping my kidneys and chest. The nausea had knitted a knot in my sternum, and it was getting tighter by the second.

This was going to be a sleepless night.

Ow!

My kidneys!

Why are they aching?

Feels like I've been punched.

Ow, ow, ow!

My kidneys are being crushed.

Someone sitting on my chest.

Not able to lie on my sides, or my back.

Owww!

The pain is excruciating.

Do I call an ambulance now, or wait?

Wait for what?

Fuck!
This is beyond painful now.
Where's my phone?
I can't move.

So hot!
So much sweat.
All my organs hurting, not just my kidneys.
Are they shutting down?

So cold!
Shivering.
Organs?
Still there, still painful.

Had I drifted off again?
Sheets so wet.
Sweat dripping.
Gross.

Is it morning yet?
Skin so cold.
Insides so hot!
Kidneys bursting.

Fuck!
Can't move.
Paralysed.
Pain intense.

So hot.
    Heartbeat slow.
    Kidneys shutdown.
    Paralysed.

I need an ambulance!
    I need to get to hospital!
    How do I get to hospital?
    Is it triple zero here?

I'm dying.
    How do I get help?
    Can't move.
    Voice not working.

What is this?
    From the rain?
    From the burger?
    From the doughnuts?

So hot and so cold. Heat stroke?
    What is heat stroke?
    What are its symptoms?
    My fucking kidneys!

Still paralysed.
    Can't move.
    Why did I lock the door?
    Who's going to help?

So hot!
> Can't be heatstroke.
> No more sun than any other day.
> *Where's my phone?*

So cold again!
> Skin on fire.
> Air conditioner burning.
> *Turn it off!*

Still paralysed.
> Can't call for help.
> Can't get help.
> This is the end.

She said the healing would change my life, not end it.
> Light at the window.
> *Moonlight or sunlight?*
> What time is it?

Maybe I was bitten by something?
> A mosquito?
> Dengue fever?
> *What are the symptoms?*

Sunset or sunrise?
> Still have a pulse. Can feel it on the pillow.
> Still alive.
> Just.

Where am I?
  What day is it?
  What time is it?
  No one helping.

How did I lose two and a half hours?
  How many more hours have I lost here?
  Why did I tell her I felt no different?
  Call her to apologise!

Still here dying.
  When is my flight?
  How will I make it to the airport?
  Will I get my money back?

This is it.
  Death is coming.
  I've lived a good life and have few regrets.
  I'm ready.

Lying on my side.
  Must have moved.
  Kidneys, not as bad.
  Chest, compressed.

Lying on my front.
  Aches, going.
  Temperature, good.
  Sheets, dry.

Enough!
Time to get up.
Daylight outside.
What time is it?

Time to get up.
Not hungry.
Not thirsty.
Don't need the bathroom.

Time to get up.

I rolled over, feeling like I'd been in the ring with a boxing champion for a full twelve rounds. My body was aching, but the sharp pains from last night had gone. I was battered and bruised and had no idea of the cause, or what had happened to me.

I swung my legs over the edge of the bed and used them as a counterweight to lever myself into a sitting position.

"Ow!"

My phone was where I'd left it, still plugged in on the bedside table, and I reached over and unlocked it.

The home screen displayed icons for fourteen messages, and the time read 11:11am. Not too bad; I'd been bed ridden for longer.

"Nice."

I brought the screen closer to my face to focus on the day and date listed under the time.

Thursday.

Thursday?!

I hadn't lost a morning; I'd lost two days!

How?

I retraced my days, in case I was getting this trip confused with the one before it. I'm sure I arrived on a Sunday and had my chakra appointment on Monday; so how could it be Thursday?

How could I have been in bed for that long, and why had no one checked on me?

No food, no water, no bodily functions, just aches, a fever, paralysis, and unconsciousness.

First, I'd lost two hours on Monday, and now I'd lost two days since!

How?

I collapsed back onto the bed and stared at the ceiling, expecting my mind to go into overdrive, and for my panic to kick in.

As the seconds ticked away, neither happened.

I was calm and it seemed I was staying that way. My heart rate stayed at a steady fifty to sixty beats per minute, and my breathing stayed slow and deep.

This was new. Normally I'd be overthinking a situation like this, but now I merely felt curious, and a little discombobulated.

Interesting.

Was I concerned about losing the days?

Not really.

Was I worried about being so sick?

A little.

Was I interested in knowing what had happened to me?

Sure!

Was I concerned that I could have died? Reality check: *No, as I wouldn't have remembered it anyway, and we wouldn't be having this conversation.*

Was I worried about being out of contact with friends and family back home?

Nope, and if they were worried, they would have called the villa and had someone check on me.

Was I annoyed that no one had checked on me?

Not in the slightest.

My answers to my questions felt like mini epiphanies, each making me feel even more relaxed about the situation.

I had no idea what happened to me during the past two and a half days, and I didn't feel all that concerned about it.

This was a new feeling I hadn't had before.

What was it?

Was this peace?

Chapter 11

My slow and painful flirtation with death behind me now, I felt as if I was reborn into a new day. Curiosity abounded but knowing or not knowing what had happened to me, wasn't going to make a huge difference to the rest of my time here.

I had five remaining days in Bali, and I was prepared to enjoy them – with a little extra wariness of heat, rain, mosquitos, burgers, and doughnuts.

I levered my torso upwards and swung my legs over the side of the bed, cautioning myself as I did so.

Easy does it, there's no rush. No where to be and no timeframe to be there.

I hoisted my body into a standing position, taking extra care to feel my weight in my knees, consciously feeling balance through my ankles, thighs, and feet. I was somewhat dissociated from my body, as if I were a marionette pulling my own strings.

The fatigue that draped itself over me at Kayu Aya Beach three nights ago still weighed heavily on me.

My brain hurt in the way it did at the end of a migraine, but the pain felt just out of reach, as if it was a memory, and not quite mine.

Was I awake?

Or was this a fever dream?

Should I call a doctor, or an ambulance, or just ride it out?

Ride it out.

I set my course for the shower, for a rinse and refresh.

Blink, I was out of the bedroom.

Blink, I was in the shower.

Blink, I was finished and drying myself off.

I knew what I was doing, but I couldn't *feel* it, as if my mind was on a five-minute delay; my senses holding back information from my brain until they no longer made sense.

My consciousness was still out of reach.

Blink, blink, blink … I was dressed, outside the villa on the street, and walking towards the wellness centre.

Why was I going there?

Surely, I needed something to eat and drink, but any thought of eating scrambled eggs or any of its traditional sides caused the feelings of nausea to return.

My legs were taking me somewhere, but where?

As if on autopilot, I was soon seated in a café halfway between the villa and the wellness centre, with a fresh coconut in front of me, ordered sometime during the past five or fifteen minutes.

I hadn't taken a sip yet, and I wasn't sure I was capable, without it being regurgitated all over the table and floor.

I leant back on the cushioned bench seat and stared out the window.

My phone was on the table, face down, so I flipped it over to check the messages that were still unread.

There were five from my friend who'd made me promise to get a chakra healing, one from each of the past three days:

- Hey, how did it go? Has your life changed yet?

- Checking in. Let me know how it went.

- Hope you're not too unwell, take care of yourself.

Two more from this morning.

- Sorry if you're still not feeling well, take care, and drink lots of coconut water.

- You'll be fine, I promise. Rest up!

Coconut water? If I could just start with this one …

I typed my reply with uncoordinated thumbs.

- Sorry I've been offline. Might have picked up a bug or heatstroke, so been in bed for a while.

I put my phone down face up and leant forward to take a long sip through the wide paper straw wedged within the coconut.

She'd received my message and was typing her reply.

- Do you think it was a bug or heatstroke, or could it be something else?

- Like what?

- Did you see an energy healer?

- Yes. Chakra. Story for another time …

- Maybe not. I didn't want to put you off because it doesn't always happen. Healings can cause a break. They can break your stasis; your mind–body–spirit stasis and can break you apart. Good news is that you can put yourself back together however you want.

…

A pause, and then she continued.

- I'm sorry I didn't say anything.

I didn't know what she was talking about.

- Nothing to be sorry for. I'm not sure what you mean, but I'm fine now.

- Good to hear, she replied. *I spent a day in bed after my first healing, with nausea, fever, and the feeling of my chakras bursting.*

Bursting chakras? Was it my chakras that were hurting rather than my organs? I decided to be honest.

- Had the same, and felt I was going to die :-)

- And now? How are you feeling?

- Hungover. But coconut is helping.

It was. Each sip shot straight into my veins, reanimating my limbs and extremities.

- Look after yourself and we'll talk more when you're back.

I flipped my phone onto its screen and refocused on the streetscape outside the window.

People walked past going about their everyday business, talking, exercising, listening to music, and who knows what else. I felt oddly disconnected from them. Were they real or were they shadows inside my cave?

"Would you like something to eat?"

Where did you come from?!

"Yes, please. Do you have something fresh and healthy?"

"Yes! Our dragon bowl is fresh and healthy!"

"Okay, I'll have one of those please."

"Would you like to see the menu; to see its ingredients?"

"No, thank you. I trust you."

My friend's text came to mind: *mind body spirit stasis.*

What does that even mean?

I flipped my phone over and saw a new message from an unknown number starting with +62. *Indonesia.*

- How are you? Are you ok after chakra? Drink plenty of water and go with the flow.

Based on the words 'chakra' and 'flow', I assumed it was from Monday's 'thrapist'.

Nice of her to reach out. I didn't hesitate to reply.

- Thanks again for Monday. I've been unwell since but am up and about now and I think I'm at the café just down the road from you. Take care and see you again soon.

Now that I had her number, I could withdraw my statement about not feeling any different, and replace it with something better, but that could wait for later.

"Your dragon bowl boss."

A waitperson appeared to my side with a large shallow timber bowl and spoon, placing both in front of me. The contents, a work of art.

"Thank you. It looks delicious."

A quadrant was filled with a mix of seeds and granola, with a second quadrant containing chopped mango, strawberry, and banana. The remaining half of the bowl was filled with a bright fuchsia-pink paste, most likely puréed dragon fruit.

So that's why they call it a dragon bowl …

The ingredients awakened my appetite, and I scooped half a spoon of purée into my mouth.

"Yum!"

As I finished the last piece of fruit, the haze of disassociation started lifting, and my body started feeling like mine again. My heartbeat felt stronger, and my blood was flowing more freely.

I was waking up.

Remnants of my nausea and aches were slowly being consigned to memory, but the idea of ordering a coffee was still too risky.

As I continued to tune into my body, I could see a familiar face walking towards the café. She was craning her neck left and right and shielding her eyes with her hands to see through the window's reflections and into the dining room, searching for someone.

It was the chakra therapist.

She spotted me and waved, opened the door to the café and walked directly to where I was sitting.

"I am glad I found you. Are you okay?"

She took the seat opposite me.

"Hi, nice to see you again! Yes, I'm okay. I just finished a dragon bowl and a coconut and am feeling much better."

"Ah, yes! The chakra bowl! Seven colours for the seven chakras."

"I didn't know that! It was a suggestion from the waitperson. What are you up to today? Do you have any appointments?"

She looked concerned. "No, not today, but I wanted to check on you."

"Oh, thank you, but why? I'm fine!"

"How do you feel after your chakra?"

I smiled. She'd provided me the opportunity to redeem myself for my previous rudeness.

"I've definitely felt different during the past three days, and I feel much better now, but I haven't had time to process it all. I'm optimistic that it will be good for me, even though I've been a bit sick since Monday and haven't really been in a state to pay attention to it."

"I am sorry, but I did not know for certain if this would happen to you. It does for some people, and not for other people. Your throat chakra was especially blocked, so I used an ankh to help energise it. It is a new technique I am learning, and good in certain situations like yours."

She seemed much warmer and kinder today, and more pleasant to talk to.

"What's an ankh?"

"Ankh is Egyptian, like a staff with a cross and a loop on the end. She mimed the loop with her left finger. "It supercharges chakra for a far more powerful effect."

"And you used it on me?"

"Yes. You asked me to. The ankh gives chakras more energy than traditional chakra and the effects are better, but new energy can take time to get used to. It will rebalance your body, and your mind, and spirit. I did not know if it would do this for you as everybody is different, but you were receptive."

"I was receptive?"

"Yes. When I asked you if you wanted me to try the ankh, you were happy to try it."

I had no recollection of her question, or my answer.

"Are you talking about stasis?"

"What is stasis?"

"I'm not sure, but I think it means harmony or balance."

"Then yes, I am talking about harmony and all your chakras now being in better balance than before. They are connected. If they are not in alignment, or not spinning freely, then the rest of you will be out of alignment too. When I re-energised your chakras, they will realign too."

Her description of what may have happened, connected with what my friend had just texted me. Perhaps there was something in all of this?

"Are you saying that you broke me?"

I gave her my biggest smile to let her know I wasn't concerned.

She smiled back. "I am just a conduit for energy, and I did not do anything except give you what you needed. This is something you did and received for you. Your soul was stuck and needed to be released."

"My soul?"

"Yes, your soul is in your stomach, and I massaged it loose when you were lying on the table. It rose high; high above you. This is why your stomach was making all the gurgling noises."

"Oh, I don't recall."

"Be gentle with yourself during the next few weeks and everything will be better."

I wasn't sure what to say, so I just smiled at her again.

I still wasn't sure I believed what she was saying, but I didn't feel the need to not believe it either.

"You said at the end of our session that 'for sure I was an empath' but what does that mean?"

"I thought you knew what it means as you mentioned it at the start."

"I am new to this, and I don't really understand any of it. I don't understand empaths, chakras, energies, or any of what you did in that room. In fact, I don't remember much of what happened whilst I was in there!"

"It is okay. You went into a trance so I could work with your subconscious. I thought it was not your first chakra."

Trance?

"It was my first, but I don't remember the trance. I hope I didn't say or do anything weird."

She laughed. "Clients always ask me that! No, not at all. You were receptive and followed instructions."

Nothing of what she was saying was causing any of my normal reactions. I felt no panic, no elevated heartrate, no increase in blood pressure, and no hamsters on running wheels connected to my overthinking.

I was going to take this opportunity to ask her a different question though.

"May I ask you, if I am an empath, what is your advice for me?"

"For sure you are an empath, but you must learn to go with the flow, and you must trust the universe. Not all energy is yours and not all feelings are yours. Know what is yours and what is not. Everything happens for a reason, and you must trust it, and go with it."

"I get that, but how?"

Did I get that?

"Do not resist life. Do not control it or let it control you. Flow with it. If something makes you happy, do it. If something does not make you happy, then do not do it. It is very simple to be happy. To be happy, you just have to be happy!"

"If something doesn't make me happy, don't do it?"

"Yes, of course!"

"I don't think I've considered that before. Life is full of sacrifices."

"Why does it have to be? Keep it simple. If there are people or situations or experiences you do not like and do not make you happy, then do not do them. It is simple."

"But it's not that simple, is it? Sometimes we have to do things we don't like, for money, for food, or for family."

"If something is causing you pain, and you do not like it, then why do it? Life is too short. Why not find another way that is better? If you must do something you do not like, then find a better way. Your body will tell you if something is good for you or not. Tune into your body. All your answers are there."

Her advice was appealing and felt consistent with Luxembourg's, and my revelations in Allestree.

"Thank you. You've given me something new to think about. I'm still not sure about the whole stasis thing, but I will keep an open mind."

Could this be what flow was all about?

Could my version of 'going with the flow' be as simple as keeping an open mind and testing experiences that felt good, and not so good?

What if I didn't need to understand the words and concepts to benefit from them? What if I didn't need to believe in stasis, chakras, empaths, or any other label I didn't understand?

What if all I needed to do was keep an open mind, and try to be who I wanted to be, rather than who I thought I should be?

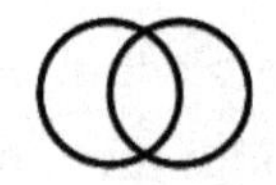

Chapter 12

I was back, sitting on the middle cushion of the three-seater black leather couch in the counsellor's living room, ten weeks since my first visit, and nine weeks since my last. My time in Allestree and Seminyak had provided me space for new ways to think, and for new answers to present themselves, even though I was no longer sure of the questions.

My head had stopped spinning from the uncoveries during the past few months, and the reliving of my relationships, beliefs, thought patterns, actions, and behaviours had started to evolve rather than revolve.

I couldn't distinguish between my experiences, memories, and the conclusions I'd made up since my last visit, but I wasn't sure it mattered. The not-Dutch counsellor's concept of storylines had weaselled its way into my brain and had become all-encompassing. They were all I saw, and all I noticed, and I was still having difficulty dropping them.

Each event had more than one, it seemed. If a driver cut me off in traffic, they were either a selfish so-and-so, or in the midst of a personal emergency. If people dawdled in front of me on the footpath, they were either inconsiderate arseholes, or lost, and didn't know where they were going. If couples were scrolling away on their phones whilst at a restaurant or bar, they either had nothing to talk about to each other, or were trying to find something interesting to show their partner.

I couldn't just let anything be. My existence was still consumed by narratives, about other people, and about myself. It was how I made sense of what I witnessed.

But somehow, whether by chance, or on purpose, the not-Dutch counsellor had given my overthinking a name and had brought it out of the cave and into the open.

Storylines.

I'd spent the six years after my ex-wife's breakdown, seeing her through the lens of her depression and bipolar disorder and was still seeing her that way today. My storylines about who she was, what she was going through, and what she needed from me had become my truth and my way of navigating my life, and I'd lived six years in limbo, without intention, not progressing, and not living my own life.

I'd sacrificed my time for hers, and those years were gone for good, and for what?

I believed the counsellor had been referring to this loss when she'd told me about the danger of storylines overpowering and sidelining actual experiences. It was what had happened to me.

I felt stupid for my inability to move on after so long, but I still didn't know with any certainty if I was seeing my history as it always had been, or if I was simply creating new versions to better fit my new understanding of me, my programming, and my operating system.

Before I could move forward with my life, I still needed to be sure that I could separate my fact from fiction, my experience from memory, and most importantly, my stories from the truth.

I wanted to rebuild myself into a better version, but how could I, when my thoughts and preferences seemed the same whether they were based in reality or fantasy?

The worst possible outcome in all of this was for me to re-imagine myself as the same old person I'd always been.

The counsellor had made two mugs of rooibos tea before I'd arrived, and I was cradling mine in my lap as she took her seat to sip hers.

"Thanks for seeing me at short notice."

Her smile radiated kindness and warmth.

"You are welcome. I was wondering how you were, and if you were okay after our last meeting, and then you called."

My brain was about to burst, and I didn't think I'd have the capacity to engage in small talk. "I need to know something, I'm curious, in your opinion, what's the difference between imagination and intuition?"

She pulled the mug away from her lips and blew across its too-hot surface. "Why do you ask?"

The duel of questioning my questions without answers had commenced.

"Well, the past few weeks have been really weird for me—"

"How so?"

Where do I start?!

With hating myself, or breaking myself?

"To be honest with you, I haven't stopped thinking about the three or six pieces of advice you gave me last time I was here, and whilst I thought they were a little vague at the time, and I didn't know how to apply them back then, I think they've occupied my thinking ever since."

She kept her expression hidden, her eyes continuing their steady gaze into mine.

"I got away into space, like you said, and, well, it's been like I've been hit in the head with an axe, right here in my forehead. I feel like my brain is cut in half and now I'm seeing things in at least two ways, if not two hundred ways, and I'm no longer sure what is real, or what I've imagined since. I also got away to Bali recently and had a very weird experience there, but I'll tell you about that another time."

Her smile widened. "You look fine to me. There is no axe in your head, and as for Bali, Bali is Bali, a place of wonderful energy."

"It sure is!"

"Your question is an interesting one, but I must ask why you think there needs to be a difference between imagination and intuition? Maybe they are the same thing, or maybe two parts of the same whole?"

Another riddle!

"How do you mean?"

"Well, based on your reaction during our last few sessions, I did not think you believed in intuit—"

"That's not quite true and I'm sorry if I gave you that impression. It's just that I don't understand it, at least, I don't understand how it works for me, so I don't know how to use it, or *if* I should use it, and all that aside, I don't like it, and really don't want it."

I could hear my voice rising, becoming agitated, and stopped.

Her eyes widened and she lowered her mug enough for me to see that her mouth was open. Was it a look of shock or surprise?

You did cut her off …

"I'm sorry I cut you off from what you were saying."

"It is okay. It seems you have more to say this session; quite a change from last time."

Was it a change?

"What is intuition if it is not a feeling converted to an imagined thought? Intuition and imagination do not have to be different, and can be one and the same, but I must ask again, why do you ask?"

It was as if a floodgate had opened. I took a deep breath and regaled her with tales of my drive to Allestree and my time on the beach, and my recollections of what I knew, what I thought I knew, and what I thought had happened. I told her about why I thought my relationship with my ex-wife might have started, as well as the details of our long-distance first year together. I amused her with my interaction with the seadog and the revelations that opened up for me when I found my first shark tooth and my eleventh, and I described my new recollections of what I think I knew in Tokyo and how I'd acted in spite of myself, and how I'd ignored my intuition about my marriage, in favour of my storylines of 'shoulds' and 'ideals'.

She listened intently, without interruption, only lifting her mug from time to time, to conceal her reactions, or lack thereof, to my flow of words.

"There was this moment, a split second, on our very first date when she was lying diagonally across the bed. I remember it so vividly. She'd propped herself up on her right elbow and had a cup of tea in her left hand. She was still in her work clothes, an apricot knee-length skirt and a cream coloured knit, and I was standing near her at the base of the bed. We were talking about something; I don't remember what, but at that precise moment, everything went dark, not literally, but figuratively. She looked unrecognisable, and if I'm honest, quite unattractive, and maybe even ugly. In that split second, I remember an ache in my gut, and a feeling of certainty that we were never going to work out. But it made no sense: we were less than an hour into our first date, and so I blinked, and the feeling, the darkness, and all the ugliness went away."

"It seems this feeling did not go away if you can remember it so keenly."

"It was just so contrary to everything else I was thinking and feeling at the time. Like I said, it made no sense and I think it was the inconsistency that I remember so well. I put it down to nervousness and doubt; however, now that everything has happened the way it has, I wonder if I knew all along; or if in fact, the end of our relationship was orchestrated by me, as some sort of self-fulfilling-prophecy I'd set in motion and was subconsciously working towards."

She smiled again, as if she understood what I was saying, even though I *felt* I didn't. "I think you know that this was your intuition speaking to you. You knew, even if you did not know how you knew."

"Even if I did, what was I supposed to do? I'd just flown halfway around the world to be with her! Was I supposed to thank her and say, 'sorry, my gut has spoken to me, and this isn't going to work out, have a nice life'?"

The sharpness of my words and tone did little to hide my feelings, but she didn't react to my rising pitch and stayed smiling. "My advice for you was to tap into your intuition. You need to know it is there and pay attention to it; do not ignore it, but also, do not believe it fully either. Become conscious of it, and curious about it. Let it guide you when it feels right. Treat it as a valuable resource and keep testing it by investigating your reasons, but more than anything, let it *be there* for you.

"Maybe the ugliness you saw was a manifestation of what had happened until that moment; that the weeks between her first text and you flying over had been covered in red flags and you were already feeling tormented by the way she seemed, and how she was treating you.

"Her lying on the bed, so relaxed, after you had made her a cup of tea may have been a culmination of how you were feeling; that you had flown halfway around the world to see her, whereas she had just walked down the street after work and sat herself on the bed to be waited on."

Could any of that be true?

"I guess that's the problem, and the crux of my question. Was it my intuition at the time, or is it my imagination in the here and now?

"I'm forty-one, and everything I believed to be true about my life, might not be. I still don't know how I've made it this far without understanding anything about myself, whilst at the same time thinking I understood myself perfectly!"

"Wait until you turn forty-two."

She snorted into her mug causing the red tea to spray over its edge, her comment amusing her far more than she anticipated.

I didn't flinch. "I wish I wasn't so introspective; that I could leave things as they are, without needing to think about them, or worse still, trying to make sense of them. This whole self-awareness thing is a curse, and sometimes I wish I could make it stop."

She wiped her mug down with the palm of her hand. "Yes, it can be a curse, but it can also be a cure. It may contribute to your problem, but it may also be the solution."

More riddles!

She opened her mouth to say something more but closed it again on an indrawn breath. She looked conflicted. I couldn't remember her doing that before now, and it felt a little unnerving.

Her jaw fell open again, remaining that way as she stared into the middle distance between us, clearly in deep thought.

It looked as though she needed encouragement to continue. "It's okay, you can say what you need to say; it's why I'm here."

She inhaled again. "I want to find the right words to say to communicate the message I want you to hear."

I hadn't stumped her before but was now worrying about what I'd said to have caused her reaction.

"What I want to say to you may have the opposite effect of what I would like you to do, but I do not think there is another way to say it."

"Okay, so how about you just say it and we can talk through the detail afterwards?"

"Yes, I think this will be the only way. I need you to pause for a moment and to listen, without letting the little voices in your head take over."

No chance! "Okay."

"I need you to hear what I am saying and not judge it, and not judge yourself, okay?"

She was preparing me for criticism, which I hoped I was ready to hear. I nodded.

"Okay. So, you left our previous session a little sceptical about empaths, intentions, storylines, boundaries, energy, and intuition, but I can see now you were open enough to think more about it, which is really good by the way. You seem to be mastering the concept of shoshin which is also good. After you get over the initial shock of a new idea, you treat it with eagerness, openness, and a lack of preconceived ideas. It is a great fifth dimensional skill to keep."

The shit sandwich is coming … Criticism wrapped in two pieces of praise …

"Thank you. I got out into space like you said, and all these new thoughts kept racing in with your voice ringing in my ears; it was like I was some sort of transceiver, or like one of those electronic blue lights that attract bugs—"

Her expression suggested I should stop talking.

"The advice I want to give you may sound counterintuitive, like the opposite of the advice. Does this make sense?"

No, it does not!

"No, well, no, not yet."

"Well, here it is. I am very happy you treat our sessions and our discussions seriously, but I wonder if you can benefit by taking them less seriously?"

Huh?

"I am concerned you might be too suggestible or easily influenced by new information and if I say something in a session that you may obsess over it, like it appears you have done for the past couple of months."

Obsess?

So, not only may I be on the spectrum, now I have

OCD?! Next, you'll diagnose me with adult ADHD! What's after that? Dissociative identity disorder?

The little voices were taking over.

"I am happy you are exploring yourself, and yes, it is good to keep learning and working towards the truth, but I think you need to balance this with letting things be, and living, and being who you are, and letting yourself have fun. Your whole life does not have to be about making sense of things. Sometimes, things are the way they are. Have you worked out what you would like to do, just for fun?"

She'd raise the fun thing before, and I still didn't have a better answer than last time.

"No, not really. Finding shark teeth might be fun, but also might be a waste of time—"

"Remember: if it is enjoyable, then it is not a waste of time."

"Okay, but as far as my obsession with introspection goes, it's just me being me; I've always wanted to learn and understand myself better."

"Yes, and this is okay, but like I said last time, you need to try to find the balance. You need to balance what is going on inside your head with what is going on outside in real life, and like I also said to you last time, sometimes you need to just *live* your life, not analyse it."

Had you said that last time?

"Okay, yes, I will try and find the balance. And I'll try not to be as suggestible to new ideas as you think I'm being."

She tapped the side of her mug and smiled. *Gotcha!*

"Aha! But is this not you still being suggestible?"

She'd created a clever paradox.

If I listened to her advice, I was being suggestible, but if I tried not to be suggestible, I'd still be listening to her advice.

"I don't think I can get myself out of this one, so I'll simply say that I will try to find a balance of suggestibility."

"Exactly right. Well done!"

She took a swig of her tea and shuffled back in her seat, causing me to do the same.

"I would like to tell you another little story if that is okay. It is like a fairytale, but not really."

I hope it has something to do with intuition and imagination!

"Sure, go ahead! I'm always up for one of your stories."

"Okay, thank you. This follows on from my first piece of advice for you last time about your intentions."

I felt I was mastering that piece of advice and didn't feel she needed to consolidate it any more than she had but wouldn't resist.

"I will keep that in mind."

"Once upon a time, there is a kingdom or queendom as it may be, and there is a queen that rules all the lands. This queen has everything she could possibly want, health, wealth, fine garments, expensive jewellery, fancy food and wine, peaceful subjects, and a staff of people to take care of her every need, but the one thing she is missing in her life is a—"

I jumped in to interrupt. "Husband or wife?"

"—partner to share it all with. Unlike other fairy tales of

princes and princesses; this queen has had her fair share of relationships, but none of them have worked out."

"Sounds familiar. Perhaps the two of us can hook up."

She ignored my interjections and continued. "One day, in a fit of loneliness, the queen beckons her most trusted handmaiden and sends her on a quest. The queen wants to know the one true secret to a successful relationship and wants the handmaiden to set off to survey as many couples as she can, to try and find the one true answer. In return, the queen promises her handmaiden anything her heart desires."

"Oh, this should be interesting. I want to know the answer too!"

"Everyone does! So, the handmaiden packs her essential items and rides off on her horse to travel the countryside to find the answer her queen seeks.

"As with any story about a quest, she searches high and low, from village to village, yadda yadda yadda, to ask everyone she can, about the secret to a long-lasting relationship.

"She asks old couples who have been married for decades and young couples who are newlyweds, but she cannot find the one true answer and keeps getting varied responses.

"Trust, respect, kind words, communication, physical attraction, shared hobbies, shared interests, good sex, children, and grandchildren, are just some of the answers she is given.

"During her third month away from home, the handmaiden notices a cloaked man nearby eavesdropping on her conversations, a man she has seen a few times before. She summons him to ask him why he is listening and whether he had any words of wisdom for her.

"He tells the handmaiden that he is not in a relationship, but he knows the one true secret to a long lasting and healthy relationship, but before he would reveal it to her, she would need to agree to take him back to the castle and make him her husband."

"Eek! I can't imagine forcing someone to marry you is the secret, or if he thinks that relationship is going to last very long!"

She took another sip of her tea and continued.

"The handmaiden is repulsed by the man's proposal but finds herself caught in a conundrum. For the past few months, she has had little success finding the information she seeks. She wants to please her queen but also wants to earn her reward.

"She considers the man's offer and asks him to remove his cloak so that she can— how you say— check him out.

"The man steps forward and lowers his hood, to reveal his— now this is where the story gets a little politically incorrect— reveal his deformities and ugliness. Actually, please let me modernise the story a little bit and change that to unattractiveness, as attractiveness is subjective. So, he steps forward and lowers his hood to reveal his unattractiveness to the handmaiden. Everything about the man, from his hair to his height, to his build, to his eye colour is not what the handmaiden finds attractive in a suitor. He has poor skin, and poor teeth, and other things, and I could go on, but I will not because you already get the picture, yes?"

I nodded along, intrigued about where this story was going, and if it had any relevance to me. "Ugly man, got it."

She smiled and finished the last sip of her tea.

"The handmaiden feeling sick, agrees to the man's offer and the two of them ride back to the castle.

"Later that evening, just before sunset, the two are married in a small ceremony with only a celebrant and no witnesses.

"After they proclaim 'I do' the handmaiden demands to know the secret.

"The man keeps his end of their deal and replies with a single word.

"Do you know what this word is?"

"Narcissism?"

"No! Sovereignty."

"Sovereignty?"

"Yes, sovereignty. The handmaiden pushes him away and flies into a rage as she thinks she has been tricked by such a simple answer, but as she tries to rebut and argue and think of all the reasons he is wrong, she cannot, so she runs off to tell the queen and ask for her reward."

The counsellor stopped, checking. "Do you know this word, sovereignty?"

"Yes, I think so; It's like freedom and autonomy, yes?"

"Yes, freedom, autonomy, independence, and much more than that.

"Upon hearing the single word secret to a long-lasting relationship, the queen also flies into a rage, but after calming down, she too cannot find any argument or rebuttal against it.

"She accepts the answer and asks the handmaiden what she would like as her reward, and the handmaiden asks for secret passage away from the queendom and away from her new husband to a village where she can govern with enough riches to keep her and her subjects in comfort for all her remaining days."

"Sneaky one, that handmaiden. Gets the secret and then runs off!"

"The queen agrees but needs until the next morning to make the arrangements.

"The handmaiden returns to her quarters where the cloaked man is waiting to consummate their marriage."

I brought my hand to my mouth. "Oh no!"

"As she enters the room, he removes his hood, and in place of the unattractive man she married ten minutes ago, is the most attractive man she has ever seen. He is her version of perfect, with perfect hair, perfect eyes, perfect skin, perfect teeth, etcetera, etcetera."

"What happened to the other guy?"

"She is confused and asks him who he is and what he has done with the other man.

"The man responds that he is the same man she married earlier that evening. He tells her that he was cursed many years ago by his ex-wife, and that the curse makes him unattractive during the day, and the opposite at night.

"He tells the handmaiden, that as his wife, she now has

the power to invert the curse if she chooses to, or she can leave it the way it is. She can make him attractive during the day and ugly – I mean unattractive – at night or keep things the way they are."

Interesting!

I leaned forward in anticipation of her answer.

"Her choice is between having an attractive man at night in the bedroom, and an unattractive man during the day with her friends and family, or the other way around.

"The handmaiden is saddened by his story but tells the man she cannot make such an important decision about his life. She tells him that she wished he could make the choice for himself.

"Without making a choice, the two of them go to sleep."

"So, they didn't go at it then?"

"Maybe they did, or maybe they did not. This is for your imagination and is essentially unimportant." She paused for a moment, and continued, "The handmaiden wakes at daybreak as the sun is rising, not sure if she will stay or run away. She stares at her husband lying next to her, waiting for his transfiguration back to ugliness, but as the sun rises higher and higher in the sky, there is no change.

"She shakes him awake and shows him a mirror and asks him why he made the choice he made, to be handsome during the day, and the opposite at night.

"The man replies, 'I did not make a decision. You broke the curse by giving me –" she paused again. "But you know what she gave him, do you not?"

Ding, ding, ding!

"Yes, yes, I do. She gave him sovereignty. His choice to do what he wanted to do."

"Yes, she did, and do you know what this story means and why I have told it to you?"

I leant back in my seat and took a swig of my tea.

"I think so. Is it because you're trying to tell me that all healthy relationships are built on sovereignty, and that sovereignty comes from our intentions for ourselves?"

"Correct. Yes! But what does this story mean for *you* and your relationship with your ex-wife?"

I didn't want to answer, but I knew I couldn't avoid the unpalatable truth.

Could it be that my 'shoulds', and ideals for my ex-wife had stripped her of her sovereignty, or at the very least, reduced my encouragement and support of her sovereignty? Whilst she always made her own decisions, I could see that I'd tried to coax her to do the things I thought were best for her, and best for us. She'd rarely listened, but that hadn't stopped me from trying.

I shuddered with the realisation, fumbling for the words to explain, but the counsellor snapped me back to the present with another question.

"So, can you please give me an example, so I can know you have not got the wrong end of the stick?"

I cleared my throat. "Yes, of course. I suppose the example that comes to mind is probably one of the last interactions we had, before she decided to leave me, or possibly the interaction that led to her final decision.

"We were in Naxos during the last few days of our holiday. We'd hired a car because our hotel was in the middle of nowhere, in a beautiful place near Stelida."

"I know this place. Very beautiful but very isolated."

"Yes, that's right, and because of that, we needed a car. I'd never driven on the wrong side of the road, whereas she had, so she was happy to be our designated driver. One evening – actually, it may have been our last evening there – we were meeting friends in Apeiranthos, and she drove us there. Long story short is that as she went to park the car, she forgot which side she was on, and misjudged the other cars and tore the side of the rental off, as well as the front bar off another car, and as luck would have it, the owner of the car she hit was standing up against it with two of his mates.

"She was so annoyed with herself, and me too for being there, and sat in the car furious and unable to speak, but in my own special way, I managed to make things worse."

"How did you make things worse?"

"She told me to get out of the car and to go meet our friends for dinner, and to leave her alone to sort out the accident with the men, but I refused. We were in a foreign place with foreign people, and I didn't want her to have to deal with three guys alone. I wouldn't have felt safe if it was me on my own, and there was no way I was going to leave her in what may have been a dangerous situation."

I paused for a moment to work out how to best wrap up the story.

"Go on."

"Anyway, she lost her mind at me, turned red, cried, cursed, and yelled at me to leave, saying she didn't want me anywhere near her. I refused, but rather than stay in the car or near the car, I gave her some space and sat on a wall about thirty metres away. She waited for a representative from the rental car company to arrive and survey the damage and negotiate a settlement with the locals, and in the end, they were all really good about it, and it cost us about three hundred euros."

She clenched her jaw, before releasing it to ask: "And how do you think this relates to sovereignty?"

"Well, I guess I didn't respect her right to make a decision for herself and in turn, I didn't do what she asked me to—"

"Which was?"

"To leave her alone to deal with the accident on her own."

She clenched her jaw again. "And now, after hearing my story, do you think you should have left her in a strange place with strange people to deal with the accident on her own? Do you think my story about sovereignty makes the situation any safer for her?"

I was confused.

"No, I don't think it does make the situation any safer, and even if I'd heard your story before, I'm not sure I would have changed what I did. I think I would have still stayed close by, to make sure she was safe and ensure I had no regrets."

"I think you have missed the point of my story."

It was obvious I had. "I don't understand."

"The story is not about her sovereignty; it is about yours. It is not about you taking your wife's sovereignty away, because she always had it, and was never going to let go of it. The point of my story is to show you that in your marriage, you gave away your sovereignty to your ex-wife. You stopped making decisions for yourself, and instead, you made your decisions for her benefit and for your relationship's benefit. Your ideals and 'shoulds' stripped you of your own sovereignty and your own right to make decisions that were in your best interests."

That definitely wasn't my takeaway!

"You're right, I didn't get any of that, and I may have completely misunderstood the point you were trying to make, but interestingly, I did have a similar realisation when I was in Allestree."

"You did not misunderstand me as such, but because you have such a strong and unyielding internal frame of reference; you are always blaming yourself for situations, whether you are to blame or not.

"Not everything is your fault, but I suspect you have always believed it is, and this may be the greatest storyline of your life."

Chapter 13

Her story had nothing to do with my question about the difference between intuition and imagination, but her surprise twist and appraisal knocked the wind out of me. Partially, because it was true.

I'd learnt about psychological frames of reference during my first year of psychology at university, and had quickly and easily identified mine as internal rather than external; looking inward and blaming myself for just about all the negative situations I found myself in.

I'd take one hundred percent responsibility for the things that didn't go well, but avoided all credit for when things did go well, preferring to distribute it to others.

It was part of my programming and the only way I knew how to be, and even now, if given the choice, I wouldn't choose the opposite. People who blamed everything on others without taking responsibility for their own actions and decisions were in my opinion, the worst kind of people.

"You're one hundred percent right about my internal frame of reference," I admitted. "It's one of the things that drives me crazy about the current generations. They want everyone around them to bend to their way, without wanting to bend themselves. They have no interest in meeting in the middle, or in compromising, and everything needs to be done the way they want it done, even if it is contradictory or self-defeating. They follow the loudest voice, and are constantly filled with faux outrage, and have no ability to think for themselves or be critical about issues. They care about inclusivity above all else, which is great by the way, but they actively promote exclusivity with the labels they slap on other people. They want to be treated as individuals but want to be treated better than everyone else. It's a contradiction that can't be achieved, but they don't care, because that's someone else's problem to deal with.

"I don't blame them though, as it's not entirely their fault. Our generation brought them up to be the way they are. We invented the 'everyone is a winner' attitude and now we're reaping what we sowed. This current generation wasn't taught resilience as they were shielded from needing it.

"It's quite the clusterf— I mean mess!" I corrected myself hastily. Mustn't lose my grip in front of the counsellor. "It's a mess of our own making, and I can't see how we're going to get out of it. And now they're managers, and teachers in schools, and are getting into politics, and are CEOs, so I think it is just going to get worse until it implodes and something else happens.

"It will be interesting to see how their children are raised, and the new character traits they develop. I imagine privacy is going to be of utmost importance to them."

A look of shock, or was it surprise, spread across her face, and her mouth dropped open once more, wider than before.

"Sorry for carrying on, but the frame of reference thing is something I spend a lot of time thinking about; but how can this be my greatest storyline when it is who I am?"

Her mouth remained open. "Something about you is different. Something has changed during the past two months."

"It's probably that I'm a little more relaxed. I did just return from a lovely holiday in paradise."

"Maybe, but I think it is more."

I wondered if I should tell her about my chakra clearing or my near-death experience, but she continued before I could say anything.

"Tell me, what conjures up for you when I say the words guilt and shame?"

Double bounce.

Once again she'd changed tack in the disconcerting way I now expected from her, but this time, I was ready to answer. "I don't really think about either, but I guess they're negative feelings and emotions and I can't imagine I want to revisit either of them."

"What if I were to hypothesise that guilt and shame are two of your default programs, and this is why you have such a strong internal frame of reference?"

"I would ask you what they have to do with it?"

"And I would say, everything!"

"Okay, then, so how?"

"I ask you to think about this objectively. Take yourself out of the equation for now. Think of two people, or better, think of two children. Child One is given all the things they want and need, including encouragement to strive for more, and the belief they are better than everyone else, and deserve more. Their parents provide a nurturing environment and put the child at the centre of the universe, accommodating their behaviour and demands."

"Sounds like most parents today, and what I just talked about; how about the second? I'm guessing the opposite?"

"The second child is given what they need but is witness to the sacrifices of their guardians or parents, who work long hours, or two jobs, and often go without things they need for themselves. Child Two may or may not be made to feel guilty about their own needs, but they do anyway, and may see themselves as a burden, because their needs are being met at the expense of somebody else's. The second child is not encouraged to strive for more and is made to believe they must earn everything they want."

"Okay, two children, on opposite ends of a spectrum."

"Imagine these two children meet and become friends. What do you think this relationship will look like? Which one will feel worthy, and which will feel guilty? Which will feel proud, and which will feel ashamed? Which will be the giver, and which will be the taker? Which will be the people pleaser, and which will not care what others think? Which will have an internal frame of reference, and which will have the external?"

"I don't think your questions need answers, as it seems obvious, unless you have some hidden surprises or insights?"

"No, no surprises this time. This story is as it sounds, and the rest of the children's lives will be affected by their parent's mindsets and attitudes. Without critical thinking as you put it earlier, one child will develop a strong external frame of reference based on feelings of being worthy, deserving, and entitled, and the other will develop a strong internal frame of reference based on feelings of guilt and shame. Adults who were not made to feel valued when they are children, may never feel worthy, and adults who are made to feel too valued when they are children, well, they may well become narcissists." She shot me a cheeky smile.

"Ha, that's funny!"

I knew she'd have a connection in here somewhere!

"I hear what you're saying, but I still don't like psychoanalytical psychology or the idea that you can trace everything back to your childhood. It's too simplistic."

She smiled. "I do not think it matters if you like it or not."

It was time for a comeback.

"Okay, so now I have a story for you. Have you heard the one about the drug addicted mother and her twin daughters?"

"Sounds like a variation to a story I know, but please go on."

"A drug addicted mother raises twin daughters in the best way she can. One of them is always in trouble, gets poor grades and is frequently in fights. She starts experimenting with drugs at an early age and by the time she's sixteen, she's also addicted to drugs and alcohol. Her twin is a picture-perfect student. She never gets in trouble, gets straight As, and keeps away from alcohol and drugs. By the time she is sixteen, she has graduated from high school and is applying for various jobs and university places. When the principal of their school asks the two girls why they are so different to each other, they each give the exact same reply.

"Do you want to guess what this is?"

She didn't hesitate with her answer. "Because of the mother."

"So, you *have* heard this story before?!"

"No, I have not, but I am a psychologist, and you are using this story as a reason to avoid analysing your own upbringing to avoid investigating where your programming has come from."

I sat back deeper into the sofa.

"Maybe I am, but I believe we all have choices, and it is an easy way out to blame others for the way we are."

"There is your unbreakable internal frame of reference again!"

She diverted her gaze, staring through the lead light windows above my head, before shooting off on another of her seemingly random tangents.

"Back to a question you asked earlier; I do not think it

matters which version of Tokyo is real and which is made up, and the fact that you are telling the stories, means it is a little bit of both. What is more important, is that you are seeing things in new ways you previously did not, and even more importantly, you are beginning to use this insight in the present rather than on the past.

"My three pieces of advice to you last time were not intended for you to examine your past and relive the events you have already lived."

Wish you'd told me that earlier!

"There is no point to this, as the past is already past, and there is nothing you can do about it. The future is yet to be written, so pay attention to the present, be mindful, and tune into your intuition, for the things that are happening now will affect your future."

I was pretty sure she'd said all that before.

I bit the rim of my mug before releasing it to respond. "I get all that, but I've been sitting with this stuff for a while now, and it honestly feels like I've messed up my entire life. I don't remember a time when I just let things be and wasn't on some kind of mission to change them to fit into some sort of preconceived ideal."

"So, the question for you is, how can you modify your internal frame of reference to lessen your preconceived ideals and your 'shoulds'?"

"Is that the question?"

"Did you take my advice and read about the psychoanalytical constructs of ego, id, ego, and superego, and the four competing selves?"

Oops! Forgot all about it!

"No, sorry, I didn't. I didn't want to take all your advice at once, as I didn't want to be completely suggestible!"

She giggled and touched her nose with her right index finger before pointing it my way, gesturing a respectful 'touché!'.

"Very good. I like this; I like this sense of humour. This is good to see."

She extracted the note pad and guillochéd pen from the secret compartment in the table in front of her and beckoned me to sit opposite her.

As I stood up, she drew a cross through the page, splitting it into quadrants.

"So, this is my version of the model, and I am sure there are others using different words, but they will mean the same thing."

She scribbled four words on the page, one in each of the boxes, and then spun it around as I took my seat.

"Each person has four competing selves within them."

"Only four?! I think I have four hundred!"

"Well, there may be more for some people, and some with less, but let us start here with four. They are the ideal self, the social self, the perceived self, and the actual self.

"The ideal self is who you think you should be—"

"That's me for sure!"

"The social self is who you think you should be when you are around other people, the perceived self is how you think others see you, and the actual self, is as the name suggests, the person you actually are."

Makes sense.

"Apart from ideal, which of these boxes do you think you mostly live your life?"

I scanned the page, quadrant to quadrant, repeating her descriptions in my head. "I'm definitely in the ideal box based on my discoveries – I mean uncoveries – during the past nine weeks, but now I'm not so sure anymore. There are two others on your page that resonate just as much."

"Which two?"

"In addition to ideal, I think social and perceived."

She spun the pad of paper around to face her and circled the three words I'd identified with. "Correct. All three of these are the 'shoulds' in your life."

"The 'shoulds'?"

"Yes, each time you try to live up to your ideal, social, or perceived self, you will do the things you think you should do or say the things you think you should say.

"I believe you spend most of your time trying to meet ideals. Not only your own, but the ideals and perceptions of others, and the way you think others want you to be. Even though you have made all of this up with your storylines, if we put this aside, you spend no time being your actual self; why do you think this is?"

Well, firstly, this information would have been quite helpful at our last session as I had to work some of this out on my own! Still, since she asked …

"That's easy. It's because I have no idea who that person is. I am whomever other people want or need me to be."

It was becoming more and more obvious to me. I didn't know who I was at my core and was still trying to figure that out. It was first brought to my attention by the blue-suited counsellor ten or eleven months ago, when he'd asked me the simple question about what it was I liked doing, a simple question I could not answer.

"Correct! So, what we need to do is find this actual person in you." She poked the barrel of her pen towards my chest. "In the perfect world, there are not four different selves, but just one unified authentic self. If we could be who we actually are, then we would not be at war with ourselves."

She drew multiple lines across the page to connect each of the quadrants. "There are six sources of conflict between our different selves, and when there is conflict, there is tension, and where there is tension, there is anxiety, and if this tension is left unchecked, then there will be other illnesses. Knowing where the conflict is coming from, will help you understand it, and will help you make decisions about how to resolve it."

If only it was that simple …

She must have read my scepticism because she continued in her most reasonable voice. "Your subconscious and your intuition know who your actual self is, and each time you act or behave for one of the other selves, your subconscious and intuition will let you know. You need to tune into it."

"Do they make a stethoscope for this stuff?"

She laughed out loud. "Ha, you are full of humour today!"

"Seriously though, how do I tune in?"

"This part is easy. All you need to do is tune in to what makes you happy and peaceful, *and* tune into what does not."

It was similar to the advice I'd received in Bali from her doppelganger.

"Each experience is a test. Each time someone asks you something, do not analyse it. *Feel* whether it makes you feel good or not good? To understand your actual self; who you *actually* are, is to recognise when you feel good and peaceful and when you do not. When you identify the feeling, you can make a conscious decision about what to do next. *Listen* to your body, tune into your good feelings, and feel your peace. It is that easy."

"It's interesting you raise this now as during my time in Bali, I had many memories of not feeling good during my marriage, or in any of my other relationships after the first three months. After my ex-wife's breakdown, I frequently imagined what it would be like to be on my own again. I'd fantasise about where I'd have lived and what I'd be doing if I were on my own, down to small details like where I'd put furniture, what artwork I'd have on the walls, and how I'd spend my time if she hadn't been there. And I felt *happy* in each of those thoughts. It was almost as though I subconsciously manifested our breakup, without consciously wanting it. All these memories seem at odds with how hard I fought to try and save the relationship. Was this my actual self, competing with my perceived or social self and possibly even my ideal self?"

Her face turned serious, and her voice deepened. "Possibly, no, probably, yes. Your ideal, perceived, and social selves come from your programming. Keep interrogating your programming, and you will find your actual, or higher self."

Higher self? This was new.

She continued. "I read a word the other day which I quite liked. It is 'automaticity', which describes our auto pilot, or the way we do things because we always have. I think it is another good word for programming."

Automaticity. Sounds like me.

"I think that is what makes this stuff so challenging. If it's automatic, how do we notice it?"

"All you need to do is take a moment to be who you are. To feel what you are feeling without judgement and without it taking over. What did you say last time? 'Let your feelings sit next to you on the park bench, and do not do anything with them'."

"Yes, that was something I heard in New York, but I struggle to do it."

My body relaxed and I exhaled some of the tension I'd been accumulating since arriving here. Letting myself be who I wanted to be right now, was letting myself slouch.

I slid down into the chair and into the worst possible posture.

"Tell me, are you sleeping? You look tired."

You too with the compliments! I needed to change the subject.

"Another funny story for you. After you had me do all that stretching last time, I've realised that I have been holding my breath and limiting my movement when I go to sleep, so as to not disturb anyone else."

She slapped her left hand on her knee. "Oh, you have met someone new!"

"Ha, ha, no, that's the thing. I haven't, but I still go to sleep each night like I'm sleeping next to someone else. As though I'm trying to be quiet for them. I've been holding my breath and clenching my hands into fists when I get into bed for almost ten years, and I've only just realised it! So, to answer your question, no, I'm not sleeping well! And the other thing I've noticed because of you, is just about everything!"

"Oh, how so?"

"Ever since you alerted me to my hypersensitivity, I've become overly conscious of it; and not just to my hyper-sensing senses, but to me noticing me noticing them. It's like having a double consciousness!"

"What things are you noticing now?"

"Everything! But right at this moment, I can feel that a few of my eyebrow hairs above my right eye are out of place. I can feel my breath causing a burning sensation on my upper lip. I can smell the ink from your pen, and the paint in this room, even though it probably hasn't been painted for four or five years …"

"Six, actually." She smiled and touched her nose again. "What else are you conscious of?"

"The brightness and colours in here are changing with the movement of the clouds outside, and I can hear three different types of birdcalls in your garden as well as your fridge compressor switching on and off; oh, and that lamp in the corner has a low frequency buzzing sound.

"I can taste my mouth and smell my nose, and as I say all of this, I can feel my ears heating up and sweat starting to bead on the back of my neck. I'm guessing these sensations have always been there for me, but since you brought them to my attention, they are louder, clearer, and brighter, and I'm no longer sure that other people sense the world around them in the same way I do."

She nodded her head and smiled. "Maybe they do, or maybe they do not. Maybe it is normal, or maybe it is not, but what is important, is that it is normal for you. What is normal anyway? Sensations, like many other things, exist on a spectrum and different people are on different parts of the spectrum. Some will have more, and some will have less."

"These days, I think I've started wishing for *less*. How can I tell someone that I want to run screaming out of a room because I'm overwhelmed by the flickering lighting, the kettle whistling, a dog barking, the air-conditioning being too cold, and my eyebrows not sitting right?"

She shook her head. "I am sorry to say this, but as you pay more attention to yourself, and become more deliberate and conscious, you will notice many more of these sensations. Your hypersensitivity has been this way since you were a child, but your subconscious has filtered it out. Keep paying attention and keep questioning everything to uncover your programming, and so you can get further out of your cave, but at the same time, please be careful of sensory overload as your synaesthesia will give you a flight or fight response, like wanting to run screaming out of a room."

"Synaesthesia?! I'm pretty sure I don't taste sounds or hear colours but based on everything else I've learnt in this room, what would I know?!"

"Synaesthesia is more than this; it can be feeling sound as pain, especially loud or unexpected sounds, and specific frequencies might set you off. It can be feeling light and colours in your body, some pleasurable, and others painful. If you have sensory overload, your senses will become confused. This is important for you to recognise."

"How can I be careful of overload, when my senses are all turned up to eleven, and are constantly overloaded? I think I now better empathise with children with ASD and can understand why some of them don't want to be touched, or don't want to talk, or why they lash out when the inputs become too much."

"Yes, but the difference is that you do not do these things. Take time for yourself, and excuse yourself if you need to. It is the only way."

Is it the only way?

I tried changing the subject again to help supress my overloading senses.

"If we rewind to your earlier story about sovereignty for a moment, I still think that some of my thoughts and actions did not respect the sovereignty of my ex-wife, and quite possibly, some of my ex-girlfriends before that. I don't think this is just my storyline, and I don't think it's just because of my internal frame of reference."

She adjusted herself in her seat, appearing frustrated.

"I am sorry to ask, but how would you know if it is not just your storylines, and not because of your internal frame of reference?"

It was the first time she'd challenged me so directly.

"Well, I am trying to look at it factually. They came into my life looking for support and whilst I tried to do my best, I don't think I respected their decisions, if their decisions were at odds with the support I was trying to provide them with. I don't think I supported them fully when I didn't like a decision they made, or when I thought they should be making a different one. At the very least, isn't that a bit hypocritical?"

Her body seemed to deflate a little as she acknowledged my question.

"We are all hypocritical, and we all have duality, but I think you still have the wrong end of the stick. Tell me honestly, did you ever use physical force on your ex-wife, or any of your partners to do something against their will; or more to the point, did you ever coerce them with some sort of control, like withholding something from them, or keeping them from their freedoms?"

"I'm sure I did. My ex-wife for example didn't want to go to Tokyo, or to Greece, or to couple's counselling, but I coerced her to go to all three."

"I think you do not understand the word 'coerce'. Let me find a better word— let me try 'intimidate' or 'pressure'. Did you ever intimidate or pressure your partners to do something against their will, things they did not want to do?"

"No, never! Look at me! I couldn't intimidate a fly!"

I didn't have the physique or the personality to bully or intimidate anybody.

"Exactly. And did you withhold money or affection, or anything else as a means to force your partners to do something they did not want to do?"

"Never! I never shared a bank account with any of them. Their money was always their money, and I didn't want a say in how they spent it; and as for the other things, who would do such a thing?"

"If your ex-wife told you definitively that she did not want to go to Tokyo, or to Greece, or to couple's counselling, what would you have done?"

"Pleaded some more, I guess."

"And beyond that?"

"Nothing. What could I have done? In the end, she did walk out, and I just let her. I didn't stand in her way or try to hold her back. I think I was sitting on the bed at the time and just watched her walk past me and out the door."

"You need to stop gaslighting yourself about this. You did not take her sovereignty, but she did take yours, or at a minimum, you gave it to her willingly.

Perhaps I did, and perhaps I finally needed to admit it out loud.

"By the time I kissed her goodbye at the gate and boarded my flight, I'd handed her full power and control over me and my life. From that day forward, she took charge of me and my decision making."

Game, set, match, Luxembourg.

Chapter 14

I skolled the rooibos in my mug without taking the time to savour its rich smoky flavour before setting my cup down on my lap.

What was the point of that?

Mindful, not mindless!

She got up from her seat and gestured for me to follow her, towards the entrance hall, turning right into a corridor, which led to her kitchen.

"Same again?"

"Yes please, and maybe this time I'll take the time to taste it."

"Sorry?"

"Sorry, nothing."

Her kitchen was at the back of the house and overlooked the greenest of gardens. There was no open plan here. This was an old-fashioned country kitchen with a broad central entrance and cupboards and benches lining its perimeter.

The entire room was dedicated to food preparation. A huge farm-style sink sat opposite the entry and an old-style wood burner stove was installed into the wall to the right. It was cast iron and looked heavier than a car.

"How did they get that in here?" I asked, pointing.

"Through the roof." She pointed upwards. "They needed to crane it in, but I had to have one. It is what we use in Europe in winter to help heat the house. It is connected to the radiators in the other rooms and gives me a taste of home."

"How long have you been here?"

"About thirty years."

It was another similarity between her and her 'sister from another mister' in Bali.

She put fresh teabags into our mugs, and poured the water, watching me as I watched her, careful not to scald her hand, all the same.

Rather than head back into her living room, she handed me my fresh mug of tea and leaned against the sink to face me.

I had a sudden urge to know more about her.

"So, what's your story? Partner, children, how did you end up here?"

She smiled. "Who is counselling who now?"

I smiled back. "Sorry, it just feels weird talking about me all the time."

"This is your shame and guilt again making you feel uncomfortable."

Shame and guilt? I said nothing, waiting for her to answer my question.

"I have one daughter and was married to her father up until recently, but it is the cliché story of him leaving for a younger model."

"I am so sorry. I didn't mean to—"

"There is nothing for you to be sorry about. You did not do anything; it is a natural question. His leaving had nothing to do with me and is not a reflection on me. His decision was his own, as his life is his own, and it also is not a reflection on me. We both had our sovereignty to do as we pleased, and even though I did not like his decision, it was still his to make."

"I am sorry for bringing it up, but may I say, I aspire to achieve your level of maturity and Zen."

She chuckled at my compliment and shifted her weight on to her other leg, resting her hand on the sink, way too close to her mug. I tried not to think about it, as she continued to speak.

"There is another way for us to approach your programming, and I think I mentioned this at our last session. What do you know about shadow work?"

"I think I've heard the term before and may have done some of it during my university days, but I'd prefer not to guess and look like an idiot, so please tell me."

"There is that shame again, this time about looking foolish. I think shadow work may be helpful to work out where it is coming from. It is a method to investigate your programming and to build awareness, but I must warn you, that you need to be ready in yourself, because if you are not, or if you go too deep or too fast, then you may do more damage than good."

Nothing ventured … Count me in, lady!

"I don't think there's such a thing as too deep or too fast for me, and right now I want to know more so I can sort myself out."

"Ah, except this is not the aim of shadow work. The aim is to build awareness. Shadow work does not solve problems; it can only show you where they came from. Trying to use it to solve problems is counterintuitive and will strengthen the shadow."

She rocked herself off the sink to stand up straight and picked up her mug. Her movement suggested it was time to leave her kitchen.

I led the way out, but she overtook me in the hall, leading me into the counselling room, before taking a seat in 'my' chair, and motioning for me to take hers opposite.

"Changing things up, are we?"

"It is an easy way to get some new perspectives. To learn new habits, we need to break old habits. Changing the way you look at things, may just change the way things look."

"Is this the nature of shadow work? To get you out of your comfort zone?"

She rubbed her chin and looked through the stained-glass windows to her left.

"Maybe, but let me start at the beginning, with another little story – yes, I think that will be best.

"This one is about two wolves. A parent explains to their child that they have two wolves inside of them doing constant battle. The first wolf contains all the goodness; things like kindness, love, respect, compassion, generosity, and altruism. The second wolf contains all the badness, all the selfishness, and things like greed, temper, impatience, and hate."

I thought there was no good and bad …

"The child looks concerned and asks the parent, 'which of the wolves inside of me is going to win?' to which the parent replies, the one you care for, and the one you feed."

"That's a nice little anecdote!"

"Except, it is not nice and is not the lesson for the child, or for you, or for anyone else to learn."

She'd built my intrigue yet again.

"How so?"

"It is important to be kind to, and to care for both wolves so they can coexist in harmony together. Starving one will make it more desperate and more unpredictable."

"I'm not sure I've ever thought of it that way."

"Most people do not. Most people try to starve and ignore the wolf they do not like. The shadow self is this wolf. It is the part of ourselves we suppress and hide away in the shadows, and which in many cases, cast a shadow over us, and who we really are—"

"Is this in addition to the ideal self, social self, and all that?"

"In a way, it is, as our shadow selves will rarely appear in social situations, however, let us talk about shadows in isolation from the previous discussion. Let me also distinguish these shadows from the shadows on the cave wall – remember those? – although, they may end up being the same thing."

So many shadows …

I nodded. *Go on …*

"The shadows are traits we try to ignore about ourselves; the things we do not accept about ourselves. They are the parts of us which we are shameful and guilty about, although shame and guilt may themselves be parts of our shadow self.

"The shadows are our alternate personality; not our opposites as such, but the personality traits we do not want to admit to, or that we despise or reject about ourselves. What sort of things do you think are contained in your shadow self?"

I straightened up in my chair.

"Oh, my goodness! Where do I start?!"

"With something simple."

"Intolerance, impatience, anger, hypocrisy—"

"And do you believe that supressing something like anger makes it go away?"

"Yep! So far, so good!"

She smiled. "I am afraid not. Supressing anger or any of the traits you mentioned does not make them go away; rather, when they are ignored or starved, they will become more desperate to burst out."

I nodded to demonstrate my agreement, feeling a little lightheaded. Viewing the room from this perspective felt weird and uncomfortable, and having the bay window to my right, rather than to my left was making me feel strangely detached from my body.

I blinked it away, focussing once more on her.

"I think I understand."

"In shadow work, we must remain kind to ourselves and show ourselves the same compassion and empathy we show for other people. Shadow work is not easy, and requires honesty, kindness, and then … more honesty and kindness.

"These lines of inquiry require you to shine a light into the dark parts of yourself to see what is hiding in there. It requires you to accept those parts with compassion without repressing them further.

"Shadow work is about understanding *why* your shadows were created; it is not about getting rid of them or rejecting them further.

"If you reject what you find, then whatever caused your shadow self may be retraumatised and you will only strengthen your shadow self, making things worse.

"You must be ready for this process in your own time.

"If you do this, please go slowly and do not rush."

If I do this? I thought we were doing it already!

"I'm confused. Is this something we do together, or is it something I do alone?"

"Alone is best, as it is easier to be honest with yourself, but I can offer some support and guidance, if and when you need it.

"The most important thing is that you must not be judgemental when you do shadow work. Do you understand?"

"Yes, but I'm not sure how to turn that off. Aren't we all judgemental to some degree? Some more than others?"

"Yes, of course, but judgement is easily overcome by curiosity. If we try to squash – or is it quash? – our judgement, then our judgemental side will end up in our shadow self." She smiled. "Do you see how this work has the potential to do more damage than good?

"Shadow work requires you to be open and curious. As I said, curiosity will override judgement, so you personally will not have to worry about being judgemental. But speaking of judgemental people, shadow work will usually show that the people who are most judgemental, are the same people who most fear being judged."

"Ha! Simple as that then?!"

"To start your own shadow work journey, some questions to ask yourself are, what parts of yourself do you keep hidden from others? What did your ex-wife not know about you? What do your parents not know about you? What are you in denial about? Do you feel worthy of love? What causes you shame? What do you feel guilty about? What makes you angry? Why do you have no boundaries?"

Boundaries? Where did that come from?

I looked up to see her smiling again.

"I put that last one in there to see if you were listening, but for you it is a question you could investigate. And another thing," she smiled again, "if you answer these questions based on how you think you *should* answer them, then you are not doing shadow work. These questions may take you fifty years to answer truthfully, and each time you ask them, you may receive a different response. If you listen to your intuition, you will get closer to understanding your own programming."

Fifty years?

"Pay attention to your reactions. What are you intolerant of, or impatient with, and investigate your storylines about these reactions.

"How critical are you? How likely are you to blame others or be defensive; as these are indications of something lurking in your shadow self."

Noting my confusion, she stopped, and said: "Let us have a quick go, with something simple. Tell me about something small that bothers you, or you wish you could change about yourself, and we will see if it leads you to a shadow."

How could I choose just one? There was so much that bothered me!

"There is something small that irritates me beyond logic, and as much as I've thought about it, I can't rationalise it, or make it go away."

Her expression invited me to tell her what it was, but I was embarrassed by it.

I steeled myself. "It's slow walkers, or worse than that, people who walk on the wrong side of the footpath, especially when I'm out walking my dog, who I have specifically trained to walk on my left side, so she is out of the way of oncoming pedestrians.

"And before you say anything, I know that walking on

the left side of a footpath is an Australian thing, and not necessarily *wrong*, and that people have the right to walk as fast or as slow as they want, but these rationales don't prevent me from wanting to hip-and-shoulder them out of my way!"

My right shoulder lurched forward as if possessed by the thought of it.

"Okay, so let us start with some simple questions. Try to be honest with your answers.

"Why do you want to shove them out of the way?"

"To teach them a lesson; to stop them from doing it again."

"A lesson about what?"

"A lesson to be more considerate."

"So, are they inconsiderate?"

"Yes, but not on purpose."

"And what effect is that having on you?"

"I am forced to move."

"And why does this bother you?"

Why should I move if I'm doing the right thing? They are obstructing me and are forcing me to do something I don't want to do or be somewhere I don't want to be."

"So, is this about right and wrong?"

"It *might* be."

"And how does people doing the wrong thing make you feel?"

"Annoyed, and also a bit anxious that they are going to bump me out of the way if I don't move, or turn the tables on me, and abuse me for doing something they don't think is right."

"And how old does that make you feel?"

"What?" I wasn't sure I'd heard her correctly.

"How old does that make you feel?"

"That's a weird question!"

"How old?"

"I don't know … eight?"

"Okay, so maybe now we are getting somewhere. Something may have happened when you were eight related to right and wrong, to have caused this part of your personality, but I will not ask you about it, as I know you do not like talking about your childhood."

She gave me a playful wink, knowing she'd set me off.

What happened when I was eight?

"As you can see, delving into the cause of your shadows may bring up many different things. In this example, your intolerance for people walking on the *wrong* side of the footpath may be caused by your feeling of moral or ethical righteousness, so then the next part of the investigation is to try and work out where this righteousness came from, and so on, and so forth.

"One investigation will lead to another which will lead to another which will lead to another."

Another journey without end! I tried not to let my disappointment show, but I imagine she picked up on it anyway.

"Regardless of your answers, the purpose of shadow work is to try and uncover the origin of your feelings and thoughts. Sometimes these origins will be recent, but a lot of the time, they will have formed a long time ago. Remembering what was happening to you when you were eight years old may give you an answer, or it may not, but let us not delve into that now, as the purpose of what we just did was to show you one of the methods of shadow work. It is not the only way, but it is a good way to try and get past your immediate thoughts on things, and to try and get in touch with the way you *feel* about them. Your brain can rationalise just about anything, but your heart and gut cannot."

"I'm still struggling with that concept."

"And this is okay. There is no rush." She a smiled again, before continuing. "Another way of approaching shadow work is to think about a person you do not like and would not want to spend any time with. Or think of a person who brings out the worst in you, and then ask yourself why, and then ask yourself why again. Keep asking.

"These people are sometimes referred to as our shadows as in many cases they exhibit the traits we do not like in ourselves.

"They are also sometimes called mirrors because they reflect the parts of ourselves we do not like.

"Speaking of mirrors, did you know that mirrors do not show us an accurate picture of ourselves?"

Another seeming non sequitur. Why was she now talking about mirrors?

"Are you left-handed or right-handed?"

"Right-handed."

"Did you know that a mirror will show you as being left-handed. Did you know this?"

I stared into the space between us and imagined she was a mirror showing me my reflection, and sure enough she was right. My right hand would appear as my left in the reflected image.

How had I not noticed this before?!

"So, if your reflection is not real, what is? Use this visualisation to challenge the image you have for yourself; the image you take for granted, and as you go through the process, remember this; as it is of utmost importance!"

As she spoke, she waved her index finger at me, drawing circles in the air, over and over, again and again. "Remember the spiral." She drew the circle in the air a fifth time, and a sixth. "Maybe this makes more sense to you now?"

What was she talking about? What had I missed?

"I'm sorry, what's the spiral? We've covered a lot of stuff in here, but I don't think we covered anything about a spiral."

"Are you sure? We must have!"

"No, I don't think so. I'm pretty sure we haven't."

"But this is very important for shadow work, and for everything else we have been talking about! Are you sure we have not discussed it?"

"No, I don't think I know what you're talking about, and if we have, I'm sorry for not remembering it."

She looked a little flustered.

"Sorry! Let me rewind. When we talk about opposites on spectrums, how do you see them, or how would you draw them on a piece of paper?"

It was a strange question, as how many ways were there to draw a spectrum?

"I see them as opposite ends of a straight line, and I draw them that way too. Don't we all, or is there another way? That's what they are, aren't they?"

She brought her right hand to her chin again. "Yes, most people think of opposites as being at either end of a straight line, but there is another way to see them, a more helpful way, at least more helpful in my opinion."

She waved her finger in the air again, in the shape of a circle. "Try visualising the spectrum as a spiral or coil; not a complete circle as such, as the two ends do not meet. Think of a spectrum as a single loop of a spring where one ends sits just above the other."

I wasn't quite following.

She picked up the notebook and pen from the table between us and flipped to a new page. She then sketched an oval, carefully and lightly, so its end point sat a few millimetres below her starting point.

The shape looked three-dimensional, and if she'd repeated the pattern and kept drawing downward, she would have drawn a picture of a spring or a spiral.

She used the tip of her pen as a pointer to explain. "See here?" She tapped on the starting point of the oval, which was at the top of the single-loop-spiral. "Imagine this is one end of a spectrum; and here— she tapped on the end point of the spiral— is the other end."

She traced her pen over the oval again, and again, backwards and forwards. "See how far apart these two points are" —she tapped the start and end points again— "but at the same time they are close together? They are maybe two inches apart, but at the same time they are only a tenth of an inch apart."

"Yes, I see, but how is that a spectrum if the ends are so close together?"

"This is exactly my point! The spiral spectrum is a model I developed many years ago when I was doing my PhD thesis. It is an alternative way of viewing spectrums or dichotomies or oppositions, as it shows how close two ends of a spectrum can be, but at the same time how far apart they are. The two ends are not in the same place and cannot be in the same place, as they remain different and opposite, but at the same time they are far apart and are close together. Does this make sense?"

No, it does not!

My head nod turned into a shake. "Yes, kind of, but no, not really."

"Okay, think about this. Imagine for a moment you are a really good, devout, holy person; the best person in the world, who never does anything wrong or bad."

I grinned at her. "Are you saying I'm not? Besides, I thought there was no such thing as good or bad?"

"And this will better explain why.

"To be this really good person who never does anything bad, you need to have a very good understanding of what bad is. Good is a comparative word, and it sits on a spectrum of good and bad, so you need to know what is bad, so you do not do anything bad, because if you do not know what bad is, then how do you know what to do, and what not to do, so you can be good?"

It was another wordy tongue twister for my mind, but as her words rolled around and settled into place, they seemed to make sense.

"Or think about a considerate person, the most considerate person you know."

"I try to be that person!"

"Okay, so if we use you as an example; you will need to know what it is to be inconsiderate, so you do not say or do things that are inconsiderate; things like walk on the wrong side of the footpath."

She slapped her hand on her notepad and let out a laugh, and then pointed at me.

"You must know one to know – and be – the other."

Click!

"I see now—"

"Good! But you must know that this spiral spectrum does not work the other way around. If you are a really bad person, you do not have to understand what is good to be bad or do bad. Being bad is not always a conscious choice, even though people on the opposite side of the spectrum think it is. The same goes with people who you see as inconsiderate. Maybe these people are being inconsiderate because they are not aware, or because they have not thought about it."

It wasn't a good enough explanation.

"But isn't a lack of awareness, or not thinking about it, part of the problem? Can't they just spend a little more time thinking about consequences before doing what they are doing?"

"Maybe they do, but not to the level *you* want them to. Are you not being inconsiderate by thinking other people are being inconsiderate on purpose? Are you not considering the possibility they have a different level of awareness, and that different is not necessarily better or worse?"

On snap! She'd got me.

"You know what, it's a fair point."

"Not fair, or unfair, just a different way of thinking about it, and the spiral spectrum helps explain it. Another problem with society today is that we think we know other people more than they know themselves. So many people think other people do bad things on purpose, when in fact, many are simply unaware, and do not know what the alternative is. Lack of awareness is not the same as negative intention, but we think it is."

It was another good point.

"It is why I think feminism is stalling at the moment. Women have become too preoccupied with tearing other women down for the choices they make; and for exercising their feminist right to sovereignty. Feminism must be about choice, but when some women do not like the choices of other women, they turn on them, or turn on the men who are sometimes innocent bystanders. We are losing our cause and in some circumstances – rare, but still … have become the bigger misogynists."

She was still holding her pen above the spiral, tracing it back and forth, back and forth.

"In our discussion last time, you were worried about gaslighting, but you need to know what is gaslighting, so you know what not to do; and then you choose not to do it. Understand?"

Click! Click!

"This is the nature of shadow work; to become more aware of ourselves and our whys." She sounded disappointed. "I am sorry. I thought we covered this last time when we were talking about psychopaths and empaths."

I bolted upright in my chair, my skin tingling.

"Psychopaths and empaths? How does this relate to psychopaths and empaths?"

Almost reluctantly, it seemed, she drew an 'E' next to the starting point of her spiral and a 'P' next to its end.

"Imagine this is empath, and this is psychopath." She tapped her pen on the E and the P, and then traced her pen over the oval again, backwards and forwards. "See how far apart these ends are" —she tapped the 'E' and the 'P' again— "but at the same time how close they are?"

"Yes, I see, but we've been speaking about singular personality traits; how does what we've just spoken about relate to entire personalities, or personality disorders?"

"Do you remember we discussed psychopaths having no conscience for others, and empaths having no conscience for themselves?"

"Yes."

"Well, this explains why. Empaths and psychopaths are at two different ends of the spectrum, but at the same time, they are close together, so empaths possess some of the same traits as psychopaths, and vice versa but with opposite differences. For example, psychopaths have great empathy towards themselves, but not towards others, whereas empaths have great psychopathy towards themselves, but not to others."

I leant forward, drawn into her spiral.

"Empaths know psychopathy, sociopathy, and narcissism better than people at other places along the spectrum – possibly better than some psychopaths, sociopaths, and narcissists themselves; but the difference for most empaths is they have a conscience, and most will actively choose to be the opposite of a psychopath, or at least their subconscious conscience makes this choice for them."

"Most?"

"Yes … some empaths go through dark periods where they use their empathic nature, knowingly or unknowingly, to take advantage of others. It happens rarely, but it happens."

Her description was confusing.

"Aren't these empaths psychopaths then?"

"No. The difference between the two is still conscience. Empaths in dark phases still have a conscience and feel bad for what they are doing. Psychopaths and narcissists never feel bad for what they are doing."

I cleared the obstruction building in my throat.

"I think your explanation helps me understand this a bit better now. I don't think I am always a good person, and I am really not happy with the person I was in my late teens."

"Is this anything you would like to talk about?"

"No, not really, but thanks, and thanks too for sharing your spiral spectrum with me. I haven't seen anything like this before and have not heard of dichotomies described this way. I wish we had gone through this during our last session!"

"I am sorry. This is my own mistake. We covered so much ground and I thought we did cover this before you left."

But I knew she had nothing to be sorry for.

"We're covering it now and it makes a lot of sense. You should share this with the world!"

She gave me a wink. "I am sharing it with the world; one person at a time. Do you remember I mentioned a number of psychopaths in our last session?"

"Yes; not by name though!"

"Can you see how this spiral explains how people with the same INFJ traits and preferences, or any sets of traits and preferences for that matter, can end up being on opposite ends of a spectrum?"

"I can now!"

She traced her pen over the oval again, backwards and forwards.

"There is a little bit more to this spectrum. Let me ask you, are you interested in the people and events I mentioned last time and why they did what they did?"

"Yes, absolutely! I spend a lot of time thinking about anything and everything that is happening in the world right now, and how we all got to this place. Are you familiar with those old crime shows, the ones before the fancy touchscreens and see-through whiteboards, where the cops used corkboards, pins, and red string to connect suspects and events and evidence?"

She nodded. "Yes, I know the ones."

"Well, that's what my brain looks like twenty-four-seven. It's a tangle of a million miles of red string, connecting everything with everything. It's a web within a web within a web. I can't explain why it happens, but like I've said before, I'm really interested in knowing why people do what they do, and the context for those decisions, and I guess I'm always looking for those connections.

"My opinion is that words or actions are the very last part of a process, with a million parts happening before. I also believe that most actions are reactions. I'm not all that interested in what they've done. I want to know their motivations and the possible alternatives to their choices.

"Some people think they have no choice if there is a gun to their head, but they still do. They can live and do the bad things they've been asked to do, or they can take the bullet, and die with their integrity intact."

"I know what you mean, but you may want to keep that last thought to yourself as it makes you sound like a psychopath." She laughed and slapped her notebook against her knee.

"Do you imagine that a psychopath is interested in anyone else's intentions?"

"I guess not, not unless they were using that information to fulfil their own."

She laughed again. "I think you are beginning to better understand this now."

Her spiral spectrum had me hooked.

"I think your little spiral may help me understand why I sometimes feel like a narcissist or even a psychopath. But I'm still not sure I understand what it is to be an empath."

She smiled. "You still have not made the link, have you?"

"The link?"

"Yes, there is something in this diagram that has not yet clicked into place for you, and I am wondering if we should let it sit, or if I should tell you."

I didn't want to go home without knowing. "Tell me! Please!"

I stared at the oval, and at its start and end points, its E and its P.

"Apart from what you've told me, what have I missed?"

She smiled at me in silence, building the suspense for an agonising few seconds before coming to a conclusion.

"Okay, I will tell you, but either this is going to make sense for you, or it is not, and I will not be able to explain it any more than I can."

"Okay, I can live with that."

"Remember last time, I told you an empath was like an emotional sponge, and that an empath feels the emotions of others like it was their own?"

How could I forget?

"Yes, yes I remember."

"And do you remember me saying that unknowing empaths would not be able to distinguish between their feelings and someone else's?"

I nodded.

"Well, this is why."

She planted her elbows on her knees and leant forward.

"The very nature of being an empath means you will feel the feelings and emotions of everyone along the spectrum. You will feel the feelings at every point along every spectrum, and there are countless spectrums. An empath has no choice but to coexist at both ends of whatever spectrum we are talking about, but not only at the ends, at each and every point between the two ends. Whether there are ten points, or a thousand, or a million, or even seven billion, we feel the feelings of every person at every point between the two ends, and sometimes we will feel them concurrently.

"In short, empaths are empaths for everyone, regardless of who they are, or what they have done. Empaths will be empaths for people you admire and want to emulate, *and* people you do not. You do not get to choose.

"It is not possible for empaths to be any other way. If you feel like you are two different people, or two opposing points in an argument, it is because you are. To be an empath is to feel multiple and opposing feelings and to know multiple and opposing perspectives, simultaneously.

"Empaths feel an infinite number of feelings and emotions, and as a result have an infinite number of thoughts. We are reflections in a mirror being held up to another mirror. Each reflection is a reflection, but each is not the same as the other."

She was building me up with another drumroll.

"You asked me in our last session whether you could be the opposite of the empath, and my answer to you is yes, you are; not at the core of who you are, but at the core of what you think and feel when you are in contact with your opposite, whether it be in person, or on TV, or on a stage, or written about in an article.

"The link you have not yet made is that it is not possible for you to tune into who you are without distinguishing from the noise of who you are not."

She paused and kept her eyes focussed on her pad of paper and traced her pen over the oval, back and forth, over and over again, rhythmically and hypnotically.

"Our curse is that our empathic connection is to everyone; regardless of who they are. Put us in a room full of psychopaths, sociopaths, and narcissists and we will feel what they are feeling. We will not like it, and we will not act on it, but we will feel the turmoil and we will try to process it towards some sort of reason."

I felt myself slipping. I'd thought she'd pushed me into the deep end of the pool during our last session together, but it now felt as though she was going to plunge me into the ocean from a helicopter.

She adjusted herself in her chair to again face me front on.

"It is not possible to live our lives as empaths, without

feeling the feelings of everyone else who is, and everyone else who is not. We are the one percent of the population who feel the feelings of the other ninety-nine percent.

"Whether we like it or not, we feel the empaths, the altruists, the selfless, the philanthropists, the misanthropes, the greedy, the selfish, the sociopaths, the narcissists, and the psychopaths.

"We are psychopathic empaths and empathic psychopaths, but more than all of that, we are everyone in between."

The Opposite of a Psychopath

Part 3

About the Author

Charles Tyler lives in Victoria, Australia. Since childhood, he's been fascinated by psychology, spirituality, and the power of identity. Charles started his career as a corporate trainer, before moving into management and leadership roles in Australia and overseas. In addition to writing, Charles consults, coaches, mentors, and provides advice on organisational strategy and service design. In 2010, Charles founded an art gallery for aspiring and emerging artists, and in 2020, he put pen to paper to write his first novel, *The Opposite of a Psychopath*.

The Opposite of an Empath is part two of *The Opposite of a Psychopath* trilogy.

charlestyler.com.au